Egret's Loft Murder Mystery Series

Unnatural Causes

The Dead Men's Wife

Serial Seniors

Raven's Wing Murder Mystery Series

Strange Winds

This is a work of fiction. Names, characters, places, and incidents either are the product of the author's imagination or are used fictitiously. Any resemblance to actual persons, living or dead, events, or locales is entirely coincidental.

Copyright © 2023 by T.E. Harkins

All rights reserved. No part of this book may be reproduced or used in any manner without written permission of the copyright owner except for the use of quotations in a book review. For more information, contact: teharkins@teharkins.com.

Cover design by Joe Montgomery

SERIAL SENIORS

An Egret's Loft Murder Mystery

T.E. HARKINS

CHARLES
FORT
PRESS

One

Deep breath in. Deep breath out.

The English muffin I had for breakfast sits like a bowling ball in my stomach. It seems to sway from side to side as my grandson and I walk, hands entwined, across the parking lot to the River Club. Equal parts excitement and terror war against each other inside me, and I can't help but reconsider this foolish plan to tackle my deepest fears head on.

"It follows sound logic, though—" my grandson, Curt, lets go of my hand briefly to scratch the tip of his nose, "—that mechanical factors should be assessed in order to determine the best use of positive fluid dynamics through the water."

"Of course, dear," I say, digging through the contents of

my oversized beach bag. "Did we put your arm floaties in your bag?"

"Yes, Grandmother." Curt nods his little blond head. "I ran through a full checklist of necessary items before we left the house."

Curt is six years old, but he has an IQ of 185. He is adorable and brilliant and curious.

He's also afraid of his own shadow, spiders, large bodies of water, and everything else that falls outside his cerebral comfort zone. So, when the daughter of one of my neighbors offered to give Curt swimming lessons, I thought his answer would be a resounding, *no, thank you.*

To my surprise, he'd agreed. But to make matters worse, he'd convinced me to take the lessons with him. At the end of last year, I'd nearly succumbed to my worst fear—drowning—in an attempt to avoid being murdered by a psychopathic serial killer. I survived, but now Curt has convinced me that, at nearly seventy years old, it's high time I learned how to swim.

Which is why, on this warm and sunny February morning, we're headed to the swimming pool at Egret's Loft, the upscale West Florida retirement community I moved into several months ago.

Curt had insisted on applying waterproof SPF 50 sunblock before we left my house, so there is nothing to do once we reach the sun loungers except set down our bags and stare, terrified, into the achingly blue, chlorinated abyss.

Out of the corner of my eye, I spot Curt rummaging around in his Iron Man backpack. I turn my head in time to see him snapping on a pair of too-large rubber gloves and pulling what looks like a remote control out of his bag.

"What do you have there?" I ask.

Curt's eyes sparkle as he retrieves a blister pack from the front compartment of his bag. "This is a pool water photometer. By dipping it into the water and using the receptacle located at the front of the device to dissolve the various reagent tablets, I can accurately ascertain the levels of chlorine, bromine, and cyanuric acid in the pool water. It also measures pH and alkalinity, but those are somewhat superfluous, as I already have test strips that serve the same purpose."

Another thing that terrifies Curt is allowing anything dirty to touch his skin.

"Did your father buy you that?" I wonder aloud.

Curt shuffles his feet and stares down at the ground. "Yes."

I frown. "Did your father *know* he was buying you that?"

"Technically, no," Curt admits. "But if he didn't want me to use his Amazon account, then he should seriously consider making his passwords more of a challenge!"

"Curt—" I begin, but my grandson is spared my lecture by the arrival of Savannah Jeffers.

"I'm so sorry I'm late!" The beautiful twenty-two-year-old sets down the large piece of foam she's been carrying and swipes a lock of fiery red hair out of her green eyes. "The roads out there are busier than a moth in a mitten!"

"You're not late," I assure her, though technically she is. Knowing she has a tendency to show up tardy for everything, I purposefully didn't arrive on time either. "But, yes, the place has been packed since I got back from spending the holidays in DC. I've never seen so many golf carts!"

"Me neither! Back home in Alabama, folks like to drink a can of Bud after each hole," Savannah says in a soft, melodic Southern drawl. "Country clubs wound up having to ban golf carts, on account of too many folks driving 'em drunk. So, you don't see 'em around too often."

The color on Savannah's cheeks deepens after what is, for her, a lengthy monologue, and her eyes shift to the ground. Shy around most people, Savannah has been warming up to me slightly in recent days. But Curt, whose intelligence and mannerisms tend to put most people off, really brings Savannah out of her shell.

"Hey, little man," she calls out to my grandson, a smile gracing her naturally ruby lips. "You ready to swim?"

"Good morning, Savannah." From his perch at the side of the pool, Curt nods his head in the young woman's direction. "All the chemical levels appear to be acceptable, and, at eighty degrees, the water temperature is within recommended guidelines. So, yes. I suppose I am prepared to follow through with our lesson."

"Excellent!" she exclaims, pulling her sundress off over her thin frame to reveal a one-piece bathing suit underneath. "We're off like a herd of turtles! Everyone into the pool."

"Oh, no!" Curt and I cry out in unison. He looks to me to lead the opposition.

I oblige. "We're not ready just yet. We have to put on our arm floaties and—"

"Oh, you don't need floaties, Miss Madeline. I brought you this here kickboard to use." She holds up the large piece of foam, smiling. "You know, just until you're comfortable."

"Thank you. That's very kind." I return her smile. "But I still have to put on my swim cap. And Curt needs his goggles…"

"If I didn't know better, I'd think the two of you were tryin' to stall." Her emerald eyes narrow as she accurately assesses the situation. "How about I do a few laps while you settle yourselves? Five minutes?"

Suddenly wishing I was still home in bed, all I can do is nod my head.

A rush of blood temporarily deafens me, and my fingers shake as I tuck my shoulder-length, whitish-blond hair inside the plastic swim cap my son, Ritchie, purchased for me online. My lungs have also joined in on the bodily rebellion, curtailing my efforts to blow up Curt's inflatable Batman arm floats.

"The psi is still not optimal, Grandmother," Curt repeatedly tells me. It's his version of Goldilocks, with me unable to find the pressure per square inch that's *just* right. We're both stalling. And we both know it.

Finally, we can no longer postpone the inevitable.

With Curt clutching my finger so tightly it feels like my pinky finger might snap, we plant our feet on the first step of the pool, and I feel the water rise to my ankles. Savannah glides effortlessly through the pool to join us.

"I was thinkin' we could start with a game," she says. "What do you think?"

"Will it be in shallow water, so we can stand up if we need to?" I ask, while Curt simultaneously demands to know, "Is there a prize for whoever wins?"

Savannah giggles. "Yes, you'll be able to stand up. No, little man, I don't have any prizes for the winner. *But* you would walk away with braggin' rights."

Curt looks at me, then back at Savannah. "I suppose that will be sufficient."

"Great! The game is called red light, green light," Savannah explains. "You'll float on your bellies. Don't worry none, I'll get you into position. Then when I say, 'green light,' you start kickin' your legs like a sprayed cockroach. When I say, 'red light,' you stop. We'll keep on doin' it until we get to the other side of the pool. Got it?"

"The rules seem rather simplistic," Curt complains.

"Well, maybe they are. That doesn't mean it won't be fun!" Savannah picks up Curt and pulls him deeper into the water. "Miss Madeline, you grab the kickboard there, hold onto it in front of you, and then just kind of fall onto it."

Holding Curt under the armpits and keeping an eye on me, Savannah calls out, "Green light!"

Curt bites down on his lower lip, as he and I frantically begin kicking our legs.

Before long, the pool deck is thoroughly soaked, and our earlier fears are, at least partially, forgotten. Our laughter even draws out an Egret's Loft staff member, keen to capture our enjoyment on her cell phone's camera. The attractive young woman, who I would guess is roughly the same age as Savannah, has long black hair, parted down the middle and large, black-framed glasses that swallow a good third of her thin, alabaster face.

"Hey, Sydney!" Savannah calls out to the woman. "Are we disturbin' you?"

Sydney smiles. "Not at all! Just keep doing what you're doing. This is perfect for TikTok!"

"Tick, tock?" Curt looks up at Savannah, his small body tense during the red light. "Is this a timed competition?"

Savannah laughs softly. "No, little man. TikTok. It's a

social media thing. People put up videos, and other people watch 'em."

For all his intelligence, Curt seems as oblivious about social media as I am. The thought brings me comfort until something else occurs to me.

"Oh no! Other people will be able to see me in my bathing suit?" I start to panic. While I have managed to retain my slender figure into my advanced years, I don't relish the thought of anyone seeing the way the skin on my arms and legs has begun to crepe. "Who would want to watch *us*?"

"Anyone interested in moving here!" Sydney chimes in. "We haven't met. I'm Sydney Walsh. I do PR for Egret's Loft."

"It's nice to meet you. I'm Madeline Delarouse. Are you new here?" I ask, wondering why I haven't seen her around before now. Having worked in marketing myself before retiring, I would have thought that having three people murdered in the community a few months ago would have been a bit of a public relations nightmare. Then again, a bunch of dead residents probably wouldn't be the kind of relations the community would want to make public.

"No, I've been here about a year," she explains. "But I took some time off in November to do some traveling. When did you move in?"

I nod. "That's why we haven't met before. I moved here

in November, and I've been out of town, with family, for a few months over the holidays."

"Green light!" Savannah interrupts us by announcing.

Curt and I flail our legs for all we're worth. I can hear my little grandson roaring with laughter, and any tension I'd felt from my aquaphobia melts away.

My children and grandchildren will all be in town tomorrow for a special family weekend hosted by the staff at Egret's Loft. It feels like the perfect opportunity to relax, kick back, and put murder out of our minds.

I couldn't possibly know, as Curt and I frolicked in the swimming pool, that, by this time tomorrow, another one of my new neighbors would be dead.

Two

Through the accordion-style, glass doors, I watch as the sun melts into the horizon, painting the sky in a kaleidoscope of magnificent oranges, reds, and magentas. The sound of glasses clinking, and laughter fill the air, and I can still smell the residue of chlorine on my skin from this morning's swimming lesson with Curt.

A feeling of bittersweet peacefulness settles over me.

It occurs to me, as we wait for our drinks at the Golf Club bar, that Clint would have really loved this place. My late husband, a detective with the Washington DC Police, died suddenly nine months ago. If he'd survived, we would have been enjoying our retirement together.

"A white wine for you," my son, Ritchie, interrupts my thoughts, handing me a stemmed glass. "And a strawberry margarita for the best-looking man in the room." Ritchie kisses his husband, Craig, on the cheek.

Craig scoffs. "You're only saying that because I'm the only guy in the room not old enough to be your father!"

"Maybe." Ritchie winks. "But it's still true."

"What about me, Daddy? Do you have my Yoo-hoo?" Curt, who insisted on wearing a bow tie to this evening's community-wide get-together, demands.

"I sure do, buddy! But first—" Ritchie holds the promised beverage just out of Curt's reach, "—since we're here at Egret's Loft, do you know why the egret is the symbol of the National Audubon Society?"

Craig smacks Ritchie on his arm. "Won't you just give him his drink?"

"You needn't worry, Poppa. I know this," Curt reassures Craig before turning back to Ritchie. "The answer is because, in the late 1800s, John James Audubon visited the Everglades and saw that populations of egrets, which had been nesting in the region for thousands of years, were dwindling, due to mass commercial hunting for the plume industry."

Craig frowns. "The *plume* industry?"

Curt sighs. "Feathers. They were primarily used to adorn women's hats at the time. Egret's feathers were the most popular and, thus, became the symbol of environ-mentalists' efforts to protect all wading birds." After Ritchie hands him his drink, Curt adds, "That was too easy though, Daddy. Everybody knows that."

I take a sip of wine to cover the fact that I, as it happens, did *not* know that.

Ritchie pats his son on the head and begins walking out onto the club's back patio where a large crowd has gathered.

"Hey, honey," Craig calls after him. "Don't you need to pay for the drinks?"

"Nope. We got them free because you're so handsome." Ritchie smiles, his big blue eyes twinkling.

"Don't pay any attention to him," I tell Craig. "The whole community is cashless. Everything goes onto my tab, which Ritchie pays. Feel free to order whatever you'd like!"

"Thanks a lot, lady!" Ritchie whines. "Give Craig another way to bleed me dry, why don't you?"

"Oh, I'm sure I'll be paying for it in other ways," Craig teases his husband right back.

The truth is, neither of them have to worry about finances. Ritchie is a successful and highly sought-after brain surgeon, despite being only thirty-five years old. Craig is a rocket scientist and works at NASA. It's no surprise, really, that their progeny is a prodigy.

"It's a shame Eliza couldn't make it tonight," I lament the absence of my daughter as we all walk away from the bar, into the humid air outside. From the club's large, brick patio, there's an excellent view of a putting green and a driving range that both sit at the edge of a large, man-made lake.

Craig turns to his husband. "You said Emmy swallowed a Lego person?"

He's referring to Eliza's youngest daughter. At three years old, she is adorable, precocious, and puts everything she sees in her mouth. A few months ago, Eliza had to take her to the hospital, after Emmy swallowed the battery from a greeting card.

"Just the head, I think. Not the whole Lego person," Ritchie clarifies. "But yeah, Eliza said the doctor told her to wait until Emmy poops it out before traveling. They'll all be here tomorrow." Ritchie glances in my direction. "Hey, lady. Isn't that Gina over there? Who's she talking to?"

Gina Wilson has become my best friend in the short time I've lived at Egret's Loft. A forceful New Yorker with a thick accent, a beautiful singing voice, and a nasty penchant for forgetting everyone's name, Gina has helped me solve three murders at Egret's Loft. We've both nearly died doing it.

Currently, she's resting one hand on her husband's arm, while wildly gesticulating with the other. The recipients of her seemingly enthusiastic conversation are an older man with an egg-shaped head and a much younger, exotic-looking woman.

"That's Gina, alright," I confirm. "She's talking to Fred. I met him right before the holidays. Oh, you might know him, Craig. He used to work at NASA too. Fred Burrows is his full name. I think he was an engineer or something. Do you know him?"

"Umm...no. Sorry," Craig says.

"I haven't spent any time with him, but Gina says he was blinded in his left eye by a laser. Are you sure you've never heard of him?" I press.

Craig's thick, dark eyebrows bend in consternation. "You do know that NASA has about eighteen thousand employees, not to mention contractors and partners—"

"Jeez, lady. You spent years at the Treasury Department. Did you know everyone who worked there?" Ritchie defends his husband by challenging me. "Why is it that old people always think, if people have *one* thing in common, they must know each other?"

"You're not supposed to call me old," I remind him. It's one of the rules at Egret's Loft. You can't refer to anyone as "old" or "elderly." Terms like "active elders" and "persons with advanced life experience" are acceptable.

"Alright, alright!" Ritchie holds up his hands in surrender, but he's smiling. "What's my punishment? Are you going to take away my bingo privileges?"

I glare at my son. "I sometimes forget how *charming* you can be, dear."

Ritchie, ignoring me, focuses on Gina's group. "Who's the woman with Fred? Is she his daughter or something? Should we rescue her?"

"Oh, no." I lean in conspiratorially. "That's Svetlana. His wife. She's originally from Lithuania, I think. Gina thinks he ordered her from a catalog."

Some of Craig's margarita, which he'd been sipping when I spoke, spews out of his nose. As he doubles over coughing, an attractive, "active elder" gentleman approaches us.

"Does he need help?" the man asks in a polished, British accent. He's tall, but I get the impression he was taller when he was younger. If he didn't have a thick, white beard, he would remind me of Anthony Hopkins. Not a *Silence of the Lambs* Hopkins, though; he has too many lines on his face for that.

Still, I find myself checking his glass to make sure he's not drinking chianti.

When none of us immediately responds to his offer of assistance, the man adds, "I'm a doctor. If the young man is in distress, I may be of some assistance."

"Don't mind him." Ritchie squeezes Craig's shoulder. "He's never been able to handle his liquor. But thanks, anyway! Are you new here? Do you know my mother?"

The man turns his cornflower blue eyes in my direction. "I haven't had the pleasure. My name is Hugh Darcy. I've been a resident here for the past four years, but I split my time between Florida and London. Still, it's a wonder our paths haven't crossed before."

"No need to wonder about that," I assure him. "I only

moved here—onto Cypress Point Avenue—late last year and have been gone for two months over the holidays. I'm Madeline. You've been speaking to my son, Ritchie. This is his husband, Craig, and their son, Curt."

"You live on Cypress Point? So do I! Well, it's a pleasure to meet all of you." Hugh takes a moment to shake everyone's hand. "Are you enjoying the party?"

"We just arrived," I speak for the group. "There are so many people here! And a lot of new faces. I didn't realize how many residents only spend half the year here!"

"Oh, yes. There are quite a few on our street. Have you met Viviana Arenas yet? I believe she usually returns to Egret's Loft after the New Year."

There is quite the cast of characters living on my street —a black widow, a former US Marshal, a retired NFL quarterback, a dead drug lord's wife, and an artistic hippy who paints nude people, to name a few. And, because I've had to determine whether most of them were murderers or not, I've gotten to know them all relatively well. But no one has ever mentioned Viviana before.

"No. I haven't heard the name," I tell him, having to speak louder to rise above the sound of Marjorie's new battery-operated mobility scooter. I turn to watch as she drives back and forth along the buffet table.

Marjorie Higginbottom, who also lives on Cypress Point Avenue, is the neighborhood's pink-haired Betty Crocker. Her house perpetually smells like cookies, and she always carries around a plastic bag of fresh-baked treats wherever she goes. Since I'd been away, she'd decided to trade in her old walker for a flashy, new cherry red scooter. It looks like a four-wheeled Vespa and is just as loud.

Hugh, catching me staring in the direction of the buffet, asks me if I would like to get something to eat. Curt happens to overhear.

"Grandmother, no!" Worry floods my grandson's blue eyes. "Buffets are breeding grounds for viruses and bacteria. Eating spoiled or contaminated foods, which I highly suspect that buffet contains, significantly increases your risk of getting norovirus or rotavirus, not to mention E. coli or Listeria. And I shouldn't have to tell you that, in your age group, foodborne illness has a greater likelihood of resulting in hospitalization, or even death."

Hugh looks, open-mouthed, at Curt, then at me. I shrug.

"I'm sure the food is fine." I lean forward, addressing Curt. "But I'm not hungry. So, there's nothing to worry about."

Slightly off balance already from bending over, I'm knocked off my feet by the sideview mirror on Marjorie's scooter as she zooms across the patio. Hugh manages to grab me from behind before I hit the ground and, as I recline briefly in his arms, I catch sight of another one of my neighbors, Jinny Myrtle, about ten feet away. She's staring angrily after Marjorie. Which strikes me as odd. I thought the women were good friends.

"Are you alright?" Ritchie asks, pulling me back onto my feet. "Good catch, Hugh! You probably just saved my mom from a broken hip!"

Hugh brushes aside the compliment. "I suppose management should consider posting a speed limit next to the buffet."

"What's she doing now?" Craig asks, pointing to Marjorie, who now appears to be in an altercation with a young, Hispanic man dressed in a white chef's apron.

A few seconds later, the young woman I met earlier in the day, Sydney, approaches them. She's not filming now, but it looks like she is trying to restore peace. All the party-goers are staring, their conversations turning to whispers.

We're too far away to hear what Marjorie and the chef are saying, but they both look angry. The chef throws his hands up in the air and retreats into the kitchen. Marjorie speeds away on her scooter. Sydney chases after her.

"Never a dull moment here at Egret's Loft!" Ritchie jokes.

"I wonder what's gotten into Marjorie," I think out loud. Not only did she neglect to offer me a cookie, she also nearly ran me over, and then accosted a cook! That doesn't seem like the Marjorie I know.

"Everyone's entitled to a bad day, I suppose," Hugh says.

"Would anyone care to mingle with me? I'm afraid I'm rubbish at making small talk with most people."

As Hugh, Ritchie, and Craig agonize over the prospect of socializing, my attention is elsewhere, staring into the distance.

For a fraction of a second, as Hugh was speaking, I thought I saw Clint on the other side of the patio. He was shaking his head, the way he always had when he thought I was out of my depths.

Then he was gone.

I can't escape the feeling that my dead husband is trying to warn me. But what is he trying to warn me about?

Three

"Did you know that more than half of Americans don't know how to swim?" Curt asks from the passenger seat of my golf cart.

"No, dear. I didn't." The roads are empty of traffic this early in the morning. Everyone seems to be sleeping in late after attending last night's party, so it should be a relaxing ride to the River Club for our second swimming lesson. But I can't seem to shake a deep sense of unease.

"Which means, as a non-swimmer, I'm currently in the top fiftieth percentile of the population," Curt reasons. "If the majority of society views learning to swim as inconsequential, perhaps I need to reconsider whether these lessons are the best use of my time."

"The time? Don't worry, we'll make it there in plenty of time," I say, not really having heard anything he's just said.

I want to pay attention to Curt, I do. But my mind is racing.

This should be a good day. The whole family will be together again in one place, for the first time since Christmas. With both of my children leading extraordinarily busy lives, there's not much more a mother could hope for than to spend a long weekend with her kids and grandkids. So why do I feel so anxious?

"Then again," Curt continues, "the sport does have historical significance. Were you aware that the first known depictions of people swimming date back to the Neolithic period? Cave drawings, estimated to have been created eight-thousand years ago, were discovered at Wadi Sura in the Gilf Kebir plateau of the Sahara in 1933."

He looks at me expectantly. I was barely listening. I try to home in on the last few words he'd said. "I'm sorry, dear. The wadi what?"

"Wadi Sura." When I don't respond instantly to words that have no meaning to me, Curt sighs. "It's in southwestern Egypt, near the Libyan border, in an area that's now arid, but was once home to lush vegetation and access to freshwater lakes." The way he recites the fact, I'm certain he's citing it verbatim from somewhere. "Anyway, I suppose if cavemen learned how to swim, there's really no excuse for me not to, is there? What do you think?"

I'm spared a response by our arrival at the River Club. There's a car parked near the entrance to the club and an attractive, young black woman is climbing in. Getting closer, I think I recognize the woman as Detective Samantha Baptiste, a recent transfer from the Miami Police Department. I can't imagine why she would be here now.

Intrigued, I pull my golf cart up alongside her.

She exits her vehicle and leans down to see under the cart's plastic canopy. I stare back at my own reflection in the lenses of her polarized sunglasses. "Mrs. Delarouse? What brings you here so early in the morning?"

"I might ask you the same thing," I retort. "Has something happened? Where's your partner?"

Her partner and senior officer, Detective Pete Fletcher, has become something of a friend. He's woefully inexperienced at investigating homicides, so I've helped him solve several recent murders. In return, he's saved my life on at least one occasion. Detective Baptiste, on the other hand, has always treated me with a high level of unwarranted suspicion.

"Nothing's happened, as far as I know," she says. "I came by to meet someone."

I look around at the empty parking lot. "Really? I don't see anyone else here."

"Yes, well—" she pauses, "—I'm not at liberty to discuss police matters."

"So, something has happened?"

She frowns. "I didn't say that."

"You didn't need to," Curt tells her. "By stating that you

can't discuss police matters, you've already implied that something of concern to law enforcement has transpired."

Detective Baptiste lifts her sunglasses, revealing her big, brown eyes, and stares at Curt. "How old are you, son?"

"I'm six, but I'll be seven next month," Curt proudly states. "That said, I would appreciate you refraining from referring to me as your genetic offspring. I may have been conceived in a test tube, but I do know whose eggs were utilized in the process—and they were not yours."

I cough to cover the impulse to laugh.

Detective Baptiste recovers quickly, letting her sunglasses fall back to the bridge of her nose. "Yes, well. Alright. Do you mind telling me your purpose in being here this morning?" She pulls a notebook out of her back pants pocket.

"By pulling out that notebook," Curt observes, "you're either reinforcing our belief that some sort of violation to the local penal code has occurred or you're attempting to intimidate us. Do you mind telling us which, so we can respond in the proper manner?"

Attempting to end a conversation that is going nowhere fast, I climb out of the golf cart, an unintentional grunt escaping my lips. Detective Baptiste stands up, as well, so we're now looking at each other over the roof.

"We're just here for a swim lesson, Detective," I tell her. "Our teacher should be here shortly, and we don't want to be late. Come along, Curt!"

Detective Baptiste slides the notebook back into her pocket and returns to her vehicle. "Enjoy your swim," she calls out before slamming her door and firing up the car's engine.

Even though my knees are acting up, I stride quickly toward the side gate to the swimming pool, eager to distance myself from the young woman's unpleasantness.

Curt has to run to keep up with me. "I hope I still have time to check the pool levels before Savannah arrives!"

"Don't worry," I assure him. "We'll make time."

There's no one in sight as we approach the pool, but the deck seems wet in patches. An abandoned pink flamingo pool float bobs on the surface of the water.

As we make our way to the sun loungers to set down our bags, Curt warns, "Be careful around the edge of the pool, Grandmother. I noticed yesterday that the tiles along the border have a low coefficient of friction. I'm still waiting on parts for my x-ray machine, so it would not be the ideal time for you to slip and fall."

My grandson had convinced me, in a moment of weakness, to allow him to build an x-ray machine in my garage. He really does have me wrapped around his little finger. I smile. "You be careful, too, dear."

With our eyes focused on the wet tiles, we gingerly make our way to the sun loungers. Once there, Curt quickly unzips his backpack and pulls out his pool disease detector monitor. I can't for the life of me remember what he called it yesterday. Nor can I recall what I need from my bag. Oh, yes! I need to put on sunblock before we swim. My dermatologist back in DC had warned me about melanoma.

"Uh, Grandmother," Curt interrupts my thoughts. "I don't think we'll be able to swim today. In fact, I've just decided the cavemen can retain their swimming superiority."

In the process of squirting sun cream into my hands, I don't bother facing Curt when I say, "I'm sure the levels in the pool can't be *that* much different from yesterday."

"Oh, I'm quite confident the bacteria levels will be outside acceptable parameters, but that's not the problem. Perhaps you'd like to see for yourself?"

I sigh, walking over to join Curt at the edge of the swimming pool. "What's the problem—*Oh my goodness!* Curt, don't look!"

I pull Curt's little body into mine, tearing his eyes away from the sight of Marjorie Higginbottom. The pink flamingo pool float has moved, revealing her body. She's at the bottom of the deep end of the perfectly blue pool, still sitting on her mobility scooter, almost like she drove it into the water on purpose.

Even if I was a confident swimmer, I wouldn't jump into the pool to try and save her. It would be a waste of time.

Staring into her vacant eyes, it's abundantly clear that Marjorie Higginbottom is dead.

Four

"It could just be an accident," Ritchie says, not for the first time since Curt and I returned to the house half an hour ago. He's been pacing the floor in the kitchen for the past five minutes.

"Yeah, right!" Eliza disdainfully replies from her seat at the kitchen table. "She just drove herself into the pool and drowned! That's what you think happened?"

Eliza, her husband, Tom, and their two beautiful, blond daughters, Tory and Emmy, arrived at the house while Curt and I were still at the pool, awaiting the arrival of the police.

My daughter's family had been expecting a relaxing weekend. They should have known by now, no such thing exists at Egret's Loft.

Sensing the brewing family discord, Tom and Craig

took the kids out back to play in my small pool. From my seat at the kitchen table, I notice Curt hasn't gotten in the water with his younger cousins, despite Craig's best efforts to convince him.

"The scooter was relatively new, right? I mean, maybe she just couldn't control it," Ritchie argues.

"And then she just stayed, sitting on the scooter, while water flooded into her lungs?" Eliza demands, then runs a hand through her long blond hair. "No, mark my words, she was murdered. And, if I'm right, it's time to move Mom. This would be the fourth murder at this place in less than four months! Enough is enough! Mom isn't safe here!"

"You know," I cut in, "I'm actually quite happy—"

"*We* chose this place, remember?" Ritchie interrupts, responding to Eliza, and ignoring me. "We did a lot of research, and *you* wanted her here because it was two hours from your house in Miami. She's made friends. It wouldn't be fair to uproot her now!"

"I'm sitting right here—" I try to remind them.

Eliza doesn't let me finish. "Well, none of the brochures or Yelp reviews happened to mention this place is swarming with psychopaths, now did they? She can make new friends somewhere else!"

"I like my friends here—" I begin.

This time, Richie cuts me off. "Oh sure! First, we pull her out of the house she and Dad lived in for decades, then plop her into a fancy retirement community that's supposed to be one of the best in the country. Now, just when she's getting settled again after the holidays, you want to make her move again? Don't you know that relocation stress syndrome in older people can lead to a decline in physical and emotional well-being?"

"My well-being is just fine," I object. Neither of my children pay me a bit of attention.

"That sounds like something Curt would say," Eliza speaks over me. "Are you taking advice now from your six-year-old?"

"Curt's a genius," Ritchie points out. "I could do worse."

"True." Eliza softens her tone. "You know, I'm not trying to be a jerk here. I'm just really worried about Mom. Aren't you?"

"Of course, I am. But Mom has proved herself to be pretty capable in dealing with the last couple of murders. All that time solving cases with Dad seems to have rubbed off on her. She's become quite the detective. Did you ever stop to think that maybe this is a good distraction from focusing on losing the love of her life?"

"Again, I'm right here!" I remind them, but they continue to act like I'm not even in the room.

"Seriously?" Eliza takes a deep breath. "Look, I'm all for Mom having hobbies too. If they help her cope with losing Dad, even better. But solving murders is not a *hobby*! Need I remind you, she's almost been killed *twice* already?"

"*Almost killed* is a bit of an exaggeration—" I try to argue.

"That was because she tried chasing after the murderers." Ritchie leans across the kitchen counter to look at Eliza. "We just need to teach her that it's alright to investigate, but she needs to refrain from following up on her hunches. That needs to be handled by a real policeman."

Eliza rolls her aquamarine eyes. "You're being naive if you think that's going to happen."

As my children continue to bicker between themselves over the fate of my future, the doorbell rings. So absorbed in their argument, neither of them notices.

"Why don't I get that?" I say aloud. "Hopefully, it's not a psychopath here to try and kill me."

There's no response. It's like I'm talking to myself.

I can still hear their raised voices when I open the door to Detective Pete Fletcher.

"Good morning, Detective Fletcher," I warmly greet the policeman. "It's good to see you again. I want to hear all about how your wedding plans are coming along, but for now, can you do me a favor and just please tell me if Marjorie was murdered?"

"It's nice to see you too. Even under the circumstances. Regarding the manner of death, we'll have to wait on the autopsy to confirm anything," he says, then leans in. "But between you and me, the coroner's pretty confident it was a homicide. Her head was bashed in before she and her scooter ended up in that pool."

I grimace. "Ritchie's going to *hate* that Eliza was right again."

"Eliza?" Detective Fletcher stands up taller, a frown line appearing between his eyebrows. "Is she here?"

The detective has held a grudge against my daughter since the moment the two of them met. On paper, Eliza works for the Internal Revenue Service. In reality, she's far too well informed on, well, pretty much everything, not to be somehow involved with one of the national security agencies.

I suspect Detective Fletcher's dislike stems from professional competitiveness.

She just thinks he's an idiot who gets in her way.

"Of course, my daughter is here," I tell him. "It's a family weekend. The staff have planned loads of events!"

Detective Fletcher scratches an imaginary itch on his bald head. "Right. Yeah. I'd heard about that. Well, I guess you don't have to come in now. The officer you talked to made some notes, so I can get your full statement later. But since you know a lot of people here, I just wanted to see if you had any thoughts. You know. On who might have killed her."

My children are still arguing in the other room, but on the off chance they start wondering where I went, I grab my hat and step out to join the detective in my driveway.

"Have you found the murder weapon?" I ask, positioning the hat to block the sun.

"Not yet. We found some blood on an inflatable pool toy. But there's no way that's what killed her," he states the obvious. "The killer might have taken the murder weapon with them."

"Well, I have no idea who killed her. But if I were you," I advise the detective, "I'd start by talking to the new guy that works in the kitchen. I don't know his name. Good-looking young man. Hispanic, I think. He and Marjorie had words last night. I couldn't hear what they were saying, but they both looked upset."

Detective Fletcher frantically scribbles in the little notebook he always carries on him. When he's finished, he looks up. "Anything else?"

"Depending on when Marjorie died," I say, "there are two people who might have been the last people to see her alive."

"Great. Who?"

"One is a young woman named Sydney Walsh. She does PR for Egret's Loft. She seems nice enough," I tell him. "Anyway, after the fight with the chef, Marjorie drove away on her scooter. Sydney chased after her."

"Right. Sydney Walsh," he repeats. "And the other person?"

"This one's a little tricky," I admit. "It's your partner, Detective Baptiste."

His eyes flash up from his notes. "Sammy? What does she have to do with anything?"

"I saw her at the pool this morning. She was getting into her car when I arrived for a swimming lesson," I explain. "When I asked her why she was here at Egret's Loft, she was kind of cagey. There was something she didn't want to tell me. I couldn't get it out of her."

"What could she have not wanted to tell you?" he asks.

It's difficult not to sigh. "I don't know. She wouldn't tell me."

"Yeah. Right. Of course," he says. "Well, I guess I better get going to chase down these leads. Thanks. When do you want me to come by to get your full statement? I don't want to interrupt your family weekend."

"Tomorrow will be fine," I say, then remember my overprotective children will probably spend the next few days clinging to me tighter than Saran wrap. "Why don't I come to you? Sometime in the morning?"

He nods. "Sure. Sounds good."

"Great. I'll see you then and thanks for coming by to tell me the news."

I've only been outside for a few minutes, but that was long enough in the humidity to make me perspire. When I step back into the air-conditioned house, goosebumps rise on my flesh.

Ritchie and Eliza are still arguing when I walk into the kitchen. Recognizing that they won't listen to anything I say in their current state, I put two fingers in my mouth and whistle loudly. Aside from a faint murmur of conversation on the television, silence ensues, with both of my children clutching their ears.

"I hate it when you do that, Mom!" Eliza complains.

"It was the only way I could get the two of you to listen to me," I explain. "First, I want to tell you both that whether I stay at Egret's Loft is *my* decision, and I've made it. I'm staying. Second, that was Detective Fletcher at the door. Marjorie's head was bashed in. Her death is being investigated as a homicide."

Eliza glares at Ritchie. "I told you!"

No one says anything more for a full minute. Ritchie, looking annoyed that his little sister was right again, turns his fury on the television. "Can we turn off the Weather Channel, at least? Do you really need it on? We're in Florida. Spoiler alert: today is going to be sunny. Again!"

Ritchie really, really hates being wrong.

Five

Heavy, tropical rain knocks ferociously against the glass walls of the Golf Club dining room, as we all sit down for the special family dinner the staff planned for this evening.

The table, large enough to seat twelve adults and four children, is adorned with half a dozen battery-operated tealights and several large bouquets of tropical flowers. Ritchie had arranged for us to share the table with my friend Gina's family, though they have yet to arrive.

"Look at all that rain!" Eliza says while helping her youngest daughter, Emmy, into a booster seat. "Maybe we should have left the Weather Channel on, after all. Don't you think, Ritchie?"

Ritchie, seated to my left, pretends not to hear her. He focuses his attention on her husband instead. "We haven't had a chance to chat since you arrived, Tom. How're things?"

"Not bad," Tom replies. Tall and handsome, more than one stranger has asked Tom for his autograph, thinking he's some Australian actor who plays a Norse god in films based on comic books. He's smart, too, founding a successful engineering company in Miami. "Business is good. Just hectic. We're lining up a ton of projects throughout Florida and South America. How've you been?"

"Yeah, living the dream," Ritchie responds. "When I'm not in surgery, I'm down here trying to make sure my mom doesn't get herself killed."

I smack my son on the arm. "I saved *myself*, thank you very much. You had nothing to do with it."

Craig, sitting across from Ritchie, sighs. "Can we please have one night when we're not talking about murder?"

Before any of us can respond, Gina arrives, alone, at the table.

"Hi, Gina. Where are Leon and your kids?" I ask.

"Oh, they're right behind me." She waves her hand as if her family's absence is a trivial matter. She slides into the vacant seat next to mine. Her soft, brown eyes, which are the same dark amber color as her skin, look frantic. "I need your advice on something, hun. I don't know what to do!"

Ritchie leans around me to ask, "What happened? Is everything alright?"

"Everything's fine. I'm just confused as heck. As we were leaving the house, my older daughter, Nicole, asked me if I wanted to come to a—" she lowers her voice, "—sex party she's having next month!"

"A sex party?" My loud exclamation draws bizarre looks from Jinny and George Myrtle, a Canadian couple, whose entire family is seated at the neighboring table.

"Would you keep your voice down?" Gina demands. "You want everyone here to know my kid invited her mom to an orgy?"

Curt turns to Craig. "Poppa, what's an orgy?"

"I'll tell you when you're eighteen," Craig tells him, then turns to Gina. "Are you sure that's what your daughter was talking about?"

"Young man, my knees might be creaky, but there's nothing wrong with my ears," Gina chastises Craig. "Yes, I'm sure! She asked me to a sex party and said I could decide if I wanted to be on Team Pink or Team Blue. What does that mean? Do I even want to know?"

Ritchie starts chuckling. "Is your daughter pregnant, by any chance?"

Gina stares at Ritchie as if a third eye has just materialized on his forehead. "Now, how would you know that?"

Craig smiles in Ritchie's direction. "Of course! A gender reveal party!"

"A what?" Gina and I ask in unison.

"It's a party where expectant parents reveal the *sex* of their baby," Ritchie explains.

Gina looks hopeful. "So...nothing like the parties I may, or may not, have gone to in the '70s?"

Across the table, Eliza laughs. "Not even close. It's like a baby shower, except you find out too late whether to buy a gift for a girl or a boy."

"Oh, thank the Lord!" Gina closes her eyes and leans back in her hair. "I felt like I had to say yes, when she asked. But I could feel my blood pressure going through the roof!"

"You said yes when you thought it was a sex party?" I tease.

"She's my daughter. What was I supposed to say?" Gina defends herself, then glances behind me. "Oh, hello, my precious girl."

I turn and see a heavily pregnant, thirty-something woman standing behind me. She has Gina's stunning features and Leon's height. "Umm, hi Mom...I just saw you like two minutes ago. But hello again, I guess."

"Sorry we're late," Leon apologizes, taking the empty seat next to Curt. A little girl with tawny skin and onyx curls climbs onto his lap. "Let me introduce you to the rest of the family. That's our youngest daughter, Chantelle. That's our other daughter, Nicole, with her husband, Glen. And this little bundle of joy is my grandbaby, Sabina."

The next few minutes pass in a flurry of shaking hands,

kisses on the cheek, and Curt frantically sterilizing his hands. The appetizer course is being served by the time we all take our seats.

While everyone else focuses on their food and making small talk, Gina leans closer to me. "So, I hear you were the one who found Marjorie's body in the pool this morning. Were you ever going to mention it?"

I look around to make sure no one is eavesdropping. "Of course, I was going to tell you. But you know how both our families get when we're talking about murder!"

"You didn't even last five minutes." Ritchie shakes his head.

"Five minutes before what?" Craig asks.

"Before they started talking about Marjorie's murder," Ritchie snitches.

Leon sets down his cutlery. "I thought we agreed on this, Gina. No talking about dead people during dinner. You promised to, at least, wait until dessert."

"Why can't she talk about it?" Gina's daughter, Chantelle, whose gorgeous halo of black, spiral curls has a streak of purple in it, asks. "I thought her suspicions about that NASA guy were pretty interesting."

I turn to Gina. "Fred Burrows? You think he may have been involved?"

Before Gina can answer me, Nicole confronts her younger sister. "Mom was poisoned not so long ago. She could have died! I don't think it's right to even be thinking about any of this stuff. Mom, I think you need to come and stay with me in New York for a while."

Eliza, finding someone who speaks her own language, decides to chime in. "I completely agree with Nicole. This is too dangerous. Mom, maybe you should come stay with me and Tom too."

Ritchie, ignoring Eliza, speaks across the table to Chantelle. "What about that new cook? He got into a fight with Marjorie the night before she died."

"Did the police say if she died last night or this morning?" Tom asks, drawing a sharp glare from Eliza. He winks in response. She grudgingly smiles and winks back.

"Detective Fletcher said she had trauma to the back of her head," I tell the table's occupants. "But he didn't say anything about the time of death."

"She wasn't floating, though, right?" Chantelle asks. "I mean, don't bodies float after a certain period of time?"

"I'm trying to eat my stuffed mushrooms," Leon complains. "Do we need to be talking about floating bodies?"

"The time frame is too narrow to consider putrefaction," Curt announces. "It would take about two or three days for the metabolic activity of bacteria to produce enough carbon dioxide, ammonia, and methane to bloat the body sufficiently to facilitate flotation."

Chantelle, Nicole, and Glen stare, open-mouthed, at my six-year-old grandson.

Looking at Craig, Gina says, "He knows all that, but he doesn't know what an orgy is?"

Craig throws his hands in the air. "He will now! Because of you, he'll be googling it as soon as he gets back to his iPad."

"Is that spelled with a 'g' or a 'j'?" Curt asks Gina.

"See what I mean?" Craig glares at her. "Ritchie, we really need to set the highest level of parental controls on that thing."

"Sure, babe. Whatever you say." Ritchie turns to face Gina. "You were saying something about that Fred guy. What's his deal? Why do you think he might have been involved?"

Nicole throws her napkin on the table. Eliza rolls her eyes.

Gina speaks in an exaggerated whisper. "Well, hun, before Forest—"

"His name's Forest?" Tom asks. "Like Forrest Gump?"

All the other adults at the table, all too familiar with Gina's inability to remember people's names, say in near unison. "His name's Fred."

Gina glares at all of us. "Can I finish my story or what?" After getting nods from all of us, she leans in and continues. "So, before F...the guy from NASA...ordered himself a bride through the mail, he and the recently deceased were an item. The relationship didn't end on the best of terms, if you know what I mean."

"Fred and Marjorie dated?" I ask, surprised. Though, looking across the room and seeing Fred with his much younger, bored-looking wife, it does seem like Marjorie would have been more suitable as a partner. "Do you know why they broke up?"

Before Gina can respond, Sydney Walsh walks up to our table.

"Hi, everyone!" She greets us with a big smile. "I'm taking some videos and pics for Instagram and TikTok. There are so many attractive people at this table—" she sneaks a sideways glance at Tom, "—I'd love to use some shots of you guys for our socials."

Eliza stares at Sydney, as if daring her to compliment Tom again. An oblivious Tom wipes some food from Tory's chin.

Gina and I look at each other, both trying to prompt the other to come up with an excuse to make Sydney leave, so we can continue our conversation.

It's Leon, annoyed that his wife broke her promise about having a murder-free meal, who finally speaks up. "Sure. Why not?"

"Great! Everyone just act natural," Sydney says, not seeming to notice the tension her presence created. Kids these days have no concept of how to interpret social cues.

Painting smiles on our faces, the conversation shifts into superficial territory as Sydney's camera rolls.

The more we all ignore the subject of Marjorie's

murder, the worse I feel. Looking over at the empty table where her family had planned to sit, I'm filled with a combination of anger, aimed at her killer, sadness for those left to mourn her, and, if I'm being honest, I also feel a little guilty. Not that I would ever want another one of my neighbors to die, but I can't deny that I've missed the thrill I'd experienced a few months ago when I was solving murders.

Gina, sensing a shift in me, puts her hand on top of mine and squeezes. When my eyes meet hers, she simply nods. I nod back.

We're partners in a crime, and we've set our sights on catching another criminal.

Six

Gritting my teeth and squeezing my eyes shut, I inch open the sliding glass door that separates my bedroom from the back patio, praying it won't squeak. Once there is enough room to slide my narrow frame through, I step outside and ease the door shut.

When they were kids, I would have grounded Ritchie and Eliza if they snuck out of the house. Now, with them sleeping inside with their spouses and children, I'm the one slinking away in the pre-dawn hours.

It's terrifying and liberating at the same time.

With the sliding door firmly closed, I check to see if any lights came on in the house during my surreptitious exit. The only light I can see is from the alarm clock on my nightstand, its bright green digits telling me it's just after five o'clock in the morning.

Fortunately for me, it seems that everyone who doesn't need to get up every twenty minutes to use the toilet is still asleep. Since it's Saturday, there's a good chance they might all sleep in a little later today too.

With one hand on the side of the house to guide me in the dark, I slowly walk toward the mesh door of my screened-in patio. Upon reaching the door, I gently lift the gate latch and replace it just as quietly when I've reached the other side. Satisfied with my own stealth, I'm smiling when I turn around and bump into an unknown stranger.

"*Aaah!*" I scream, swatting blindly at the shadowy figure.

"Would you shut your trap? It's only me, hun," Gina stage whispers.

"You're going to give me a heart attack one of these days, sneaking up on me like that!" I warn her as I try to breathe my way through an elevated heart rate.

Next to our heads, a light comes on in the guest room where I'd put Eliza and Tom.

"We need to move. Now!" I grab for Gina's hand but connect with her elbow instead. I use that to drag her away from the window and onto the lake path behind my house. Once we're a safe distance away, I turn to Gina. "I thought we agreed to meet out here."

She nods. "I know. That was the plan. But I woke up

early and didn't want to just stand around in the dark. There's been another murder here. I'm not about to make myself a sitting duck!"

"Yes, I suppose I can understand that," I grant her. "I still can't believe that four people have died here in the past few months."

"Actually, considering the average age of our residents, four deaths in four months isn't so bad." Gina, the loyal wife of an Egret's Loft board member, defends her community.

"If they'd all died of natural causes, perhaps." I glance out at the central lake that sits at the heart of our street. The moon, no longer shielded by the thick palm trees on my property, illuminates the concrete path around it. I begin to walk. "But what are the odds we'd have had two murderers living on our street?"

She shrugs. "Maybe it's the heat? It can make people crazy if they're not used to it." When I look at her as if the humidity might be having an impact on her brain, she feels compelled to add, "How could the board have known they were bad people? It's not like they wrote 'psychotic killer' as a former occupation on their applications to live here."

"Well, if we make it out of *this* investigation alive, I think we need to seriously consider making psychiatric evaluations mandatory for all prospective residents," I suggest.

"What do you say we focus on not getting killed now

instead?" Gina counters. "You said that your late husband, Clive—"

"Clint," I correct her.

"Yeah, yeah. Fine. He said the first thing is to make a list of the suspects, right?" When I nod, she continues. "I think Forest deserves to be on that list."

"Who's this now?" I can't remember who she's renamed Forest.

"You know." She throws her hands in the air, palms facing upward. "The NASA guy!"

"Oh, you mean Fred," I say, back on the same page. "You mentioned last night that he and Marjorie had been an item, before Fred found his young, Eastern European bride. You said it was a bad breakup?"

"Bad would be an understatement," Gina confides. "Forest lives two doors down, but Leon and me could hear the screaming from our back patio."

"Could you hear what they were saying?" I ask.

"You're forgetting the best part about having a hearing aid."

"What's that?"

"You can turn the darn thing off! Why would I want to listen to all that yelling?" she asks. "I think she mentioned something about Fred giving her a present. Apparently, she didn't like it. I don't know. I had no way of knowing it'd be part of a murder investigation. It was long before people started dying up in this place."

"How long ago?"

She scratches at the white streak in her otherwise dark gray hair. "A year ago? Two years ago? I didn't write it down on my calendar."

"If it was so long ago, and you didn't hear why they broke up, what makes you think Fred had anything to do with Marjorie's death?"

"Because of how she acted after they split up. She did everything she could to make his life a living hell."

"Marjorie?" I try to reconcile this vengeful version of our neighbor with what I knew of the treat-wielding grandmother who couldn't leave her house without a walker. "What did she do? Put laxatives in his oatmeal raisin cookies?"

"Ooh-wee!" Gina chuckles. "That woulda been a good one. But, no, it went way beyond that. She was breaking in and hiding dead fish around his house. You wouldn't believe the stench. And she sent him chocolates from an anonymous admirer—"

"Oh, now, that sounds nice," I interrupt.

"Sure. It might seem that way. Except she sent him chocolates with tiny pieces of nuts. He's deathly allergic to nuts."

"Oh, my goodness," I exclaim. "She could have killed him!"

Gina nods enthusiastically. "She very nearly did. They had to take him off in an ambulance."

"Why wasn't she arrested?" I ask. "That sounds like attempted murder to me."

"She denied sending them, and he couldn't prove it was her."

"So, how can you be sure she did it? Maybe she was falsely accused."

Gina waves off my concern about upholding Marjorie's innocence. "She admitted doing it. She told Janine she sent the chocolates."

"Janine?"

"Yeah, you know. The one always dressed in pink. I used to think her husband was mute, but then I realized he just couldn't get a word in edgewise."

"Oh, you mean Jinny."

"Yeah, that's what I said," Gina insists.

I don't bother correcting her. "Marjorie and Jinny did seem pretty close. Do you think Jinny would know why Marjorie and Fred broke up?"

Gina shrugs and tilts her head. "Probably. It's worth asking...if you don't mind listening to her jabbering away for an hour while you wait for her to get around to answering."

"She's not that bad," I defend Jinny, even though I've been on the receiving end of more than one of her endless soliloquies. While she may be a talker, she's also kind. More importantly, she has a talent for, eventually, providing useful information.

"Whatever you say, hun." Gina shrugs. "Should we swing by her house now? See if she's awake?"

I'm tempted to say yes. Instead, I say, "We should probably give her a little time with her family, while they're in town."

"But they could be here *all weekend*," Gina complains. "My kids aren't leaving for days!"

"Good point. My kids are here through Tuesday too." I consider our options. "Curt had asked me to go to the Sunday morning Scrabble game. Jinny always does the moderating. Maybe we could try catching up with her then?"

"Yeah, okay," Gina agrees. "But what are we supposed to do in the meantime? Is there anyone else we can check out?"

Detective Baptiste springs immediately to mind. Something about her presence at the River Club, right before Curt and I found Marjorie's body, is still bothering me. But if Clint taught me anything about investigating murders, it was to tread carefully when officers may be involved. They have everything to lose, they're armed, and they're trained in how *not* to get caught.

Which is why I say nothing about my encounter with Detective Baptiste to Gina. Instead, I say, "I think we should start by talking to the chef that Marjorie yelled at during the party on Thursday night. See if he threatened her...or vice versa."

"Good thinking. I don't think his shift starts until the afternoon," Gina says. "I can probably come up with an excuse to get away from my family after lunch. How about you?"

"Eliza will probably see right through me." I sigh. "But let's do it."

We've walked halfway around the lake and are approaching the section of the street where Gina lives. The sun, though not yet visible, is beginning to chase away the shadows of the night. It won't be long before our families notice our absence. Not to mention, my ankles are starting to swell from a combination of the humidity and my heart medication.

I check the time on my cell phone. It's still well before six o'clock, but I don't want to take any chances. "Tory's an early riser. I should probably get home before she wakes her mother."

"Yeah, I need to get back too," Gina says. "Nicole's been pretty hormonal. I don't know from one minute to the next whether she's going to burst into tears or tear my head off. I don't want to give her any excuses to go with option number two!"

I chuckle. "Funny, isn't it?"

Gina glares at me. "What's funny about my kid going on an estrogen-fueled rampage?"

"That's not what I meant," I assure her. "It's just, when I moved here, I thought I'd die of boredom. But I've almost been killed twice. Now, there's another killer on the loose. And, you know what? I've never felt more alive!"

Gina glances over my shoulder, then looks back at me. "You better hold on to that feeling as long as you can."

"Why do you say that?"

She angles her head across the lake, toward my house. "'Cause your daughter's standing in your backyard staring at us. And it looks like she's mad enough to kill you herself."

Seven

"Are you sure you don't want us to wait for you?" Ritchie shifts in the driver's seat of his rented Jeep Wrangler to look at me.

We're parked outside the Calusa Police Department. Its hunter green and white walls, with a large emblem of a police badge, sit in stark contrast to the tropical pastel buildings that inhabit the rest of the upscale strip mall. There aren't many people around for a Saturday morning.

"I'm sure, dear," I assure him. "I know how much Curt has been looking forward to checking out all the little toy trains."

"It's a Lionel train museum, Grandmother," Curt corrects me. "I can't believe they have a multilevel train display, with at least nine model trains operating simultaneously at any given time! How soon will we be there, Poppa?"

"Relax, buddy." Craig ruffles his son's hair. "They don't even open for another half an hour."

"I better let you guys hit the road," I tell them, knowing it'll take them at least that long to drive to the museum. "Besides, Detective Fletcher asked me to be here at nine-thirty to give my statement, and I don't want to be late. You boys have a nice time."

I open the passenger door and, holding onto the roof railing, I stretch my right leg as far as it will go and swing it around, searching for the ground. The Jeep sits too high for my feet to find purchase, but I figure the ground must be close. I lean out onto my right leg and tumble out of the vehicle.

"*Oof,*" I grunt as my rear end hits the pavement. My sun hat lands beside me in a puddle.

"Lady!" Ritchie cries, jumping out of the Jeep.

Before Ritchie can get to my side of the vehicle, a young-looking man with brown hair and a clean-shaven face kneels beside me.

"Are you hurt? Should I call for a paramedic?" There's a slight nasal quality to his otherwise comforting voice.

"Thank you, but I'm fine." I grimace as I try to put pressure on my right ankle. The pain momentarily outweighs my embarrassment.

Ritchie kneels beside the stranger and begins feeling the bones in my lower leg. "Can you move your toes?"

It hurts, but I manage to wiggle them.

Curt rolls down the window in the back seat. "See, I told you an x-ray machine in Grandmother's garage would prove beneficial. It's a shame the parts haven't all arrived yet."

I hear Craig tell him, "I don't think that's helping, kiddo."

The stranger picks up my sun hat, shaking off the water before handing it back to me.

"Nothing seems to be broken," Ritchie tells me, though I'm not sure I believe his assessment. "But we should go to the hospital, just in case."

"No, I'm fine. Just help me up, please." With Ritchie on one side, the stranger on the other, and my sun hat in my hand, I'm lifted to my feet. I turn to Ritchie. "Maybe next time, rent a car that's a little closer to the ground?"

"Whatever you say, lady." Ritchie smiles nervously. "Why don't I stay with you? Craig can go to the museum with Curt."

"Nonsense, dear," I tell him. "You run along. I'm sure Detective Fletcher will take good care of me. Have a good time with all the trains."

"Let me help you inside, at least," Ritchie says.

"I can take her. I'm headed inside anyway," the young

man cuts in. When we both look at him skeptically, he adds, "My friend's a cop. I stopped by to say hello."

"Are you sure you don't want to go to the hospital?" Ritchie asks me.

I wave off his concern, settling my sun hat back onto my head. "I'm sure. The door's only a hundred feet away. The detective will be waiting for me. In the meantime, I'll try not to be too much of a burden on this nice young man."

After several more minutes of assuring Ritchie that he doesn't need to babysit me, he finally climbs back into the Jeep, honking as he drives away.

"Be careful stepping up," the stranger says, his forearm pressing against my armpit as he helps me scale the curb.

"You're very kind to help me." I pat his hand. "What's your name?"

"The name's Brock. Brock Leitman." His mouth opens in a wide smile.

I return his smile. "It's nice to meet you, Brock. My name is—"

"Madeline Delarouse," he answers for me. "I can't begin to tell you what a pleasure it is to meet you."

My mind races, trying to figure out how this stranger knows my name. Have we met before? Maybe he's related to one of my neighbors. Or maybe he works at Egret's Loft. But his face, babyish and inviting, doesn't look familiar.

Not being able to place a connection, I ask, "How do you know my name?"

He chuckles. "I've been learning a lot about you lately. You were mentioned in one of the local papers a few months back, about some murders you helped solve in your retirement community."

I find myself in a quandary. I want to push him away, but without his arm to lean on, I might fall over. "Are you really here to see a policeman friend of yours?"

"You got me! No, I'm not." He laughs. "I mean, I've talked to some of the cops before, and it *has* been friendly. But I'm really here to talk to you. I heard there had been another murder at Egret's Loft and that you were coming by to give a statement today."

The hairs on the back of my neck stand at attention. News does travel fast. "Why would you want to talk to me?"

He leans in closer. With my arm on his, I can feel his pulse speed up. "I know you were the one who reported finding the body. And I want your side of the story, of course."

"What story is that?" I ask, confused.

"The twisted and homicidal underbelly of a premier American retirement community. Four murders in as many months. Multiple killers. And, from what I hear, you've been at the center of all of it!"

I blush, wondering if Detective Fletcher has been bragging about my contributions to the investigations. "I wouldn't say I'm at the *center* of anything. I've just helped out where I can."

"Don't be so modest," he teases. "You're a critical part of this whole story! Which brings me to why I'm here. I'm an investigative reporter. My last podcast, *Everything's Deadlier in Texas*, won a few awards. Maybe you've heard of it?"

"Your pod-what? Is that some kind of new show on Netflix?"

"No, it's a *podcast*. You know, a personal on-demand broadcast. Podcast." When he realizes that I still don't have the foggiest clue what he's talking about, he adds, "It's an audio series you can download from the internet."

"It's an audio show. Like on the radio?" It seems odd to me that this new generation, with their fancy, color flatscreen TVs, would want to go back to listening to programs on the radio.

"Kind of like that, sure," he dismissively concedes. "Anyway. I'm starting a new series about Egret's Loft. And I want you for the pilot."

I frown. "You want me to be your pilot? But I don't know how to fly a plane."

"No, no!" He shakes his head, then takes a deep, steadying breath. "The show pilot. It's what they call the first show. Never mind. What I'm trying to say is, I'm making a new…audio show…and I want to interview *you* for my first episode. What do you think?"

Clint was interviewed about his cases more than once by the media. He liked to say that, while there were some good reporters, most thought that the "facts" they printed were too good to be double-checked. He also thought that crime reporters focused far too much on the killers and far too *little* on the victims.

"If it's a show about the murders, wouldn't it be better to interview Detective Fletcher? Or one of the victim's family members? I mean, they're their stories. Not mine."

"I am going to interview them," he insists. "Later. But for the first episode, I really need you."

"Surely you don't need me." I glance at the door to the police station, worried that I'm now running late for my appointment with Detective Fletcher. "I'm sorry, but I really need to get going. Would you mind helping me to the door?"

His body doesn't move, but his facial expression becomes more intense. "You don't understand. I *do* need you. The show is called, 'The Mysterious Stranger.' Which means I need to *talk to* the mysterious stranger!"

"Are you saying that's me? This mysterious stranger?" I ask.

"Yes!" He grabs my hand. "Exactly! Now you get it!"

I tilt my head to the side and frown. "But what's mysterious about me? I do like my privacy, mind you. But my life is an open book. Always has been."

He leans in closer, and when he speaks, there is a theatrical quality to his nasally voice. "I'll paint the picture for you. Are you ready? Here we go. From out of nowhere, a stunning older woman moves into a luxury retirement community—"

"Out of nowhere?" I cut him off. "I moved here from Washington, DC!"

He ignores my interruption. "Less than a day after she moves in, people who live on her street start dying. She entangles herself in the police investigations, claiming a tenuous link to law enforcement—"

"Tenuous?" I stutter. "My late husband, may he rest in peace, earned his shield before you were even born."

"Shhh." He puts his finger to his mouth. "You're not listening. You're not paying attention to how all of this looks from the outside. I mean, there were zero murders reported at Egret's Loft, until last November. Until you moved in. Now, there have been four in as many months. You found this latest body, *and* you've been leading the police around by the nose. *You're* the one who *solved*—" he makes air quotes with his fingers, "—the earlier murders. You really didn't think that would start to make people suspicious?"

I have no idea what he's driving at. "Suspicious? Of what?"

The look he sends me can only be described as patronizing. "I hate to be the one to break this to you, Madeline, but there are a lot of internet sleuths out there who think you may be the *real* killer. And that you're using your Helen

Mirren looks and June Cleaver wholesomeness to dupe the police by framing innocent people for *your* crimes."

"My crimes? What are you saying? That I killed them all and then somehow convinced the police that other people were guilty?" I exclaim. "I'll have you know, I was almost killed last year. Twice!"

His eyebrows shoot up toward his widow's peak. "Oh my gosh! What happened?"

His sudden change in tone draws my suspicion. "Are you recording me right now? For your radio show?"

"It's called a podcast," he corrects me. "And it wouldn't be against the law if I was."

I fume silently. "What's it called? This show of yours."

"The working title is *Serial Seniors*. Why?"

"Well," I huff, "now I can tell all my friends *not* to listen to your little show. You should be ashamed of yourself. Trying to trick an older woman into talking to you so you can accuse her of murder. If you were my son, I'd take you over my knee this instant!"

"Yeah, right. Good luck with that," he scoffs.

"There's no reason to be rude!" I scold him. "I would appreciate it if you would delete any recording you may have of me and never speak to me again."

"Fine." He shrugs. "Not being willing to talk only makes you look guiltier."

"The only thing I'm guilty of is thinking you were a nice

person," I say, still clutching his arm for support. "Now, help me to the front door or, so help me, I'll track down your mother and have a word with her about the deplorable way you treat your elders!"

Eight

"A reporter wants *you* to be his first interview about the murder?" Detective Fletcher barely tries to hide his disappointment.

"Don't worry. I told him in no uncertain terms that I wasn't interested," I attempt to reassure him. "I value my privacy."

He raises one eyebrow. "It's just other people's you don't mind invading?"

I frown. "Now, I know you're upset at not being asked first, but that's no reason to be snarky. I get enough of that kind of behavior from my children."

"Sorry, Madeline." Detective Fletcher sighs. "It's just that I'd never been involved in a homicide investigation until recently, and I was hoping some positive press about solving the cases would help my book sales."

In his spare time, Detective Fletcher writes murder mysteries. I'd actually read one of them before we met.

"I understand. Weddings aren't cheap. I suppose a little extra income wouldn't hurt in covering some of the expenses." I hazard a guess at his unspoken feelings.

Detective Fletcher runs a hand over his bald head. "It's not the wedding I'm worried about. Nancy's fine with tying the knot at the courthouse. But she mentioned once, when we first started seeing each other, that she's always wanted to go to Tahiti. I want to be the one to take her. On our honeymoon."

"I had no idea you were such a romantic," I tease.

"Yeah, well. Don't go spreading it around. I'm pretty fond of my privacy too."

"Privacy about what?" Junior Detective Samantha Baptiste surprises us both by saying. She must have returned from her coffee run while we were deep in conversation.

"Nothing." Detective Fletcher swivels his desk chair to face his computer. "Madeline's here to give her statement about Friday morning. I'm just going to fill in the top of this form, and then we'll get started."

"I'm glad you're here," Detective Baptiste says to me, pulling up a chair alongside mine and sitting down. "I had a few questions of my own about Marjorie's murder."

Detective Fletcher glances up from his computer

monitor to scowl at his partner. "I've got this covered, Sammy."

Her eyes widen, and she puts a hand over her chest. "I'm sure you do, boss. It's just, when I ran into Madeline at the pool yesterday morning, she said she was waiting for her swim instructor to arrive." Her eyes harden as they settle on my face. "Was it Savannah Jeffers you were waiting for, by any chance?"

"Yes," I confirm, not wanting to give any more information until I know where this line of questioning is headed.

"What time were you supposed to meet her there?" she asks.

"Eight o'clock."

"And she wasn't there when you got to the pool?"

"No. Why?"

Detective Baptiste leans back in her chair, but her muscles remain tense. "I just can't help wondering if maybe she didn't arrive before you. You know, to get set up for the class."

"You would have seen her if she did, wouldn't you? After all, you were there before Curt and I arrived," I gently remind her. "Why were you there, again? I'm sure you said something about meeting someone. But I can't remember who you said that was."

Her dark eyes narrow. "As I said at the time, that's police business."

I turn to Detective Fletcher, eager to watch him grill his

junior detective about what she was doing at the crime scene before the body was discovered. For whatever reason, he chooses not to. He just stares at his computer keyboard, biting his lip as he uses his right index finger to type in the letters that spell out my name.

"Back to the point." Detective Baptiste leans forward, resting her arm on the corner of her partner's desk. "How was Savannah acting when she arrived at the pool? Was anything off about her demeanor?"

"Savannah?" I ask, somewhat perplexed. "You can't be serious. I may not know her well, but I do know that she's late for absolutely everything. Don't get me wrong, she has a great work ethic. It's just paired with a horrible sense of time. I can't picture her arriving anywhere *ahead* of schedule. Not to mention, the girl only moved here a few months ago with her mother. Why on Earth would she want to kill Marjorie?"

"Helen's like an aunt to her, right?" Detective Baptiste counters. "And, from what I hear, even after Helen was cleared of her husband's murder, Marjorie still went to the board, trying to get Helen kicked out of Egret's Loft. That must have made Helen pretty upset."

Helen Richards, a sexagenarian Southern belle fond of skintight clothing and plastic surgery, lives across the street from me. A widow eight times over, her real name is Doreen Deluca, and she's from New Jersey. We only discovered that she'd been living under a secret identity when she was recently accused of killing husband number eight.

During the investigation into his death, it came out that she'd been in the Witness Protection Program for decades after the mob murdered husband number two. Savannah's mother, Jolene, had been Helen's case agent, and the two women became good friends.

But this is the first I've heard anything about Marjorie trying to have Helen evicted from the community.

"You're very well informed," I remark, wondering where Detective Baptiste has been getting her information. "It's curious you've taken such an interest in our little community."

"I'd take an interest in any community with a murder rate as high as Egret's Loft's."

I can't deny the logic of her statement, but it still doesn't explain what she was doing at the River Club on the morning Marjorie died. Who could she have possibly been there to meet? Was it the same person sharing gossip about Helen's near eviction?

"Well," I say, clutching the handles of the handbag in my lap a little tighter. "Unfortunately, after I saw you in the parking lot, I didn't see anything suspicious. Except, of course, for Marjorie's body in the swimming pool. And that's what I'm here to give my statement about. The sooner I can do that, the sooner I can go home and leave you fine detectives to do your jobs."

Detective Fletcher snorts, then quickly clears his throat to cover his involuntary derision.

"I hope you *will* leave us to do our jobs," Detective Baptiste says, standing up and looking down at me. "You should know by now, trying to catch a killer can be hazardous to your health."

With that, Detective Baptiste turns, walks across the large open-plan office, and heads into the break room.

"Was she threatening me?" I whisper to Detective Fletcher once his partner is out of earshot. "That sounded like a threat."

"To be fair, two killers *have* tried to do you in," he points out, while continuing to slowly type.

"Yes, yes. But doesn't it seem a bit odd that your partner was at the River Club Friday morning? Right before Curt and I found Marjorie's body? I mean, she keeps falling back on her presence there being due to police business. You're police too. Has she told *you* why she was there?"

His fingers hesitate above the keyboard. "I can neither confirm nor deny—"

"So, she *did* tell you!" I interrupt. "Come on, then. You can tell *me*."

"I just said I couldn't—"

"And we both know that you can. And will. Eventually. So why not just tell me now? It really will save us both so much time," I argue.

Detective Fletcher turns to face me. "You're impossible sometimes."

"Was she really meeting someone there?" I ignore his comment. "And, if so, who?"

He sighs, glancing quickly toward the break room before whispering. "Marjorie. Alright? She was there to meet Marjorie."

I hadn't been expecting that. "She was supposed to meet the dead woman?"

Detective Fletcher nods, warming to his subject. "Apparently, Marjorie sent Sammy a text the night before, saying she needed to speak with her right away about something of 'vital importance.' They agreed to meet, at the pool, first thing on Friday morning."

"Why would Marjorie text Detective Baptiste?" I ask.

"You remember back in November, when Sammy was interviewing everyone at Egret's Loft who had items stolen from their homes?"

"Of course." My own security camera had been taken by thieves who'd been sneaking into residents' homes in search of jewelry and electronics.

"She gave Marjorie her business card. It had her cell number on it." Detective Fletcher shrugs. "I guess that's why Marjorie texted her."

"Have you seen the text messages? What time was their last communication? What else did Marjorie say?"

"I don't know," he admits. "I haven't seen the messages."

"Don't you have a right to see them? I mean, it could help with determining the time of death. Not to mention, there might be clues about what Marjorie wanted to talk to Detective Baptiste about. Maybe it was something that relates to her murder."

"Don't you think I know that?" he demands, still whispering.

"Then why haven't you forced your partner to show you the messages?"

He rubs his thumb and middle finger across his temples, like he's trying to massage out a gnawing headache. "Because I can't. She deleted them."

"Deleted them?" The words come out louder than I'd intended them. Lowering my voice, I ask, "Why would she do a thing like that?"

He exhales deeply. "Sammy said she always deletes messages from her sources right away. That it's her way of protecting them, apparently. I guess it makes sense."

"Protecting them? Or herself?" I wonder aloud.

Detective Fletcher looks up at me from under the hand kneading his forehead. "What is that supposed to mean? I know she can be super annoying and…overeager…at times, but you can't think Sammy had anything to do with this!"

"No. Of course not," I say, though I'm not convinced. If she had considered Marjorie a source, then it makes sense that Detective Baptiste was cagey with me at the River Club about who she was planning to meet. But it does seem strange that, if Detective Baptiste took Marjorie's messages seriously, she didn't walk around the River Club looking for Marjorie when she was late for their meeting. When I saw the detective, she'd been climbing into her car to leave. "What about Marjorie's phone? Wouldn't she have a copy of the message?"

"We can't find Marjorie's phone. It wasn't at the pool, and the family says it's not in her house either."

For now, at least, the text message is a dead end.

"And Detective Baptiste has no idea what Marjorie was planning to talk to her about?" I press.

Detective Fletcher shakes his head. "Sammy says she doesn't. Now, can we get on with taking your statement? I have to meet with the coroner in an hour."

As I recount the events of Friday morning to Detective Fletcher, my mind hums along in the background.

If it's true that Marjorie tried to meet with the detective before she died, it's possible whatever information she'd wanted to pass along got her murdered. Which means discovering Marjorie's secret could lead us straight to her killer.

NINE

"Detective Fletcher's tryin' to stitch me up for *another* murder?" Helen shakes her head, her bleached blond hair flying. "Why, that man couldn't find his own butt with two hands in his back pockets!"

"Hold on a minute, Helen," I caution my neighbor. I'd walked over to her house immediately after Detective Fletcher dropped me off at mine. I wanted to warn her that she might be on the local police's suspect list once again. "It's not Detective Fletcher asking questions, it's his partner. She knew that Marjorie tried to get you kicked out of Egret's Loft."

"That silly old cow," Jolene, Helen's friend and former Witness Protection Program case worker, chimes in. "I know it's not becomin' to speak ill of the dead, but Marjorie was stuck up higher than a light pole! What right did she have to try and kick Helen out of her home?"

I hold up my hands, seeking calm. "Be that as it may, Marjorie's actions could appear to have given Helen a motive to kill her. Did you and she...have words...before she died?"

It's a loaded question. As I've experienced firsthand, Helen has a bit of a temper.

"We sure enough did!" Helen confirms. I wince. "Now don't go makin' faces at me, Madeline. I wasn't supposed to confront the woman who was spreadin' lies about me to everyone in town? But you know what she said?" Without waiting for a reply, Helen continues, "She told me she didn't know what I was talking about. Can you believe the nerve? Lyin' to my face like that. I told her, I said, 'Marjorie, don't pee down my leg and try to convince me it's rainin'!' She seemed to think I was born yesterday."

"Did anyone witness your...altercation?" I ask.

"I was there," Jolene says. "There wasn't nobody else 'round though. And, if you ask me, Helen was mighty restrained in how she dealt with the old bat. I wouldn't've been so nice."

"Thank you kindly, Jolene, but even my own mama wouldn't accuse me of being nice to Marjorie. I admit to that," Helen says. "But I wasn't the only one who had an ax to grind with the ole coot. Marjorie had a knack for rubbin' people the wrong way. Has your detective friend talked to Jinny at all?"

"Jinny?" I frown. "She and Marjorie were friends, weren't they?"

Helen tilts her head, and her forehead shifts slightly. I get the impression she's trying to raise her eyebrows, but multiple Botox injections prevent any actual movement.

"They *used* to be," Helen says. "Up until Marjorie accused Jinny's grandson, Paul, of not returning somethin' he stole from her house back in November. There was an awful fierce dustup about that."

In an effort to help a friend through tough financial times, the teenaged Paul had pilfered items from multiple houses throughout the community. Though misguided, he was a nice boy, and no one had opted to press charges against him. Provided all the stolen items were returned.

If Marjorie had claimed her items weren't returned, the possibility existed that Paul could go to jail. Jinny would have been none too happy about that, which would explain the hostile look I'd seen pass between the two women during the party at the Golf Club on Thursday night.

"Did anyone else see them fighting about it?" I ask, knowing the detectives wouldn't take Helen's word alone that there was bad blood between Jinny and Marjorie.

"Let me think for a minute." Helen pauses, her eyes squinting, as she stares at nothing in particular. When she snaps her fingers, it startles me so much I think I may have peed a little. "That's right, it was at the River Club! The two of 'em were down there on Wednesday for lunch. Not together. They were eatin' separate. But when it kicked off —" she whistles, "—well, they made such a ruckus it would wake a possum."

While I'm generally fond of Helen's eccentric Southern phrases, right now, they're eating up precious time. I have to meet Gina at the Golf Club in half an hour to size up another suspect. But I try to swallow my impatience before asking again, "Was there anyone else there?"

Helen twirls a strand of platinum-dyed hair around her finger. "Come to think of it, I think that handsy golf pro was at the bar orderin' an iced tea."

"Dom Skellig?" I want to clarify, since Dom only seems to be handsy with Helen.

"Yeah, that's the one. Shorts so short you can practically see to the promised land," Helen confirms. "I think the Russki was there, too, havin' lunch."

"Natasha, my Russian neighbor? Or Fred's wife, Svetlana?" Though I think the latter is actually from Lithuania and probably wouldn't appreciate being referred to as Russian.

"Naw, not that one. It was your new neighbor. Natasha." Helen's nose flares slightly. I can't help but wonder if Helen's not a little jealous of the beautiful and effortlessly graceful Natasha. "I reckon she saw the fight too."

"I'll be sure to pass that along to Detective Fletcher," I

say, trying to calm Helen. "To be honest, though, Jinny doesn't strike me as the killing kind. She's just so...so...pink."

Jolene nods. "I know what you mean. Does the woman not own anything in another color?"

Helen leans in closer. "Once, I saw her wearing a tracksuit...in salmon!"

I frown. "Isn't salmon just another shade of pink?"

"She only wore it once?" Jolene barrels over my question.

Helen shrugs. "Yeah. And she only wore it in the mornin'. She'd changed by the afternoon. Told me she thought the color made her look like a harlot."

Jolene, whose own clothes are slightly worn, shakes her head. "Rich people are so wasteful."

Checking my watch, I remember there's one more question I wanted to ask. "I heard that Fred Burrows used to date Marjorie before he married Svetlana. Apparently, it wasn't an amicable breakup. Do you know anything about that?"

Helen's blue eyes widen. "You're right! It clear slipped my mind. Fred. That's who the police should be talkin' to! Why, Marjorie tried to bump him off not so long ago. Sent him chocolates with nuts, even though he's allergic. His throat closed up tighter than a bullfrog's butt."

Gina had mentioned the same incident to me earlier this morning. She also said the breakup had something to do with Fred giving Marjorie a present she didn't want. Maybe Helen knows more about what the gift was and why it made Marjorie so upset. "Do you know why Marjorie and Fred broke up?"

"Well," Helen considers. "I don't want to be the one spreadin' rumors…"

"Of course, you don't," I assure her. "But it could help with the investigation."

"In that case, I don't repeat gossip. So, listen carefully." Helen, who doesn't need much prodding to spill the beans, leans in, conspiratorially. "You didn't hear this from me, but I heard he gave her a little more than a good time in the bedroom. If you know what I mean."

I wait for Helen to say more. She doesn't. I look at Jolene. She shakes her head.

"I'm sorry. I'm afraid I don't know what you mean," I admit.

"An STD!" Helen blurts. "He gave her an STD. Quite frankly, I wouldn't have thought he had it in him to court two women at the same time. The man has the personality of a dishrag."

Realization dawns, and warmth floods my cheeks. Before I moved into Egret's Loft, Ritchie had left a pamphlet on the table of my Washington, DC, house warning that sexually transmitted diseases were on the rise in retirement communities. I'd promptly put the pamphlet in the trash and neither of us ever mentioned it again.

Fortunately, Helen's front door opens, and I'm spared the embarrassment of any further details of Marjorie's "gift" from Fred. Savannah and Sydney, both giggling and excited, enter the living room.

"Miss Helen," Savannah practically curtsies. "We were wonderin' if we could borrow some beach towels."

"You sure can. But why do y'all need towels? Can't you just get some from the pool?" Helen queries.

"We were actually thinking of going to the beach for a little while," Sydney answers for her friend. "I have the rest of the afternoon off, and we thought a little change of scenery might be nice."

Jolene scowls at her daughter. "You told me you were goin' to spend the day lookin' for a job. You can't just rest on your laurels, missy. You need to start payin' off your student loans."

Savannah notices I'm in the room and blushes. She can still be painfully shy around me, especially when her mother is scolding her.

An uncomfortable silence descends. Eventually, Helen excuses herself to go find some beach towels for the girls.

"I actually do have work, Mama," Savannah finally says. "Sydney asked me to help her do some content writin' for the Egret's Loft blog. And I'm gonna help out with an interactive marketin' project she's workin' on."

Sydney rests a hand on Savannah's arm for support.

"I'm sure I have no idea what any of those words mean,"

Jolene says, then a smile breaks out on her face. "But if you're gettin' paid for your writin', sweetpea, then all I can say is I'm proud of you."

Desperate to change the subject and even more eager to get information, I turn to Sydney and say, "Terrible thing about Marjorie Higginbottom, isn't it?"

Sydney looks down at her flip-flops, her cheerful smile disappearing. "It's super sad. I still can't believe she's really gone."

"Did you know her well?" I ask.

She looks at me, the living room light reflecting off her large glasses. "I mean, I spent some time with her. She had me over to her house a couple of times. You know, for work. I used her in some promo videos, and she helped me out when I needed volunteers for my new marketing project, but we weren't particularly close or anything."

"Pardon me for asking," I begin, "but I happened to notice you followed her after she got into an argument with the new chef on Thursday night. Did she mention what the fight was about?"

"Oh, she didn't have to tell me what it was about. I heard it myself," Sydney says, using her thumb and forefinger to raise her large, dark-framed glasses higher on her face.

That's what I'd been hoping she would say. "Really? What happened?"

"Marjorie accused David...that's the chef's name," she

explains, a slight blush coloring the very pale skin of her cheeks. "Anyway, she accused him of trying to poison her."

My pulse quickens. "Poison? She thought he was trying to *murder* her?"

"David tried to kill her?" Savannah hands fly up to the side of her face. "No way!"

"Whoa! Gosh, no. Nothing like that," Sydney says quickly. "She was talking about the food at the buffet! Said it could give her E. coli or Listeria or whatever. She was going on and on about foodborne illnesses and their impact on...um...active elders."

Remembering that Curt had given me a very similar warning about the buffet that evening, which Marjorie probably overheard, I'm filled with guilt. She may have taken my grandson's slightly paranoid opinions as facts, then used them against the new chef.

"How did David react?" I ask.

"How do you think?" Sydney asks and answers her own question. "He was totally furious. I asked Marjorie if maybe we could discuss the whole thing somewhere a little more, you know, private. But she didn't want to talk. She just rode off on her scooter."

"Did you see her again after that?" Savannah, her shyness forgotten, demands to know.

Sydney shakes her head. "No. Right after the party, I went to see my parents. They live about forty miles from here. I stayed there until I had to come back here for the big welcome dinner. The board wanted me to post stuff about the meal on social."

"I got your towels." Helen breezes back into the room.

As the young girls thank my neighbor, I take the opportunity to excuse myself and slip outside into the blazing midday sun.

Gina will be expecting me at the Golf Club in a few minutes. And now, when we question David, I'll need to figure out if having Marjorie accuse him of trying to poison her was enough to make him want to kill her for real.

Ten

Gina and I lock eyes across the crowded dining room. She breaks the contact to glance at the clock on the far wall, then she looks back at me. I shrug.

Kids have a way of messing up even the best laid plans.

Ritchie, Craig, and Curt were still out when I returned from Helen's house. I'd intended to sneak into the garage and steal away on my golf cart before the others realized I'd returned, but Eliza anticipated me.

Throwing open the side door leading from the house to the garage, she'd loomed on the step above me like an avenging angel, insisting we go to lunch as a family. I couldn't refuse. I did try, but my granddaughters were having none of it.

Their mother trained them well.

Gina had arrived without her family, which tells me that her time here is limited. Sooner or later, someone will come looking for her. Hopefully, we'll get a chance to talk to the chef before that happens.

My attention is drawn back to the table when Tom's phone starts to ring.

"Ugh, this guy again," Tom complains.

Eliza stops short of putting a forkful of salad in her mouth. "Who is it, babe?"

Tom silences his phone. "Some guy named Brock Leitman. At first, I thought he was an especially persistent telemarketer. But he's been calling all morning and leaving voicemails, asking me to call him back. I have no idea what he wants."

I set down my own salad fork, my appetite gone.

"Brock Leitman?" Eliza's eyebrows draw closer together. "Why does that name sound familiar?"

"He's a reporter," I explain, my stomach feeling queasy. "He has a radio show."

"Oh, right," Eliza says. "Except it's called a podcast, Mom. Not a radio show. Isn't he the one who did the show on the Griner case in Texas?"

I frown. "The Griner case?"

"That was the name of the couple. Really wealthy, lived outside Dallas. They were—" looking over at Tory and Emmy happily dipping their chicken nuggets in ketchup, she whispers, "—slaughtered in their house a couple of years ago, along with the husband's eighty-year-old mother, who was dying of cancer. There was an eyewitness. A woman named Denise Kramer, the hospice volunteer. Denise said the wife's sister killed them all because she was broke and needed the inheritance. The sister denied it, but she was found guilty and went to jail."

"Daddy, what's jail?" five-year-old Tory asks, her big blue eyes focused on Tom.

"Well, princess, let's just say if you always do everything your mom tells you to do, you'll never have to find out." Tom ruffles his daughter's hair. She giggles. "I think I've heard of this," Tom says after Tory has resumed eating. "Wasn't someone else arrested as a result of the show?"

Eliza nods, chewing a piece of lettuce. "Yeah. Brock Leitman did a little digging and found out the hospice volunteer was wanted in Florida on Medicare fraud, identity theft, you name it. She'd moved to Texas and started using her maiden name. Which is why the cops didn't put it together. Anyway, Brock theorized Denise killed the Griners. The mother had left Denise a little money in her will and Denise figured, if they were all dead or in jail, she'd get the whole lot."

"How awful," I sympathize. "Has the sister been released?"

Eliza shakes her head. "Not yet. Prosecutors are still building their case against Denise. She's in jail, though, on the earlier fraud charges. All because of the show. It was really popular."

"Okay, so this guy did a good thing," Tom agrees, "but it doesn't explain why he's calling me. What does he want?"

"I'm sorry, Tom. He's using you to get to me," I admit.

"Mom," Eliza draws out the syllable. "What are you talking about?"

I sigh. "I met him this morning outside the police station. He's doing a radiocast on the murders at Egret's Loft, and he wants to interview me for the first program."

Tom sucks in his breath and looks at Eliza. I can practically see the steam coming out of my daughter's ears.

"He wants to do what?" Eliza says, loud enough to draw the attention of Dr. Frank Rosen's family, who are sitting at the table next to us.

"Please, lower your voice, dear. I'm not a child," I remind her. "And there's nothing to worry about. I told him I had no interest in talking to him."

"Fine, but why is he here? Is he here investigating Marjorie's murder? I mean, coming off the Griner case, why would he care about the death of one little old lady?"

"I thought we weren't supposed to use the word 'old' around here," Tom interjects.

Eliza glares at her husband. "Tom, I love you, but don't start with me right now."

Three-year-old Emmy, sensing tension at the table, is now staring at us, tears forming in her eyes.

I keep my tone light, for Emmy's sake, as I respond. "Let's not blow this out of proportion. We all know it's ridiculous. But to answer your question, I did get the impression that Brock Leitman thinks I might be the real killer at Egret's Loft."

Tom's jaw drops open.

"*What*?" Eliza practically screams. Everyone in the restaurant is now looking our direction.

I'm wishing I could melt into the floor.

Tom tells Eliza to calm down, Eliza gets angrier at the suggestion that she's not being calm already, and Emmy starts wailing in large, distressed gulps.

"Come to Grandma, sweetie," I say, sliding Emmy out of her booster seat and onto my lap. She tucks her head into my collarbone as I whisper, "Everything's going to be alright."

"I need to call Ritchie. Enough is enough," Eliza says as she pulls her phone out of her purse. "Mom, you can't stay here anymore. This place is insane."

Tom puts his hand on Eliza's arm. "Sweetheart, I understand you're upset. But let's try to think about this rationally."

"Oh, so I'm not rational anymore? I'm sorry. An investigative reporter is planning to accuse my mother of murder! And you think I'm overreacting? Why didn't you tell me about this right away, Mom?" Eliza demands, and then her face freezes in horror. "Oh my gosh, is that blood?"

I follow her pointing finger and see an angry red stain on my white top. I feel my heart beating against my rib cage. "I don't think so. I don't remember cutting myself. But with those new blood thinners the doctor prescribed, I really bleed a lot."

"Everybody just take a deep breath," Tom advises. "It's not blood. It's ketchup. Emmy's a messy eater."

I glance down at Emmy, her eyes watery and her mouth smeared with the condiment. My pulse returns to normal. In my peripheral vision, I catch a glimpse of Gina, impatiently pacing by the door that leads out of the restaurant.

She must be nearly out of time.

Sensing I now have an excuse to sneak away for a few minutes, I say, "If I don't clean this up now, it'll never come out." Handing Emmy to Tom, I stand up from the table. "I'll be back soon."

"We're not done talking about this, Mom," Eliza warns me as I start to walk away.

Striding as quickly as I can toward the door, I avoid eye contact with Hugh Darcy, who's seated at a table across from a lovely Hispanic woman with a wide smile and kind eyes. As I'm wondering if that's Viviana, the woman he'd mentioned in our earlier conversation, it occurs to me that Gina is no longer pacing near the exit.

Hopefully, she didn't have to leave before I could free myself from the family lunch.

"*Psst*," a voice whispers from an alcove near the

restrooms. I turn, and to my relief, see Gina. She spots the stain on my shirt. "What in the heck happened to you?"

I wave away her concern. "My granddaughter's food missed her mouth. Shall we go speak to the chef?"

"I've been waiting on you. I thought you were gonna be there all day." Her voice is laced with frustration. "We've got to make this quick. Nicole expects me back to take Sabina to the bouncy castle they set up in the park."

"Alright, let's go. How do we get into the kitchen?"

Gina points at my shirt. "You sure you don't want to clean that up first?"

"Are you kidding? You know this isn't coming out with soap and water."

"True," she concedes. "What do you use? Baking soda?"

"I was thinking vinegar would probably do a better job."

"Yuck." Gina sticks her tongue out. "The smell of vinegar always makes me gag."

"Really? Fine, baking soda it is. But, either way, you know where they have baking soda and vinegar?"

Gina smiles. "The kitchen."

"Exactly! And while I'm cleaning my shirt we can try to find out if the new chef killed Marjorie."

Before I become a suspect in her death too.

Eleven

The first thing I see are all the knives. They're everywhere.

One blade, sharpened to a razor's edge, is slicing through onions that make my eyes water, even from a distance.

Hovering near the swinging kitchen door, I watch as David, the chef I saw fighting with Marjorie on Thursday night, ruthlessly savages the vegetables, his hand rhythmically rising and falling as he quickly reduces the large onion into slivers the size of grains of rice.

In unspoken agreement, Gina and I decide to begin asking questions only after he sets down the knife. The decision allows me the freedom to observe him as he leans against the stainless-steel workstation in the middle of the hectic kitchen.

He appears to be in his early thirties, with a head of thick, wavy, black hair, golden skin, and a deep cleft in his chin, partially hidden beneath a dark, five o'clock shadow. Overall, he's very handsome and it dawns on me that his good looks are probably behind the blush on Sydney's face when his name came up in conversation earlier.

Concentrating intently on his work, David doesn't even notice our presence. Other workers in the kitchen sneak glances at us but seem too afraid of their boss to draw attention to us and, by extension, themselves.

Suddenly, the door behind us swings open, bumping Gina from behind and nearly knocking her over. The person on the other side of the door, who clearly wasn't expecting resistance when they went to push it open, yelps, and we hear plates crashing onto the floor.

David whirls around, the knife still clutched in his hand, and his face stormy. "Who are you? And what are you doing in my kitchen?"

Manners dictate I should try and assist the poor young waitress, now covered in food and trying to clean up broken plates from the floor. My survival instinct, on the other hand, won't allow me to look away from the business end of the pungent blade held in David's hand.

"I'm sorry, young man. We didn't mean to cause any trouble," I begin, my hands held high as if in surrender. "I got some ketchup on my shirt, so we came in here, hoping you might have some vinegar."

Gina elbows me, whispering, "I thought we agreed it would be baking soda."

"Right. I meant baking soda," I correct myself. "I need some baking soda to clean my shirt before the stain sets in. I'm sure you, of all people, can appreciate how difficult it can be to get stains out of whites."

I try to give him my most disarming smile. He scowls at me in response.

After a brief staring match, he sighs and snaps the fingers on his free hand. "Sonya. Baking soda. Now."

A terrified-looking girl, who can't be a day over eighteen, scampers off to another part of the kitchen.

"I'm Gina. My husband is on the board here," Gina says in a way that implies she brought a figurative gun to David's literal knife fight. He lowers the blade. She smiles and adds, "You're the new chef. Darren, right?"

"David," the chef and I say in unison.

A quizzical expression briefly crosses his face, then he seems to lose interest. "Sonya will be back with your baking soda. Then you can leave."

Before he can turn his back on us, I say, a little too loudly, "It must be exciting being a chef. I bet you've worked in a lot of kitchens. I can barely manage mine. All the appliances are a lot...smarter than they were in my day. Far too smart for me, in fact."

"Uh huh," he grunts, and returns to chopping onions, thoroughly disinterested in us.

Turning to Gina, I shrug. She tilts her head, her eyes shifting back and forth between me and David, encouraging me to get back in the ring for round two.

"Are you from the area, or did you move here for the job?" I try again to engage him.

He doesn't turn around, but says, "I'm from Texas but have been working in Miami."

"Miami? That sounds glamorous. What made you come here?"

The knife halts mid-slice. "Glamour isn't all it's cracked up to be."

Something in the tone of his voice electrifies the tiny hairs at the back of my neck.

"My daughter lives in Miami," I persist. "She and her husband love to eat out. Where did you work? They've probably been there."

"Sonya," David calls out, ignoring my question. "Did you find the baking soda?"

Out of the corner of my eye, I see Gina stepping sideways, moving toward a row of shelves built into the wall, holding cooking appliances like mixing bowls, industrial-sized utensils, and a mortar and pestle shaped like a turtle. Pulling a pair of glasses out of her handbag, she leans in closer.

"I found it." The young kitchen worker returns from a side room, practically bowing as she presents the box of baking soda to David.

"It's not for me," he snaps. "Give it to those ladies and then show them the door."

Realizing that my window of opportunity to question David is rapidly closing, I attempt using the direct approach.

"Pardon an old woman's curiosity—" my use of the forbidden word is enough to make him turn around in surprise, "—but Marjorie was my neighbor. I saw you two exchanging heated words the night before she died. Do you mind me asking what upset you both so much?"

His eyes narrow. "I hardly see how that's important."

"I'm sure it's not," I do my best to assure him. "But I'd still like to know."

He grabs the box of baking soda from the hands of the young girl, then flicks his wrist in dismissal. It's enough to send her running for safety.

"If you must know," he says on a deep exhale, "she was complaining about some of the food. As if everything in the buffet should have been catered to her individual taste. She got upset when I didn't bend over backward for her, and I got annoyed by her incessant prattling. There really wasn't much to it."

I frown. "Really? I heard she accused you of trying to poison residents with foodborne illnesses and you took considerable offense."

The heat from the ovens is no match for his boiling temper. "Who told you that?"

All of a sudden, it feels wrong to tattle on Sydney. I suspect she has a bit of a crush on the handsome, if ill-tempered, culinarian. "I really wish I could remember. But that's the thing about aging. Sometimes you forget what you're thinking, even while you're thinking it."

"Then think harder," he says through clenched teeth. "I have a right to know if someone is implying that I had anything to do with that pompous windbag's death!"

"Well now, that's not a very nice thing to say about a dead woman," I point out.

He takes a step toward me, still holding the knife. "Who told you?"

The once-bustling kitchen has fallen silent, and all the workers are now blatantly staring, waiting to see what happens next.

Gina grabs my elbow and begins to gently tug me toward a side door, urgently whispering, "Let's go, Mandy."

"Can I at least have the baking soda?" I ask. "Otherwise, this stain will be impossible to get out."

"No!" Gina hisses quietly. Then, flashing a wide smile for David as she inches us backward, she says, "So nice to meet you, Darren. I really like your cooking. It's delicious. And it's never made *me* sick."

She's timed our exit perfectly. We're through the door before David can throw anything at us.

As soon as we're in a back hallway, I shake her hand off

my elbow. "You could have at least waited until he'd given me something to clean my shirt."

"Are you for real? You were antagonizing a killer in there, and you're worried about your shirt?"

I chuckle. "Don't be silly. David isn't a killer."

She raises her eyebrows. "Umm. Is it time for new prescription glasses, Mandy? Did you not see the huge knife he was wielding at us?"

"Of course, I did," I assure her. "That's precisely why I'm not worried."

Gina puts her hands on her hips. "You're going to have to explain that one to me, hun."

"If he really *was* a killer," I explain, "he'd be doing everything he could to make us think he's *not* a killer. Since he was acting exactly like you'd expect a scary killer to act, it only makes sense that he can't be a killer. Understand?"

Gina shakes her head. "Not even a little. And for your information, it wasn't just the knife that made me nervous."

I nod. "Yeah, he really needs to get a better handle on his temper."

"That's not what I mean." Seeing someone that looks suspiciously like Eliza at the end of the hallway, Gina pulls me into a small alcove for privacy. "Let me ask you, has Detective Fleishner found the murder weapon yet?"

"Fletcher," I say, not knowing why I even bother anymore. "No, not as far as I know. But it wouldn't surprise me if his partner tries looking for it in Helen's house."

"The black widow again? What'd she do to get their attention this time?"

I answer her question with one of my own. "Did you hear anything about Marjorie trying to get Helen kicked out of Egret's Loft? Apparently, she took it to the board, so Leon must know about it."

"Oh yeah. I'd forgotten about that." Gina rolls her eyes. "Leon did mention it, but it just made us laugh. Marjorie was always complaining to the board about something or other. The grass cutters are too loud. The lake is too blue. The humidity's too high." Gina clears her throat. "I know it's wrong to criticize the dead, but she was a real piece of work. If that woman had won a million dollars, she'd have just moaned about the taxes."

"Really? I thought most people liked her? They always took her cookies."

"Taking a woman's cookies doesn't automatically make her your friend."

She's right. I took Marjorie's cookies on occasion, but, clearly, I had no idea what she was really like. Then I remember what started this conversation in the first place. "Why did you ask about the murder weapon?"

Gina looks in both directions and, seeing no one, whispers, "I think I found it."

"What?" I exclaim. "Where?"

"On the shelf, in the kitchen. I saw one of those things

—well, I guess it's a set. You know, one piece is a bowl and then there's a stick to grind things with…"

"You mean a mortar and pestle?" I ask, taking comfort in knowing that Leon does most of the cooking in their household.

"Yeah, exactly. I saw one in there. Shaped like a turtle. It was actually kind of nice."

My eyebrows knit together. "What makes you think it's the murder weapon?"

"The bottom of it was stained. Granted, it could have been tomato sauce. But why would that have been on the *bottom*?"

"I don't know." I shake my head. "That doesn't seem that suspicious. Kitchens can be messy places."

"Fair enough," Gina admits. "But does that explain why I saw a clump of pink hair stuck to one of the turtle's legs?"

My pulse quickens, and I start rummaging through my purse. "I need to call Detective Fletcher. If David thinks we're on to him, he might try to destroy the evidence!"

"So," Gina says, a smug look on her face, "now you think I might have been right about him being a killer?"

"I'm not saying that. I still don't think he did it."

"If you're so sure he's innocent, why don't you just go back in the kitchen and collect the evidence yourself?" Gina taunts.

My finger hovering over Detective Fletcher's contact

page on my phone, I say, "Need I remind you, I've almost been killed twice? It's not that I'm afraid to die—" I tap the button to call the detective, "—I'd just prefer not to be responsible for it happening."

Twelve

"You really have to hand it to the staff here," Ritchie says that evening when we arrive at the potluck being hosted for all the families. "This was supposed to be at the River Club, right?"

"Yeah. But why let a little murder get in the way of a good cookout?" Eliza deadpans, as Emmy attempts to drag her toward the petting zoo set up next to the pickleball court.

As part of the weekend's activities, the planning committee at Egret's Loft had arranged a barbecue for all the residents and their relatives. Since the River Club has temporarily been designated a crime scene, the venue had to be changed at the last minute. But you'd never know it looking at the setup.

Gas grills have been rolled onto the asphalt on one side

of the pickleball court, with cloth-covered folding tables and coolers on the other, hosting a variety of side dishes, desserts, and beverages brought by residents. In the middle, there are dozens of smaller tables, where families can sit while they eat. A Latin salsa band has claimed the bocce ball court as their makeshift stage, right next to a large bounce house for kids. Nearby, there's also a petting zoo, complete with pony rides, a waterpark fashioned with sprinklers, and a few Slip 'N Slides, like the ones Ritchie and Eliza played on when they were little.

I check my phone for the fifteenth time in the past ten minutes, anxious to hear back from Detective Fletcher.

"Still nothing?" Eliza asks, handing Emmy off to Tom so he can take their two daughters over to pet the baby llamas.

"No," I sigh. "I don't know what's taking so long. The board gave the police full access to the kitchen hours ago. Maybe Gina was wrong about what she thought she saw."

"I wouldn't know. I wasn't there," she chastises me. "Just so you know, I'm still not thrilled you were in the kitchen, talking to a possible murder suspect. You need to be more careful, Mom."

"I already told you. I was only in there to ask for baking soda to clean my shirt," I stretch the truth. "How could I have known the chef might be a murderer?"

"Uh huh," Eliza tuts, not buying my explanation for a second.

Craig eyes us both warily before turning to address Curt, "Hey, buddy, what do you say we go pet the animals with your cousins?"

Shock fills Curt's young face. "You've known me my whole life. What makes you think I would want to expose myself to potentially deadly animal-borne pathogens? Are you familiar with the symptoms of cryptosporidiosis? I assure you, they don't sound pleasant." He shakes his head. "Honestly, Poppa, it's like you don't even know me."

Craig sighs. "Fine. Should we go check and see if they have any Yoo-hoo in the coolers?"

"Now you're speaking my language," Curt says, allowing his father to lead him away.

"Phew, now that Craig's gone, I can talk about Marjorie's murder without getting threatened with divorce," Ritchie jokes, before handing off our tub of potato salad to one of the employees arranging the food table.

"You're just as bad as Mom." Eliza rolls her eyes.

"Then it's no wonder I'm her favorite child," Ritchie counters. "But there's something that's been bothering me. If the mortar *is* the murder weapon, why was it in the kitchen? I mean, Marjorie was at the bottom of the pool at the River Club. The kitchen's at the Golf Club. Why go to the trouble of putting it back? Especially if it was covered in blood and hair?"

"Are you thinking someone might be trying to frame

the chef?" I wonder aloud. It would make sense. The fight he had with Marjorie was very public.

"Or it was a double blind. He put it back himself so it would *look* like he was being framed," Eliza offers, then uses the palm of her hand to softly slap her own forehead. "Why am I encouraging this?"

I rest my hand on her shoulder. "Because your dad and I raised you right."

"Madeline?" a woman's melodic voice intones behind me.

Turning around, I see the woman who was having lunch with Hugh earlier. She appears to be about my age with box brown hair and impossibly white teeth.

"Yes, that's me." I extend my hand for her to shake while introducing my children. "You must be Viviana. I can't believe you live next door and we haven't met before now."

Viviana enthusiastically shakes our hands, energy humming through her fingertips. "I always stay away until after hurricane season. I went through enough of those working in Miami."

"I hear you," Eliza says. "I had to get a new roof after last season. Are you from Miami originally?"

"No." Viviana shakes her head so quickly back and forth it almost looks like she's not moving it at all. "I was born in Cuba. But after Fidel Castro took all my family's money and arrested my late husband, it didn't feel like home anymore. You know?"

"Yikes. Your husband was a political prisoner?" Ritchie grimaces. "If you don't mind my asking, was he ever released?"

"He was." She nods, her head bobbing faster than the wings of a hummingbird. "Though, later on, I almost wished he was still locked up." She laughs. "I'm teasing. My husband and I were always joking. He loved a good ribbing."

I return her smile, though, inside, I'm missing my Clint. He always knew how to make me laugh, even when I was angry at him.

"How long have you lived at Egret's Loft?" Ritchie asks Viviana, the conversation dragging me away from my self-pity.

"Five years now," she replies. "But I spend the summers with my son in California. He's a screenwriter. He was too busy to come out this weekend, though he assures me he'll make it up to me soon."

"What does he think about Egret's Loft?" Eliza asks. "I mean, it sounds like you were out on the West Coast, but surely you both heard about all the murders here late last year."

I glare at Eliza, but she keeps her eyes trained on Viviana, ignoring me.

Viviana's energy level drops significantly. "We did. It's hard to imagine terrible things like that happening here."

"And now it's happened again," Eliza presses on. "Did you know Marjorie well?"

I want to kick my daughter, but I hold off, curious to hear Viviana's answer.

"No." She now seems subdued, almost uncomfortable. "Marjorie and I weren't that close."

"She wasn't always offering you cookies?" Ritchie jests. "Mom, didn't you say she was like the neighborhood's very own Betty Crocker?"

"She did seem to have an endless supply of baked goods," I confirm.

"That's true," Viviana acknowledges. "But you know how, as a parent, you're constantly warning your kids not to take candy from strangers? Well, it was kind of the same with Marjorie."

"Really?" I ask, wondering how I'd been so oblivious to everyone's obvious dislike of her. "You think she was putting something dangerous in her treats?"

"No, nothing like that. Except maybe one time." She pauses, glancing wistfully over to where Fred Burrows is sitting. I imagine she's referring to the time Marjorie gave him chocolates with nuts. "She just wasn't someone you could trust. Always had her hands in other people's cookie jars, if you catch my drift."

I can't say for certain, but I sense her comment is somehow linked to the look she gave Fred. If that is, indeed, the case, no wonder he gave Marjorie an STD. It seems like he's made the rounds of every eligible woman at Egret's Loft.

"No, buddy. It's not polite to point out all the different ways people can die from eating trans fats," Craig admonishes Curt as they rejoin our group. "Especially when you're at a barbecue with active elders."

"Fine." Curt's shoulders slump. "If that man scarfing down fried chicken doesn't want to know that his dinner could increase his risk of heart disease and bad cholesterol levels, I won't bother telling him again."

Viviana waves to a tall couple standing over by the grill. "I should leave you to enjoy the party with your family," she says to us. "Hugh told me how lovely you are, so I wanted to come over and say hello."

Eliza turns her head slightly to the side, blue eyes squinting at me. I shrug off her questioning look. Romance is the last thing on my mind.

I hear the beep of a text message coming in on my phone.

"It was very nice to meet you," I hurriedly tell Viviana. "I'm sure we'll see a lot more of each other."

As she's walking off, Ritchie, Eliza, and I huddle around the cell phone.

"Who's the text from?" Eliza asks at the same time Ritchie is demanding, "What does it say?"

"One day," Craig sighs. "Can we have one day without hunting for killers?"

I ignore Craig. "Give me a second. I need to find my glasses."

"They're on your head," Ritchie informs me.

"So they are." I pull the glasses down onto the bridge of my nose and peer through them. "It's from Detective Fletcher. He says it *was* blood and hair found on the turtle."

"Turtle?" Craig asks, in spite of himself. "I thought it was a mortar."

"The mortar was shaped like a turtle," Ritchie explains. "Keep up, sweetheart."

"They've tested it against Marjorie's blood and hair," I read on, "and…it's a match. Marjorie was killed with the turtle. They're waiting on fingerprint analysis before bringing David in for questioning."

"Right, so if we're thinking David didn't do it, we have to figure out why the real killer returned the turtle to the kitchen," Ritchie says.

"No," Eliza sternly replies. "*We* don't have to do anything."

Ignoring Eliza, I say to Ritchie, "Or maybe that's where she died. The turtle might have been the closest weapon. We have to consider that. But if she was killed in the kitchen, then how did she end up half a mile away, at the bottom of the swimming pool?"

Thirteen

"Grandmother, do you know that man?" Curt asks me as we disembark from my golf cart the following morning.

We've just pulled into the River Club parking lot for the Sunday morning Scrabble tournament. Since the game is played indoors, too far away from the swimming pool to contaminate any potential evidence related to Marjorie's murder, the staff figured we wouldn't get in the way of the police investigation.

"Which man, dear?" I ask, scanning the sparse crowd of would-be board game champions entering the club.

"My daddy said it was rude to point," Curt explains, "so I suppose the best way to describe his location would be to say he is in the northeast quadrant of the parking lot, roughly two hundred and fifty feet from the street."

I turn my head right, then left. "You know what, Curt? If you point him out, I promise not to tell your dad."

"Wise choice. It's the most efficient method." Curt raises his small hand toward the back of the parking lot. "He's over there, getting into the silver Honda Civic."

I follow Curt's finger and see Brock Leitman sliding into the driver's seat. I don't know how he got past the guards at the front gate. One of the other two thousand plus residents of Egret's Loft must have agreed to let him in.

Taking Curt's hand and walking toward the River Club, I say, "Come on, dear. Let's go."

Once inside, we see there's a line for the Scrabble sign-in table. Hugh stands at its end, and we take our place behind him.

"I wasn't aware you were a fan of Scrabble," Hugh greets me.

"Oh, yes, I do love to play. But I'm not that good," I admit, resting my hand on Curt's shoulder. "My grandson always beats me."

This gets the attention of Roy Everhard, a former NFL quarterback and current resident of Egret's Loft, who's in line ahead of Hugh. Curt played Scrabble against him once. Roy lost. Badly.

"Of course, you lost to the little guy," Roy cuts in. "That kid's smarter than my computer."

"Thank you, Mr. Everhard," Curt says. "That may be the

nicest thing anyone has ever said to me. I don't suppose I could interest you in a rematch?"

Roy throws back his mostly bald head and lets out a bark of laughter. "No, kid. I don't suppose you could. But I would be willing to take on your grandmother." He winks at me suggestively.

I do my best not to cringe. "Thank you for the invitation, Roy, but I won't be playing today."

"You won't?" Curt and Hugh say at the same time.

I shake my head. "I'm afraid not. I want to catch up with Jinny. Maybe Mr. Darcy would be willing to play with you, Curt."

Hugh's knees crack as he kneels down to Curt's height. "What do you say, young man? Will you do me the honor of watching me lose?"

Curt nods stoically. "I look forward to it."

The line has been progressing as we've been chatting. We watch as Roy gets paired up with Dr. Frank Rosen. It's Hugh's turn next.

Jinny, dressed in a pink sundress with pink shoes, a pink purse, and pink glasses, writes Hugh's name down on her seating chart. She looks up to assign him the next player in line and sees me.

"Hi, Madeline. George, look, it's Madeline." She doesn't wait for her husband, who's sitting silently beside her, to respond before plowing on. "We knew you were back in town. What's it been, about a week? We've seen you in passing a few times, don't you know. But we haven't had time for a good chat. How were your holidays? Ours were very busy. We ended up going to Canada to spend time with the kids and grandkids. They grow up so fast, eh? We came back in early January though. Wanted to start out the new year in the warm weather. Was it cold up in DC? I bet it was cold. That's why we're all here, isn't it? To hide away from winter. Oh look, you brought your little grandson with you. He created quite a stir the last time he was here. I'm sure you remember. But, then, Roy never did like losing. Do you two want to play together?"

Jinny pauses to inhale some much-needed oxygen. I'd forgotten how many words she can get out on one breath. But I don't want to waste time pondering the thought. If I don't speak soon, she'll step in to fill the void in the conversation.

"It's nice to see you, too, Jinny. Hugh has agreed to play Curt," I tell her, pointing at the seating chart. "I won't be partaking today. I was thinking you and I could have a chat."

"Well, isn't that nice. Do you hear that, George? Madeline wants to catch up. Let me see, I'll just write down Curt's name here. The two of you will be playing on table number sixteen. The number's on the table, you can't miss it. I see there are a few people in line behind you, so let me get them paired up, and then we can relax and have a nice double, double. Coffee with two creams and two sugars. You remember, eh? Now, I usually don't drink more than one cup a day, but this is a special occasion. What's that, George?" she asks, though George hasn't uttered a word the whole time Jinny has been talking. "You don't mind handling the rest of the line? That would be wonderful, thank you. In that case, we can leave the boys to their game, and we can go grab a coffee? Doesn't that sound just delightful?"

Jinny gathers up her pink purse, and taking my arm, we walk toward the bar.

As she opens her mouth to speak, I cut her off. "I want to hear all about your holidays. But first, I wanted to see how you're holding up. Losing Marjorie must have come as a huge shock."

"Poor Marjorie." Jinny sniffles. "It really was quite a shock, don't you know. But, of course, you would know, since you're the one who found her in the pool. What a way to go. Though I heard she didn't drown, after all. She was hit with something on the back of the head. I hope it wasn't a golf club, like poor Carlota. But then I don't think the police know yet what killed Marjorie. I hope she didn't suffer. I keep asking myself what she could have gotten herself into, to end up like that. She used to be so nice—"

"Used to be?" I interrupt to ask.

"Well, now. One doesn't like to disparage the dead. And we were friends for years. She had her quirks, and, yes, she could be incredibly rude when the mood struck her. But she had a good heart and she meant well. It all seemed to change around the time she broke up with Fred. I never did like him. Too full of himself and too charming, by half, with the ladies, don't you know."

I'm finding it difficult to form an accurate picture of Fred. At first glance, he strikes me as rather dull. Similarly, Helen described him as having the personality of a dishrag. The most interesting thing about him, as far as I can see, is how he convinced a beautiful, younger woman to come live with him in a retirement community. But Marjorie obviously had feelings for him, Jinny paints him as some kind of flirt, and heaven knows what was happening between him and Viviana. I make a mental note to have a conversation with Fred so I can draw my own conclusions about him.

"At the end there, she was getting very confused aboot what was going on and who her real friends were," Jinny continues talking, in her thick Canadian accent, which turns all of her *abouts* into *aboots*. "Old friends should be the best, because you've known them longest, eh? But Marjorie seemed to want to forget all aboot the past. No, I take that back. She did forget the fact that we were good friends, but she didn't forget the past. She'd become obsessed with it, don't you know. And not in a good way. Constantly harping on aboot her family tree. To be honest, it started to wear a bit thin hearing her brag aboot this ancestor or that. If I had to hear one more time aboot her great-grandmother who, she said, revolutionized cooking. I mean, how often—"

"Yes, that does sound tedious," I say to stem the rising tide of non sequiturs. "You say she seemed to forget that the two of you were friends. What did you mean by that?"

Jinny's hand tenses up on my arm. "The details don't matter so much as to why she started acting different toward me. And, frankly, I don't like to discuss them. That was between me and Marjorie. I just wasn't a fan of something she was doing, and I let her know. As you would, eh? Well, that only made her dig in her heels and push back harder. We stopped speaking. It was that bad. Mind you, I would never wish her harm. I most certainly would not. I'm torn up aboot what happened to her. And if you want the truth, I think Fred is to blame for a lot of what happened to Marjorie."

I jump in to clarify. "You think he might have killed her?"

"Let's just say, I think Marjorie was a much different woman before she caught Fred two-timing her. It was like she turned off her heart. She didn't want love anymore. She just wanted revenge. Which I don't agree with. Dig two graves, that's what George and I always say. It's so much better to forgive, eh? Why, about a year ago, I was talking to a young woman here, who was having an awful time with her mother. She just couldn't forgive her for putting her up for adoption—"

"Sorry to interrupt, Jinny. I was just wondering, do you think Marjorie's revenge plan might have backfired on her?"

Jinny tilts her head to one side. "Are you asking if I think Fred killed her after all the stunts she pulled on him? I'm sure I don't know anything aboot that. He was madder than a bumble bee in a jam jar, don't you know. But me accusing a man of murder? I don't think I could. Not without more than just a hunch. Not a hunch, really. That sounded bad. It's more that I have a nagging feeling that he might have been involved in some way. Though maybe not directly. Or even indirectly. Let's just say, he probably isn't losing sleep over her dying. Unless he can't sleep because he's worried Marjorie had some dirt on him. Which she probably did."

With Jinny, I find myself always trying to read between the lines. Which gets harder the longer she talks. She gives me far too many lines to keep them all straight.

"Here we are, now, at the bar," she narrates our physical actions. "I'm going to get a double, double. Will you have the same, or would you like one of those fancy drinks that end in 'cino,' like cappuccino or Frappuccino?"

As we order our drinks and begin to settle into conversation about our holidays, it occurs to me that Marjorie may have left clues in her house as to who would want to kill her.

All I need to do now is figure out how Gina and I can get inside to look for them.

Fourteen

"I didn't think it was supposed to rain here in February," Ritchie complains as he looks out my living room window a few hours later. A thunderstorm has transformed the sky from cornflower to steel and puddles have formed on the patio tiles surrounding my pool. "This is supposed to be the Sunshine State. I think they should refund some of our taxes."

"Mommy, when are we going to the carnival?" Tory asks, as Eliza cleans up the remains of our early lunch.

As part of its calendar of events for the family weekend, Egret's Loft staff have arranged a carnival in the parking lot by the boat docks. Tory and Emmy had been promised kiddie rides, bumper cars, ring toss, and ice cream. Instead, they're now stuck inside, moping.

"We'll have to wait and see if the rain stops, sweetie,"

Eliza answers Tory before turning to Tom. "I hope they don't end up canceling it. How many more episodes of *Bubble Guppies* do we have downloaded?"

"Not enough to keep them entertained all afternoon," Tom replies. "But it shouldn't be a problem. The storm is supposed to pass in about an hour or so."

"In the meantime, we could all play Trivial Pursuit," Curt offers. "But I need to be on a team with Tom. He's the only one here capable of answering the sports-related questions."

"Didn't you win at Scrabble this morning?" Craig asks. "It's just as important to learn how to lose as it is to win, buddy."

Curt squares his shoulders. "Says the man destined to lose Trivial Pursuit."

Ritchie's phone alerts him that he has a new message. Looking down at his screen, he asks, "Mom, why is Gina outside with a huge gift basket?"

The doorbell rings.

"You really need to stop spying on me with that door camera of yours," I admonish my son as I walk toward the front door. "But, to answer your question, Gina and I spoke yesterday and decided it would be neighborly to take a sympathy basket over to Marjorie's family."

"Uh huh." Eliza looks skeptical. "Just going over to offer your condolences, are you?"

"It's the least we can do," I say, before grabbing my umbrella. "I won't be gone long."

Once I'm on the front step, the door closed behind me, a raincoat-clad Gina shoves the gift basket into my arms. "I was starting to think you'd never answer the door. My arms are about to fall off from the weight of that thing."

"Nonsense. It only took me a minute," I say, trying to adjust the large, cumbersome wicker basket in my arms. "I just wish my kids had been at the carnival, so I didn't have to explain what we're doing."

"Do you think they're onto us?"

"They're not dumb, Gina. So, yes, I think they are absolutely onto us."

"Come on then." She opens my umbrella and holds it over both our heads. "Let's go before they can stop us."

We lumber down the street, leaning together so neither of us gets wet. Being a few inches taller than Gina, the plastic tips attached to the umbrella's canopy keep poking me on the side of the head. Fortunately, Marjorie's house is just a few doors down from mine.

As we approach, I notice that the driveway is empty of cars and only the faintest of light flickers inside the house.

"It doesn't look like anyone's here," I state the obvious.

"Only one way to find out." Gina strides ahead, forcing me to keep pace if I don't want to get left behind in the rain. At the front door, Gina bangs on the metal knocker.

We hear what sounds like muted conversation from behind the door, but no one comes to let us in.

I'm just about to suggest we try again later when we hear a loud, "*Aaah!*" coming from inside. Surprised, I nearly drop the basket.

"Did you hear that?" Gina exclaims.

"Of course, I heard that. I'm not deaf."

Gina begins shifting her weight from side to side. "We need to do something. What should we do?"

"Try the door. See if it's locked."

She twists the knob, and the door inches open. Gina pulls back as if scalded. "What do we do now? Do we go in? Or should we call the cops?" she asks. "What if the killer's in there?"

"If there is a killer in there, whoever's screaming will be dead by the time the police arrive. Take this." I shove the basket back at her, acting braver than my pounding heart gives me credit for. "I'm going in."

Gina shakes her head and lets the gift basket fall to the ground. "I can't just let you go in there by yourself, now can I?" Making the sign of the cross, she says, "Here goes nothing."

With me in the lead, Gina and I tiptoe into the foyer. The sound of voices is louder now and seems to be coming from the living room.

Another high-pitched scream shatters the silence. Gina grabs my hand.

Inching forward into the large, open-plan living room and kitchen area, I catch sight of movement near the side wall. A figure begins to take shape, and I recognize the person. It's a young Jamie Lee Curtis. She's screaming at some guy in a freaky white mask on the television.

Relief floods over me. "Relax, Gina. It was just the TV. But, since it's on, that probably means someone's here."

"Hello?" Gina calls out, releasing her grip on my hand. "We heard screaming and wanted to make sure you were alright."

There's no reply.

Looking around, I notice the kitchen appears to have been ransacked. Pots, pans, and muffin trays litter every surface, and a bag of poppy seeds seems to have exploded on the counter. "Oh no, it looks like someone broke in!"

"Naw, Marjorie's kitchen always looks like this," Gina says, moving toward the oven. Her breath catches and she freezes in place.

"Gina? What is it?" I ask, remembering a story I heard once about an alligator having found its way inside Marjorie's house.

Gina reaches for something on the counter, and, using two fingers, holds up what looks like the wrapper for Nestlé Tollhouse premade cookie dough. "What the heck? Her cookies weren't even handmade!"

I shake my head. "Some people have no shame."

"I mean, you think you know a person." Gina's nose

wrinkles in distaste as she drops the wrapper back onto the counter.

My eyes move to the door of Marjorie's study. "Since we're already here, I don't suppose it would hurt to look around a little. I'd like to take a peek at Marjorie's study."

"While you do that, I'll check out her bedroom. You can learn a lot about a person from looking inside their drawers."

We split up to begin our search of the house. Opening the French doors to Marjorie's office, I'm greeted by an avalanche of manila file folders that seem to have slid off the desk. Several of the folders have evacuated their contents, leaving a smattering of loose paper to blanket the floor.

Gently pushing papers aside with my shoe, I make my way toward the desk. A stack of opened envelopes sits in the center, next to a bunch of medical bills. Only the bills aren't addressed to Marjorie. They're addressed to a woman named Drusilla Hackney and were sent to a PO Box in Naples, a larger city about half an hour away from Egret's Loft.

Hearing a crinkle under my shoe, I look down to see what I stepped on and find my own name written on the tab of a manila file folder. Picking it up, I look inside and see handwritten notes chronicling my move into the neighborhood and my efforts to solve the earlier murders that rocked the community. Though there's nothing scandalous in the notes, I can't help feeling like my privacy has been invaded.

Certain that, if Marjorie had a file on me, she must have made them for other Egret's Loft residents, my eyes scan the other folders on the floor. I see the names of practically every resident of Cypress Point Avenue and many of the staff members at Egret's Loft. Marjorie seems to have kept secret files on all of us!

Just as I'm about to pick up a thick folder titled "Local Cops," I hear a sharp knock on Marjorie's door. I remain perfectly still, hoping whoever is out there will leave when no one answers. Then the person knocks again, even louder.

Silently exiting the office, I move slowly into the foyer. Gina joins me there.

"Do you think they'll go away?" she whispers. "Or should we sneak out the back?"

Before we have a chance to decide, the front door swings open. Detective Samantha Baptiste stands on the porch, rain pouring down behind her and the contents of our abandoned gift basket littering the tiles at her feet.

"We had reports of a burglary in process," she explains and smiles before adding, "You, ladies, are under arrest."

Fifteen

"It wouldn't kill them to make this place a little more comfortable," Gina complains, struggling to get comfortable on a metal bench that also doubles as a bed.

"This isn't a spa, Gina," I remind her. "We're in jail."

"I know!" Gina's lips curve upward in a smile. "Can you believe it? At our age, being locked up for breaking and entering? It's kind of exciting."

"We're not being locked up," I assure her, as I try to pick some unknown criminal's old chewing gum out of the fabric of my skirt. I should have checked the seat more carefully before sitting down. "Marjorie's door was open, and we didn't take anything from inside. They have nothing to hold us on."

Gina runs her fingers over the metal rods that separate

our cells. "Right, so I'm imagining these bars and the overwhelming aroma of urine?"

Pretending not to hear her, I glance down at my watch. After waiting in the interrogation room for nearly forty-five minutes, and then being questioned by Detectives Fletcher and Baptiste for over an hour, we'd been allowed to make one phone call, to solicit a ride home. Since Gina and I were both slightly concerned about our families' reactions, I suggested we recruit Helen to smuggle us back into Egret's Loft. I figured she couldn't refuse, considering I helped clear her of suspicion in not one, but two, recent murders. As expected, she'd agreed to come right away.

That was half an hour ago. "It shouldn't be too much longer now."

"Are you sure it was a good idea asking Holly to bail us out?" Gina asks.

"Helen." I blurt out the correction through sheer force of habit. "And she's not *bailing us out*. We haven't been charged with a crime. Detective Baptiste only put us in here while we wait for Helen to pick us up, because she wants to prove a point."

Gina raises one well-groomed eyebrow. "And what point would that be?"

"I'm not quite sure," I admit. Detective Baptiste could just be annoyed with us for finding clues that she'd missed, or she could be trying to scare us away from the investigation because she's involved somehow. Either option is equally probable at this point. "I hope Detective Fletcher went to the house, like I asked, and collected all those files."

Gina frowns. "I wonder what Marjorie was doing, collecting info on all of us like that. You said she had a file on all of us and some of the staff too?"

I nod. "Perhaps she was just being cautious about who she associated with. You have to admit, people at Egret's Loft aren't always who they claim to be."

Gina waves her hand dismissively. "That's not Egret's Loft, that's life. Everybody pretends to be something, or someone, they're not. Why, before Leon and me got married, I had him convinced I was a good cook."

"How did you manage that?" I ask, belatedly realizing the question might have sounded rude.

Gina doesn't take offense. "There was a restaurant below the apartment my sister, Phoebe, and I shared in college. The owner had a bit of a soft spot for Phoebe. Let's just say we had more leftovers than we could have ever eaten on our own."

"You exploited that young man's affection for your sister to get free food?" I tease.

She nods, her face contrite. "Sad, but true. People use other people to get what they want."

"And Marjorie?" I ponder aloud, still thinking about the folders in the dead woman's house. "Who was she using? What did she want?"

"Well, we know she wanted people to think she made her cookies from scratch."

"I hardly think someone would kill her for using premade dough." I roll my eyes.

"Alright." Gina sits up straighter. "What about Forest? She wanted him dead. Maybe he returned the favor."

"You mean Fred." The correction is already out of my mouth before I even have time to consider it. "That reminds me. Your husband's on the board of directors. Do you think you could ask him to log into Fred's online calendar? I'd like to find out what activities Fred has planned for the weekend?"

"If you want to talk to him, why don't we just go knock on his door?" she asks.

I shake my head. "If there's one thing I've learned since moving to Egret's Loft, it's to be in a public place if you plan on asking someone if they're a murderer."

"That's probably wise," she agrees, grimacing and standing up. "When is Holly getting here? This bench is killing my hips."

Just then, the door opens, and Detective Fletcher enters the holding area, scowling. "Your ride's here."

A flawlessly made-up Helen pushes him out of the way and rushes over to my cell. "Madeline, I got here just as quick as I could. I'd have been here sooner, but wouldn't you know, you called right in the middle of my weekly hair appointment."

Jolene strides into the room behind Helen but stops to confront the detective. "She's in here? It doesn't make a lick of sense, you puttin' Madeline in the cells. Why, after all she did to help you catch Carl's killer a few months back, you should be on your knees thankin' her, not treatin' her like a common criminal."

Detective Fletcher, with color rising in his cheeks, opens his mouth to speak, but Jolene doesn't give him the opportunity.

"Why don't we go ahead and call a spade a shovel. Y'all don't have the first clue about solvin' crimes. You'd still be pissin' into the wind looking for who killed Carl if it wasn't for her. I still have connections in law enforcement, and I ain't afraid to use 'em. So, I'm gonna ask you nicely. Unlock that cell this instant."

"If you're done telling me how bad you think I am at my job, let's get all of you out of my station." Detective Fletcher fumes. "As fast as possible."

Helen squeezes my hand through the bars. "We'll be right outside in the car waitin'. I spent enough time in this here cell myself to last a lifetime."

As Helen and Jolene exit, Detective Fletcher approaches the door to my cell.

While I appreciate Jolene coming to my defense, I do feel bad about the effect her words might have on the detective. He does tend to struggle with confidence about his professional abilities when it comes to solving murders.

"It's nice to see you again," I greet him, but he won't look me in the eye. "I hate to ask, but I'd really appreciate it if you don't mention this little incident to my family. I don't want them to worry."

Glancing back to make sure Jolene is out of earshot, Detective Fletcher whispers, "I'm so sorry. I had no idea Sammy was going to put you in here. I only just got back to the station myself."

Focusing on more important matters, I ignore his apology. "Were you at Marjorie's house?"

He turns a key in the lock and the door swings open. "Yeah, I went by Marjorie's place."

"And? Did you get all her files?"

"And—" he pauses to unlock Gina's cell, "—there was nothing there. I didn't find any files in her study. Not a single one."

"What?" Gina demands.

"But there were papers all over the floor," I say. "How did you not see them?"

Gina plants her hands on her hips and asks, "Were you lookin' in the right room?"

"Did I check the right room?" Detective Fletcher repeats her question with a dumbfounded expression and clenched fists. "Not that it's any of your business, but I checked *every* room. I didn't find anything. There was nothing there to find! Look, you've all made it very clear that you think I'm an idiot—"

"I don't think you—" I try to interrupt, but Detective Fletcher cuts me off.

"Stop. Between you, your friends, and your know-it-all daughter—"

"Eliza?" My stomach drops. "Does she know I'm here?"

"—I've had enough for one day," he charges on. "It really doesn't matter what you think. I'm going to find out who killed Marjorie all on my own. I'll show you. So just get out of here. Now."

The veins in his neck are pulsing wildly, and, if he were any older, I might suggest he call his doctor to make sure he's not having a heart attack.

I've never seen him so angry, and it occurs to me that he might need a little time to cool down. But, needing to make sure he's on the right track, I risk asking, "Did you do any checking on Drusilla Hackney? She has a post office box in Naples."

Feet firmly planted hips-width apart, he raises his arm to point at the door. "Out. Now!"

Already feeling awful about hurting Detective Fletcher's feelings and dreading going home to an angry daughter, my spirits sink even lower when I see Detective Baptiste leaning against her desk, waiting to watch us leave.

"No hard feelings, Mrs. Delarouse. I was just doing my job." Her smug smile tells me just how much she's enjoying this. "You be careful now. There's a killer on the loose, after all."

I'm thinking this day couldn't possibly get any worse when, suddenly, it does.

Brock Leitman is outside the station, waiting with a handheld recording device, when Gina and I exit the police station. Somehow, he found out what happened.

"Why did you break into Marjorie Higginbottom's home?" he demands. "Were you there trying to cover your tracks?"

Gina opens her mouth to speak, but, too tired for another confrontation, I silence her with my hand on her arm.

"It's not worth it, dear," I assure her.

I sure hope that decision doesn't come back to bite me.

Sixteen

There are no signs of life inside my house as I stand on the street, working up the courage to face my children. Eliza must have heard about my arrest from Detective Fletcher and, if she knows about it, Ritchie does as well. The thought fills me with dread.

Clint and I worked hard to raise Ritchie and Eliza as good, law-abiding citizens. It helped that their father was a police officer, because they knew, if they got into trouble, he'd be the first to hear about it. Consequently, they'd never disappointed us.

How can I ever face them again, now having spent time behind bars?

Looking across the street at my neighbor Phyllis's house, I'm tempted to ask her for sanctuary. But I know she wouldn't answer my knock. She'd just show up later tonight, inside my house, without me knowing how she got in, like a ninja. I don't need any more surprises today, so I just raise my hand and wave. The front windows are dark, but a light flashes in the back room, her way of returning my greeting.

With a deep sigh, I force my feet to carry me to my front door. Before I can type in the code to unlock it, the door opens. Ritchie and Eliza stand on the other side. I forgot about the camera. They've probably been watching me this whole time.

"Are you alright, lady?" Ritchie asks, concern etched in the lines of his face.

"I'm fine." I take both kids' hands in mine. "But there's something I need to tell you both. Earlier today I was arrested—"

Eliza's eyes spit fire. "We know. We are so mad—"

"You have every right to be mad," I concede. "I'm supposed to be a good role model—"

Eliza's eyebrows shoot upward. "Wait, you think we're mad at you?"

Hope flutters in my heart. "You're not?"

"Of course not, lady!" Ritchie assures me. "We've just been worried about you."

"Who are you mad at then?" I ask, confused.

"Samantha Baptiste," Eliza utters with clenched teeth. "She doesn't deserve to be called a detective anymore. Not when she's wasting time carting you and Gina off to the station and ignoring obvious suspects, like David and Fred."

"Your buddy, Detective Fletcher, didn't seem too pleased about it either," Ritchie chimes in. "He said you found a whole bunch of files in Marjorie's office, but by the time he found out what was going on, the whole lot had been cleared out of there."

Poor Detective Fletcher. His partner missed out on evidence—which it clearly was, if someone went to the trouble of removing it all—and everyone was blaming him for what happened. No wonder he was so upset.

"We would have picked you up from the station, but he told us you'd already arranged a ride. So we sent Tom and Craig to the carnival with the kids, while we waited for you here," Eliza explains. "If we'd known you'd be there so long, we would have come to get you ourselves."

"Oh, I'm only late because Helen was getting her hair done when I called her," I tell them. "But it did seem a bit excessive that Detective Baptiste made us wait in the cell."

Ritchie's eyes widen in surprise. "She actually locked you up?"

"That's ludicrous!" Eliza erupts. "What is she playing at?"

We've been standing in the foyer this whole time, with my kids' bodies blocking access to the living room. All I want to do is sit down. My heels are starting to hurt. "I've been wondering the same thing myself, but can we talk about it sitting down?"

In a flood of unexpected solicitousness, Eliza takes one of my elbows while Ritchie claims the other. Slowly, they start walking me toward the sofa.

"I'm not an invalid," I protest. "I just want to sit down."

"Yeah, yeah," Ritchie dismisses my comment. "Just sit down so you can tell us what you're thinking."

Once I'm comfortably settled on the sofa, with Ritchie beside me and Eliza on the loveseat across from us, I begin to share my thoughts. "I think we can all agree that Detective Baptiste was not happy that I solved Carl's murder after she fingered the wrong person."

Ritchie chuckles. Eliza rolls her eyes.

"Did I say something funny?" I ask.

"Just ignore him, Mom," Eliza instructs. "He's being a child."

Frowning in confusion, I realize it's easier just to move on. "She seems to have a deep need to prove herself. Which is normal, I suppose. Your father always said that women on the force had it much harder than the men. I imagine that's still true now, to some extent."

"The question is, how far do you think she'd go to prove herself?" Ritchie wonders.

"What is that supposed to mean?" Eliza asks. "Are you implying Baptiste murdered Marjorie just so she could pretend to find the *real* killer?"

"I don't know." Ritchie shrugs. "I mean, what was she doing at the River Club the morning Mom found Marjorie's body? Why was she even at Egret's Loft?"

"Apparently," I interject, "she had a text from Marjorie asking to meet. But before you go asking what the text said exactly, I can't tell you. Detective Fletcher said she deleted the message."

"Wouldn't it still be on Marjorie's phone though?" Ritchie asks.

"I don't think they've found her phone," I say.

Eliza pulls her phone out of her jeans pocket and starts typing. "Don't worry. If a message was sent, I'll find it."

As her mother, part of me wants to chastise Eliza for her ethically questionable manner of obtaining information. A larger part of me doesn't want to rock the boat. This is the first time Eliza hasn't given me grief or tried to talk me out of investigating a murder. It feels nice, for once, to know she believes in me more than the local police.

"I'm also going to talk to one of my friends at Miami PD," Eliza continues, still typing away. "It can't hurt to find out what they thought of her when she worked there."

Ritchie nods. "Good plan. Right now, my money's on her being the killer."

"What about the chef, David?" I ask, just to play devil's advocate. Even though he seems to have had motive and opportunity, not to mention a horrible temper, I'm still not convinced he's a murderer. "He did fight with Marjorie, and the murder weapon was found in his kitchen."

Ritchie takes a moment to consider. "What else do we know about the guy? Aside from the fact that he's cute. But don't tell Craig I said that."

"He also has a rap sheet," Eliza says, without looking up from her phone. "Convictions for robbery and distribution."

Ritchie's head swivels to look at his sister. "He was selling drugs? Are you looking him up right now?"

"Yes, to the drugs. No, I'm not looking him up now," Eliza answers. "I had him checked out yesterday after he threatened Mom in the kitchen."

"A drug dealer threatened Mom?" Ritchie shrieks.

"How do you know about that?" I ask at the same time.

Eliza rolls her eyes at me. "Seriously? You actually thought I'd believe you just wanted to clean your shirt? You should really tell Gina to be less obvious the next time you want to meet up behind my back."

"Why didn't anyone tell me about this?" Ritchie complains. "I'm part of this family too."

"Of course, you are." I pat his knee, like I did when he was a child. "Eliza, about those convictions. How recent were they?"

Eliza puts her phone back in her pocket. "A couple of years ago, when he was living in Miami. He did a little time. He seemed to clean himself up when he got out, on paper anyway. Which just means he wasn't caught doing anything, not that he stopped breaking the law."

"How did he get a job at Egret's Loft with a criminal record?" Ritchie, incensed, demands.

"There have been four murders here in as many months," I remind him. "I don't think this place has the best track record of checking references."

Ritchie shakes his head. "I'm starting to think Eliza was right. We should move you out of here."

I ignore his comment. "Eliza, can you do me a favor? Can you do a background check—all above board and legal, mind you—on a woman named Drusilla Hackney?"

"Sure. Who's she?"

"I don't know," I admit. "But I found medical bills in her name at Marjorie's house."

Eliza's phone is once again in her hand. "Address?"

"The bills were addressed to a post office box in Naples, but I don't remember the number."

"Fabulous," Eliza utters sarcastically. "Another possible lead we missed out on because of detective deadbeat."

"Um," Ritchie interrupts, staring down at his own phone. "I think we might have a bigger problem."

Eliza sighs. "Good Lord, what now?"

"You know how you told me about Brock Leitman trying to get in touch with Tom?"

"Yeah," Eliza warily replies.

"So, I started following his podcast home page. And this

just popped up." Ritchie turns his phone around to show a tiny alert in the middle of the screen.

Feeling on top of my head and finding nothing, I say, "I don't know where my glasses are. You're going to have to tell me what that says."

He and Eliza exchange a look before Ritchie begins to read. "Click now for a brief clip of Brock Leitman's newest podcast, *Serial Seniors*."

"But...but I didn't talk to him," I stammer. "He said he needed me for his first show."

"It looks like he made do without you," Ritchie says.

I scoot over so Eliza can sit on the sofa beside me. She pushes a button on Ritchie's phone and says, "I have a feeling this is really going to suck."

None of us disagree, as Brock Leitman's nasal voice fills the living room.

Seventeen

I'm Brock Leitman, award-winning creator of *Everything's Deadlier in Texas. Join me as my new podcast,* Serial Seniors, *investigates a series of bloodthirsty murders committed behind the palmetto-lined gates of a luxury Florida retirement community.*

It all began last November, when the mother of a Colombian politician was brutally slain inside her own home. Days later, the body of a disgraced former oil tycoon was found on the riverbank, in the jaws of an alligator. Police arrested a suspect and the peace-seeking residents of Egret's Loft—like legendary quarterback Roy Everhard—breathed a sigh of relief.

"They caught the guy. So yeah, I wasn't worried."

But shortly after the arrest, a retired auto entrepreneur was found murdered on his wedding day. A suspect was arrested, and residents were, once again, able to rest easy.

Until now.

In recent days, the sleepy retirement village has been rocked by yet another murder. A homemaker, cookie baker, and grandmother of ten, was found dead at the bottom of a swimming pool.

World-renowned forensic pathologist Dr. Frank Rosen, a neighbor of the deceased, had this to say. "Not this again. We've already gone down this road twice before."

But as local police begin the hunt for a third suspect, I'll explore a different scenario.

You see, there's another theory. That all the murders were committed at the hands of one woman—the widow of a Washington DC detective.

A lonely woman, who moved into the community mere hours before the first murder. An intelligent woman, who's used her brains to outwit the local police. And a brazen woman, who has no trouble confessing, because other people are behind bars for her crimes.

"I killed them all," she blatantly said, not knowing she was being recorded.

The worst part? Two innocent people languish in prison for crimes they didn't commit. I've had the opportunity to speak with a father and son, who insist they were framed.

It's up to us to give them justice.

Join me later this week for the first, mind-blowing episode of Serial Seniors.

Eighteen

"This is bad. This is so bad!" Ritchie is up off the sofa and pacing. "How does he have you on tape confessing to murder, Mom?"

My whole body feels numb. "I...I don't know. I never confessed to killing anybody. I haven't killed anybody! Is there some device that could, I don't know, change someone else's voice to sound like mine?"

Eliza, calm but tense, shakes her head. "No, it's more likely he edited what you did say to make it sound more incriminating—which really should be illegal. But listen, Mom, you can't talk to him again, do you understand me?"

"But shouldn't I try to explain that he's wrong?" I argue. "I can tell him—"

"*No!*" My kids scream in unison.

"Can't we sue to put a stop to this?" Ritchie asks. "I mean, it's slander!"

"Let me think for a second," Eliza says. "We know it's all a load of nonsense, obviously. But he must have *something* if he thinks he can make those kinds of accusations. Surely, he wouldn't go off half-cocked like that if he didn't have some proof."

I take a deep breath to steady my nerves. "What could he have though? I didn't do anything."

"He must have talked to Victor, right? That's the father and son he mentioned," Ritchie surmises, referring to the first murder case I solved at Egret's Loft. "So, Victor has to be the one telling Brock that Mom framed him, right?"

Eliza doesn't seem convinced. "Probably, but I don't think that would be enough."

"Yeah," Ritchie concedes. "Victor isn't exactly an unbiased party. When is his trial anyway?"

"Detective Fletcher told me it would be some time next year," I say. "But I don't understand. He tried to kill me! How can he get away with saying I framed him?"

"He said, she said." Ritchie shakes his head. "Since no one else was in the house when he almost bashed your head in, it all comes down to what a jury would believe."

I turn my attention to Eliza. "You were spying on me when I was in his house that day, weren't you? You heard him confess. Isn't that how you knew to call the police?"

"Yeah, but I didn't record the conversation."

Ritchie throws his hands in the air. "You didn't? Jeez! Some spy you are."

"I am not a spy," she enunciates each word carefully. Ritchie and I aren't buying it. "Not to mention, I was trying to save Mom's life! Sorry I didn't take the time to worry about evidence for the court case."

Something occurs to me. "Since you're my daughter, it would just look like you were trying to protect me if you said anything about the confession, wouldn't it?"

"Yep," Ritchie answers for her. "What a mess."

"It is," Eliza agrees. "So, how do we find Marjorie's killer? What's our next step?"

Ritchie and I look at each other, then back at Eliza.

"Let me just make sure I'm reading the room correctly," Ritchie says. "Are you actually now *encouraging* Mom to investigate the murder?"

"Do we have a choice at this point?" Eliza replies. "I, for one, am not willing to sit by while Mom's name gets dragged through the mud. Which means we have to find the real killer. I'll look into Samantha Baptiste. I'll also find out who this Drusilla Hackney person is. Ritchie?"

"Umm," he hesitates. "I guess I can talk to David. Find out if he's still selling drugs. Maybe he's peddling pills here and Marjorie found out?"

"Oh, that's very clever," I praise my son.

"Okay, Ritchie's smart." Eliza plants her hands on her

hips. "We all know this already. Mom, what's your plan? I know you have one."

"Well, I did ask Gina to find out what activities Fred had scheduled for the next few days. We thought we'd ask him some questions," I tell Eliza, slightly apprehensive that her sudden willingness to get involved is all part of an elaborate trap. "Marjorie tried to kill him, so we figured he might be a bit upset about that."

Eliza nods. "Good. We have a plan. In the meantime, no talking to reporters. And watch what you say around the neighbors too. It seems like Brock Leitman is trying to chat up every person in Egret's Loft, and we can't give him, or anyone else, more ammunition."

Ritchie and I both nod our assent. I pick up my phone.

"What are you doing, lady?" my son asks.

"For crying out loud, Mom. We just said to keep a low profile," Eliza moans.

"I'm texting Gina," I say. "We agreed to meet for coffee tomorrow morning at the Golf Club. I'm thinking it might be best if we meet somewhere outside of Egret's Loft instead."

Neither of them says anything.

"I can still talk to Gina, right?"

Nineteen

Gina has already arrived when Ritchie drops me off at the Starbucks just a few blocks away from Egret's Loft the following morning.

Before I exit the vehicle, Ritchie instructs me to call him when I'm ready to be picked up. I don't know whether to laugh or cry when I realize how much our roles have now reversed. How many times had I said the exact same words to him when he was younger and needed to be dropped off at his friends' houses? The unwelcome truth settles in.

I have become the dependent one in our relationship.

Lamenting the loss of my parental authority, and unsettled to know a radio reporter will soon have the world believing I'm a murderer, my patience is already on a razor's edge when Gina scowls at me.

"Why did you want to meet here?" She sounds annoyed.

"It seemed as good a place as any. Why? Don't you like Starbucks?"

"I wouldn't know. Never been to one."

My annoyance dissipates in disbelief. "You've never been to Starbucks?"

They're on virtually every other block back home in DC, and, I know from an anniversary trip with Clint, they're littered across Manhattan as well. In fact, I really have to think to remember a time before grandé caramel macchiatos.

She shakes her head. "I always got my coffee from a bodega a block away from our brownstone in New York. No point fixing something that isn't broken."

"That makes sense," I agree. "But since we aren't in New York, what do you say you give Starbucks a try?"

Signaling her reluctant assent, we enter and take our place in line.

"Did you tell your family about what happened yesterday?" I ask as we wait.

"I told Leon. At first, I thought he was angry, but then he burst out laughing. I think I would have preferred him being mad," she complains, taking a step closer to the counter. "What about you?"

"My kids found out," I tell her. "But, surprisingly, they were more upset with Detective Baptiste."

Gina leans in closer to me. "There's something not quite right about that new detective, if you ask me. I was thinking about it last night. Do you think she could have cleared out all of Marjorie's files while we were waiting in the interrogation room? We were in there a good long while before she and Detective Fleishner came in."

"You mean Detective Fletcher, and, yes, the thought had crossed my mind," I tell her. "I still think it's odd she was at the River Club the day Marjorie was murdered. My kids agree, and Eliza said she'd do a little digging into the detective's background."

Skepticism plays on Gina's face. "Your daughter wants to help now? I thought she hated us trying to solve murders!"

"Oh, she still does," I confirm. "But I think she hates the thought of her mom being accused of murder more. You may not have heard, but there's a reporter making a radio show—"

"Oh, that," Gina interrupts, grimacing. "Nicole played some of it for me when I said I was planning to meet up with you today."

Something in the tone of her voice catches my attention. "She knows it's not true, right?"

"Yeah," she says. "I mean, maybe. She's kinda on the fence. Alright. To be honest, she warned me not to meet with you in private. Just to keep the peace, I lied and told her I'm having coffee with Holly right now."

"Helen." I can't help correcting her. "This is awful. Even your daughter thinks it might be true?"

"Don't pay any attention to her," Gina tries to reassure me. "I'll be glad when the baby comes. She's bein' far too hormonal. I mean, just the other day a laxative commercial made her cry."

"It's not true. What that reporter is saying," I assure Gina.

"Don't you worry, Mandy." She pats my arm. "I never believe anything I hear on the news."

"Welcome to Starbucks, can I take your order?" the fresh-faced girl behind the counter asks with all the enthusiasm of a teenager on her first week of the job.

Gina, who spent none of our time in line looking at the menu of options on the wall, spends the next five minutes asking questions to try and figure out what she wants. In the end, she settles on a grandé black coffee.

"Can I get a name for your beverage?" the girl asks, the muscles holding up her smile flickering like a dying lightbulb by the end of the exchange.

"A name?" Gina asks.

"Yes, ma'am." The girl eyes the line behind us, its occupants getting restless.

"I don't know," Gina scratches her head. "I guess you can call it Bob."

The girl shakes her head. "No, I wasn't asking you to name the coffee." Then, in a move that makes me think she'll succeed in the working world, adds, "You know what, why not? Bob it is. You can pick up Bob down there."

After Gina is out of earshot, I smile at the girl. "Keep up the good work."

When I rejoin Gina at the end of the counter, she pulls a piece of paper out of her purse. "Before I forget, I had Leon look up Forest's schedule—"

"You mean Fred?"

"Sure." She glares at me before consulting the note in her hand. "It looks like he signed up for the line dancing lesson at the Golf Club tonight. His wife doesn't appear to be going, so I was thinking we should go. Catch him when he's on his own. He might admit to more without his wife around."

"Line dancing? I love dancing but Clint, rest his soul, couldn't keep time with a metronome." The memory of his awkward efforts brings a smile to my lips. He always tried, regardless of how embarrassing it was for him. "If we're going dancing tonight, I should probably take a nap this afternoon. Eliza's husband, Tom, and I have a golf lesson scheduled for later this morning. If I don't get some rest afterward, I'll be tuckered out when it comes time to dance!"

Gina eyes me warily. "We're not going to dance, though, are we? I thought we were trying to confront Forest in a public place."

I adopt a serious expression. "Yes, of course. We're

going to talk to *Fred* so we can find out if he killed Marjorie."

"Have you given any thought to how we're going to do that? It's not like we can just come right out and ask him."

"No, I supposed we should start with his alibi for Thursday night and Friday morning and work from there." I wish we could narrow the timeframe down a little more, but with everything going on yesterday, I didn't think Detective Fletcher would be particularly receptive to me pressing him for Marjorie's time of death. "Oh, I just thought of something. Do you know if Marjorie's house has one of those cameras on the patio?"

In my first few days at Egret's Loft, I'd learned that nearly every house in the community has a camera on the back porch that broadcasts live video to the security department—the thinking being that, if an active elder falls over and can't get up, someone will spot them on the video feeds and send help.

"Yeah, I'm pretty sure she had one," Gina confirms. "Why?"

"Do you think you could access it to see who went into Marjorie's house after we were there?"

"Darn, why didn't I think of that?" Gina complains. "That's so smart. Whoever went in after us and cleaned out the files must have killed her, right?"

"Not necessarily," I caution her. "But whoever took

those files had something to hide. We need to find out who. And what it is that they don't want us to know."

"Bob?" a bored-looking barista interrupts us by calling out. "I have an order for Bob."

"Oh." Gina snaps to attention. "Bob. That's for me."

When she returns with her drink, I have to ask. "How do you remember the name of your drink but the only people's names you remember are your kids'?"

"What do the drink and my kids have in common?" she asks.

"You named them." I smile, but my enjoyment of the moment fades quickly when I see the person seated over Gina's shoulder, at a table near the side door.

With one hand, Brock Leitman sips from a paper cup. With the other, he's typing something into the laptop that's open on the table in front of him.

Seeing my expression change, Gina turns to see what got my attention. Her shoulders become tense when she spies the smug-looking reporter, smiling to himself as he reads back whatever slanderous thing he's just written.

"Why, I oughta give that reporter a piece of my mind." Gina takes a step in his direction.

I gently grab her elbow to halt her forward momentum. "The kids warned me not to say anything to him. They said it'd only make things worse."

Gina looks skeptical. "Even if we explained to him why he's wrong?"

"I thought the same thing! It makes sense, right?"

"Yeah! So let's go talk to him."

I shake my head, not wanting to run afoul of Eliza's newfound cooperation. "No, it's probably for the best if we listen to my kids. At least for now."

"Hey, you're the one he's gunning for, so I'll respect your wishes. But what if he tries to talk to you?"

"It's best not to have to find out," I say. "I'll text Ritchie to come get us. We should go."

"Sounds good. Tell him to pick us up at the Publix," Gina instructs. "I want to buy some chamomile tea. Maybe that'll relax Nicole a little."

Seeing that Brock is intently focused on his laptop on the other side of the room, Gina and I try to slip out the front door without being noticed. The entrance to the Publix is only a few hundred feet away. With any luck, he won't even know we were here.

We arrive at the door leading out of Starbucks, relaxing slightly, when, from behind, someone reaches around us, taking hold of the handle and pulling the door open for us.

"Thank you very—" The words stick in my throat as my eyes focus on the smiling and self-satisfied face of Brock Leitman.

"Nice to see you, Madeline," he says, his voice originating from somewhere in the upper region of his nostrils. "I won't hold you ladies up. Just wanted to say I hope you enjoy the podcast."

Without a word, and before either Gina or I can slip and say something we'll later regret, I grab Gina's arm and rush her out of the Starbucks. I don't relax the pace until we're safely inside the air-conditioned produce section of the Publix.

After regaining her breath, Gina turns to me and says, "His mother should be so ashamed of him."

Twenty

The late morning February sun burns so hot it feels like the fabric of my sun hat might melt into my scalp. This is my first trip to the driving range since returning from spending the holidays with Ritchie and Eliza, and I'm disappointed to notice that structures which used to provide shade on the range have been removed.

My face, already flush from the heat, flames even further when I realize I'm likely the reason they're now gone.

"Thanks for bringing me out to practice my swing," Tom says, barely showing any strain from our heavy golf bags, which hang, like a lead balloons, from either side of his broad shoulders. "With work and the kids, I can never seem to find time to golf. For the record, that's also going to be my excuse when I play terribly." He chuckles.

"Don't worry about that." I pat his arm. "The only thing you should be concerned about is not getting hit by one of my balls."

A puzzled expression plays across his face. "What do you mean?"

"Just a joke," I lie. The truth is, my errant swings have already resulted in one ruptured breast implant and a possible concussion. I like to think it wasn't my fault, that the poles of the shade structure just happened to collide with my golf balls in a most unfortunate manner—hence, the current lack of shade. Which most definitely *is* my fault.

"Madeline! Welcome back," Dom Skellig calls out from a few hundred feet away, drawing scowls from the more serious local golfers.

Tom squints in concentration. "Is it just me, or does that guy look a lot like—"

"Tom Selleck?" I finish his question. "Yes. We all suspect it's intentional."

Tom gives a knowing nod as Dom hurries over to us across the grass.

Dom sports Tom Selleck's trademark mustache and the top buttons of his golf shirt are left carelessly undone to reveal a generous amount of chest hair. But most characteristic of the 1980s sitcom star, Dom's shorts leave even less to the imagination than Magnum PI's infamous legwear.

"You said you were bringing a friend today," Dom says, his smile faltering slightly. "I was thinking maybe you were going to get your friend, Helen, back out on the links."

"I doubt she'd want to be anywhere near me when I'm golfing," I tell him, trying to manage his disappointment. The breast implant mishap happened to involve my buxom neighbor. "No, this is my son-in-law, Tom."

"It's a pleasure, Tom. I'm the resident golf pro. The name's Dom, with a D. That's an important distinction," he assures us. "People *already* confuse me all the time with a certain Hawaiian-based private detective, if you know what I mean." He winks.

"I get that," Tom replies politely. "Nice to meet you, man."

"Well, why don't we get you both set up," Dom says.

On the brief walk to the range, Dom asks Tom about his level of experience, which Tom, humbly, describes as "limited." As they're talking, I nervously observe all the other Egret's Loft residents out practicing, spotting Hugh Darcy at the far end of the range tee. I follow one of his shots as it sails out over the man-made lake and lands in the water, just shy of the two-hundred-yard floating marker. For the sake of my own pride, I hope he doesn't notice my presence until after I've finished practicing.

"Madeline, why don't you just warm up by practicing

your stance and swinging the club," Dom tells me before turning to Tom. "Do you need any refreshers?"

"Probably. It's been a few years," Tom acknowledges. "But let me just loosen up with a couple of shots first, yeah?"

Dom raises his hands in the air, as if surrendering. "Sure thing. Just let me know if I can help you out with anything."

I pull a club out of my bag and walk over to an open tee.

"Remember what I taught you before. Keep your grip loose," Dom instructs.

I swing my pitching wedge, clipping grass as I aim for an imaginary ball. "It's just awful what happened to Marjorie, isn't it?"

Dom lowers his gaze and shakes his head. "It's a real shame. She was, um…" He pauses, searching for a compliment. "Good at making cookies."

My eyes narrow. "You didn't like her, did you?"

Dom sighs. "I'm sorry. That's an awful thing to say about someone who just died, isn't it? It's only that, well, she wasn't very nice."

"So I've been told. I heard she even got into a huge fight with her friend, Jinny, at lunch on Wednesday," I mention, trying to confirm Helen's story.

"Yeah, it was pretty epic. I was there. Saw the whole thing. I felt really bad for Jinny. She's sweet, you know. Not like Marjorie, who was always fighting with people and trying to get staff in trouble."

My interest is piqued, but I try to play it cool, not wanting to arouse his suspicion. I hear Tom's club connect with a ball as I take another swing at the grass. "Really? I saw her exchanging words with that new chef, David, at the welcome party on Thursday night. Had she tried to get him in trouble?"

When Dom fails to respond, I glance in his direction. He's looking at Tom, his mouth slightly agape.

"Dom? Did you hear me?" I ask.

"What?" Dom squints, trying to concentrate. "Um, yeah, the fight at the party."

"Do you know what the fight was about?" I ask, trying to hold Dom's attention as Tom sets up another ball.

"Yeah," Dom confirms. "She said something about how she was gonna report him to the health department for violations. Claimed his food was making people sick. I saw him afterward in the kitchen. He was really ticked off."

"Did he say anything to you?"

The thwack of Tom's five iron striking a ball pulls Dom's focus off my question and onto the ball's trajectory. The stunned look on the golf pro's face deepens as the ball soars through the air, finally landing with a splash just past the 250-yard marker.

"Um, how long did you say it's been since you last played?" Dom asks Tom.

"A couple of years," Tom replies, quickly adding, "but that was just a lucky shot. I'm sure I won't be able to repeat it."

I put my hand on Dom's arm, and he, reluctantly, turns to face me. "We were talking about what David said to you in the kitchen after his fight with Marjorie, remember?"

"Umm, yeah. Sure." He sounds distracted. "Did I say he said something? I don't actually remember him saying anything. I just remember what he did."

"And what was that?" I press, trying to get in the question before Tom hits another ball.

Dom has his eyes on my son-in-law as he answers. "He knocked a pot of boiling pasta onto the floor. I think some of the water splashed on him, but he didn't seem to notice. He just stomped his feet on the pasta and stormed out of the kitchen."

Based on everything I've seen and heard, I'm relatively convinced that the new chef has anger-management issues. It sounds like he had a tantrum in the kitchen after the altercation with Marjorie. Now the question is what, if anything, did he do about it?

"Did you see David later, after he calmed down?" I ask, belatedly realizing that I have, once again, lost Dom's attention.

As I'd been trying to pump information out of Dom, while casually practicing my swing, a small crowd of active elders had congregated around Tom. Catching snippets of their excited conversation, I can hear them all vying to sign Tom up for the next Egret's Loft golf scramble.

Dom doesn't seem to notice the group. He's staring off at the lake, in the direction of Tom's latest drive. He seems to be nearly catatonic.

"Are you alright?" I ask Dom.

He finally turns to face me. "Is this some kind of joke?"

"Is what a joke?"

He points a shaky finger at Tom. "He's a professional, isn't he? There's no way he hasn't played in years and is still that...that...good."

Male egos can be so fragile, I think to myself. Aloud, I say, "Don't worry about Tom. He's just naturally athletic. Now, about David, do you know where he went after he knocked over the boiling water?"

Dom shakes his head, frowning. "I have no idea. I didn't see him again that night. But seriously, he's just *naturally athletic*?" Dom snorts derisively. "That doesn't explain how he can drive a call that far, time after time, if he hasn't played in years!"

It's suddenly clear to me that, if I want to get any more answers out of Dom, I'll have to come back alone. Tom's a lovely man, in addition to being a good husband and father, but he's too much of a distraction. Nearly everyone who had been on the driving range is now circled around Tom, and they're all trying to engage him in conversation about his technique.

Giving up on accomplishing anything more in my interrogation of Dom, I put a ball onto a tee and take a swing. To my surprise, it sails straight and true, landing around the hundred-yard floating marker. Just my luck. That's probably the best drive I'll ever have, and nobody even noticed.

"Bloody brilliant shot," a male voice says from behind me.

Turning, I see Hugh approaching from the far end of the green. My cheeks begin to burn. "Thank you! I didn't think anyone saw that."

"Fear not, I can attest to your triumph." He winks at me. "How have you been keeping? Your family is enjoying the long weekend, I trust."

Images of being locked in a cell at the police station flood my mind, but there's no need to share any of that with Hugh. "Yes, everyone has been having a great time. They're all headed home tomorrow."

My children are all scheduled to leave on Tuesday to return to their respective lives and jobs, but I wonder if that will change now that I'm being publicly accused of murder on a radio show.

"Last night with the family then. Have you arranged anything fun?" he asks.

"Oh no, not really," I say before remembering that Gina and I do have plans for the evening. "Well, I guess there is something. I was going to see if they wanted to come with me to a line dancing class at the Golf Club."

"A dancer, are we?" Hugh smiles. "I was known to cut a rug or two, in my day. Perhaps I'll see you there."

"That would be very nice," I tell him, though I'm kicking myself for saying anything about the class. If he thinks I'm inviting him, he'll want to dance, which means less time to get answers out of Fred Burrows.

"I'll leave you to your practice," Hugh says after a moment of awkward silence. "I have an appointment with an electrician about some dodgy wiring."

"Oh, no. Were the houses here not wired properly?" I haven't noticed any problems, but with little children around, I need to be sure they're not at risk.

Hugh shakes his head. "No, nothing like that. I had some renovations done while I was away, and the contractor I hired seems to have taken a few shortcuts. Young fellow, but then he would be, wouldn't he? Young people these days all want a lot for doing as little as possible."

According to Ritchie, certain parts of Florida are a magnet for shady contractors trying to make a quick buck off the elderly, because they think we don't know any better.

I nod. "I've been warned to watch out for the contractors here."

He tilts his head and shrugs. "Not to sound paranoid, but around here, it's best to watch out for everyone."

Twenty-One

Tory and Emmy, wet and wrapped in robes, bounce over to their father's side the moment Tom and I walk through the front door that afternoon.

"Daddy, can we get a puppy?" Tory's large aquamarine eyes attempt to melt her father into submission. "I've always wanted a puppy, and we saw the cutest one at the swimming pool today. It was fluffy and soft, and it kept licking my face. Can we please get one? Please, please, please!"

"Puppy!" Emmy chimes in.

"A puppy?" Tom echoes, kneeling to look his daughter in the eye. "Just last week, you said you wanted a unicorn."

A pained expression crosses Tory's face. "I do, but Mommy says they're not available where we live."

When Emmy glances at me, I quickly move into the living room. I don't want to get drawn into that conversation. One of my grandchildren has already persuaded me to let him build an x-ray machine in my garage. I don't need the others begging me to get a pet too.

"You're back." Eliza's fingers, which had been humming across her laptop's keyboard, come to a halt. "How did it go?"

"Your husband was a hit. He got enough invitations to play golf to keep him busy for the entire year." I take off my sun hat and set it on the counter separating the kitchen from the living room. "Where are the boys?"

Eliza closes her laptop and sets it aside. "Not back from the pool yet. They still can't convince Curt to get back in the water. We had to come home early because Emmy managed to swallow a piece of foam off a pool noodle. Don't ask. Oh, before I forget, Jolene's looking for you."

"Jolene came by?" The last time I saw the former federal agent, she was railing against the local police for locking me up. I hope she's not trying to make trouble for Detective Fletcher. He really is trying to become a better detective. "Did she say what she wanted?"

"No, she didn't. But we ran into Helen at the pool, too, and she asked if Jolene had tracked you down. So, it must be important."

"Maybe I should head over to Jolene's house," I say, even though I want nothing more than to lie down and rest my eyes for twenty minutes. Spending a few hours out in the sunshine has sapped my energy, and I'll need to rest before line dancing.

"No point. She said she had to leave town for the afternoon but will be back this evening. I told her *you*'d be at the line dancing class."

Relieved that I don't have to race back out the door, I sink onto the sofa. "Does that mean you and Tom don't want to come along?"

Eliza shakes her head. "You know I'm a terrible dancer!"

She's right. She has no rhythm at all. She is her father's daughter.

"Besides," Eliza continues, "Ritchie and Craig volunteered to go with you. We'll hang back here to pack up. Tom and the girls are leaving first thing in the morning."

"You're not going back with them?" I ask, though I'm not entirely surprised to hear that at least one of my children will be sticking around to keep an eye on me.

She shakes her head but before she can answer, the front door opens. Ritchie, Craig, and Curt breeze past Tom and the girls, who are still locked in the dog discussion near the front door. As they stroll into the living room, I notice that Jinny's grandson, Paul, is tagging along.

"Daddy, can I go to the garage now?" Curt hops from foot to foot as he waits for Ritchie to reply.

"Yeah, go ahead, buddy." In response to the quizzical

expression on my face, Richie explains, "Some parts for his x-ray machine arrived while you were out."

As Curt races toward the garage, I turn my attention to Jinny's grandson. "Hello, Paul. Are you having a nice time visiting your grandparents?"

He pushes a strand of light brown hair out of his eyes. "Sure, I guess."

"How long are you staying?"

"I don't know. Maybe a couple more days."

It's been so long since my own kids were that age, I'd forgotten how much effort it takes to try and get a teenager to talk.

"What have you been doing while you're here?"

Paul looks to Ritchie, as if silently asking for assistance. Unlike Paul's father, Ritchie supports Paul's dream of becoming a Broadway singer. The two have bonded over their shared love of musical theater.

"It's okay," Ritchie assures Paul. "You can tell her. We all want to help, if we can."

"Help with what?" I can't help asking.

"I have to stay in town until, like, the police decide whether to charge me for stealing," Paul admits.

An earlier conversation with Helen comes back to me. "Oh, you mean Marjorie did file a report with the police? I heard she and your grandmother had a fight about that."

Eliza shoots me a questioning look. I'd forgotten to mention the fight. She's probably thinking I neglected to fill her in on a suspect and possible motive for Marjorie murder. But I don't feel bad about it. Eliza's spent enough time at Egret's Loft at this point to know the only thing Jinny could kill is a brisk conversation.

Paul nods in response to my question. "Yeah. It was this ugly statue, and, like, I gave it back to her myself. But she said I didn't. You know, give it back. Mémé was so mad," Paul says, using the French-Canadian name for grandmother. "She knew I'd given it back. She said Mrs. Higginbottom was just, like, trying to cause trouble."

The crease between my eyebrows deepens. "Is it possible Marjorie—Mrs. Higginbottom—forgot you'd given it back? I mean, she was good friends with your grandmother. Why would she want to cause trouble for you?"

"She didn't forget," Paul firmly states. "Mémé was always, like, trying to defend her friend. But Pépé never liked Mrs. Higginbottom. He told me she was too nosy for her own good."

"Really?" I don't know what surprises me more, that Paul's grandfather, George, actually speaks, or that he would disagree with Jinny on anything. "How was she too nosy?"

"You know, like, she was always trying to get in other people's business. Watching what they were doing all the time. Pépé called her a curtain twitcher." Paul chuckles.

"He said the worst thing was, she kept score. Whatever that means."

So, George knew that Marjorie was making notes about her neighbors' movements. That has to be what he meant about keeping score. I wonder if he knew the extent of the files Marjorie kept on all her neighbors. I don't remember seeing a file on George and Jinny, but that doesn't mean much. There were so many files, and I didn't have time to look through them all.

"Hmm," Eliza ponders the situation. Then looks straight at me when she says, "I can't imagine the police would be able to press charges *now*. Not with Marjorie dead."

Richie glares at his sister, as I quickly say to Paul, "Yes, dear. Let's hope that any talk of you going to jail dies down. I mean, goes away," I quickly correct myself.

"Exactly. Nobody's going to jail, and nobody's dying. Well, nobody *else* is dying," Ritchie tries to reassure a nervous-looking Paul. "What I'm trying to say is, everything's going to be fine."

I hope Ritchie is right.

From everything I've learned so far today, I'm beginning to doubt the wisdom of my own thinking. I'd been confident David didn't kill Marjorie, because he was such an obvious choice. But I can't deny the man exhibits some disturbing traits, like having a dangerous and volatile temper.

Then, there's Jinny. I still don't think the sweet and folksy grandmother is capable of murder. But Eliza has a point. The moment Marjorie died, Paul was off the hook for a possible theft charge. Jinny's friend had betrayed her in the worst way. How far would Jinny go to protect her grandson?

How far would any of us go?

Twenty-Two

"Does it seem weird to be learning how to line dance in Florida?" Ritchie asks as we enter the Golf Club that evening. "I mean, doesn't salsa dancing seem more appropriate?"

"We're on the Gulf Coast, not Miami," Craig reminds his husband. "You just want an excuse to shake your hips."

"True," Ritchie admits. "These hips don't lie, and they're telling me they want to salsa."

Ignoring their playful banter as they saunter off in the direction of the bar, I focus on the missing pieces of the puzzle I need to find in order to solve Marjorie's murder. But, unlike other puzzles I've built, where you have an image of what the end result should look like, this picture remains elusive. Every day brings forth a new suspect and a host of potential red herrings, mostly because I'm still trying to get an accurate portrait of who Marjorie was.

Despite my initial impression of her as a kind of benign baker, the past few days have taught me that she was actually a pretty horrible person. She betrayed her best friend, Jinny. She tried to send her ex-lover, Fred, into anaphylactic shock. She threatened the volatile new chef, David. She tried to get Helen kicked out of Egret's Loft. And she'd been keeping creepy stalker files on her neighbors.

All things considered, she kept rather busy being hateful. No wonder she needed to save time by using premade dough for her cookies.

"There you are." Gina accosts me as I cross the lobby to get to the Golf Club activity room. "Where are your boots?"

"My boots?" I ask, examining the espadrilles I took out of their box to wear tonight. "What's wrong with these?"

Gina heaves a frustrated sigh. "They're not cowboy boots. Everybody knows you gotta wear boots when you go line dancing."

"You're making that up," I insist. "Boots have horrible arch support. Your feet will be barking at you by the end of the night. And, anyway, it's far too hot for closed-toe shoes."

"You'll regret not having them when it comes time to stomp and scuff," Gina warns me before getting down to business. "Forest is already here. How do you wanna play this?"

"I've been thinking that it might break the ice to introduce *Fred* to my son-in-law, Craig, since they have the NASA connection. Craig says he's never heard of Fred, but they might know some people in common," I reason. "After he's nice and comfortable, I'll ask him to dance and find out where he was when Marjorie died."

"You think talking about his old job is going to make him comfortable?" Gina asks. "The day I retired was the last day I ever wanted to think, or talk, about work!"

Rather than admit there may be a flaw in my plan, I distract her with a question. "Were you able to get the security video from Marjorie's patio camera?"

"Yeah, but don't get too excited," Gina manages my expectations. "All you can see is someone's shadow. The security guard saved it as a movie on my phone somewhere. Shoot, I should have asked for two copies so I could give you one!"

"Do you need two copies?" I ask. "Can't you just send me the one you have?"

Gina frowns. "But then I wouldn't have a copy anymore."

"Hello, lady...or ladies. Are you ready to dance?" Ritchie joins us, carrying a glass of whiskey he got at the bar.

"I've been wondering, why do you call your mom *lady*?" Gina demands. "Does your family have some kind of old-world title or something? Was your father a lord?"

Ritchie laughs. "No, nothing like that."

"When the kids were younger, they watched this

cartoon called *Animaniacs*," I explain. "One of the characters, a little girl named Mindy, always called her mother *lady*. Ritchie started doing it as a joke. At the time, I thought he'd grow out of it, but no such luck."

A concerned expression crosses Ritchie's face. "Oh no, does it bother you? I won't do it anymore if it does!"

I take a moment to think. "You know what, I actually love that you call me lady. It's our thing and it always reminds me that, even though you're all grown up, you're still my precious little cartoon-watching boy."

Before Ritchie can reply, the high-pitched shriek of a poorly tuned microphone echoes through the building, making us all clutch our ears.

"Would all line dancing participants please sign in?" a faceless voice beckons from the loudspeakers. "This is your last call. The class is about to begin."

"I guess we'd better get in there," Craig says, taking a long sip from his wine glass. "I'll need all the instruction I can get."

Ritchie lets out a low whistle as we join a crowd of more than fifty other residents in the activity room. It's been decked out to look like a barn in rural Texas, complete with hay bales for seats, wagon wheels for chandeliers, and wooden barrels for tables. There's a beer bar and appetizer table set up on one side of the room and a small stage elevated off the ground at the front.

The room is packed with all the familiar faces. Helen,

her eyes locked on Hugh Darcy, is making small talk with Savannah near the stage. Hugh, meanwhile, is engaged in conversation with former quarterback Roy Everhard on the other side of the room. Jinny and George Myrtle are munching on finger food from the appetizer table, where an angry-looking David, the chef, is laying out a selection of cheddar wheels, pigs in a blanket, and fried Twinkies.

The young media relations specialist, Sydney, stands on the platform, sporting sparkly cowboy boots on her feet and a microphone in her hand. A woman I don't recognize, wearing tight blue jeans, a ten-gallon hat, and cowboy boots, stands next to her.

"Can I get your attention, everyone?" Sydney's voice projects from the surround sound speakers built into the walls. "This is Darlene. She's going to be teaching *y'all*," Sydney intentionally stresses the contraction, "how to dance. Before I hand her the mic, a quick disclaimer. I will be going around the room taking videos for social media. If anyone doesn't want their image used online, please see me privately. And without further ado, here's *Darlene!*"

"How y'all doin' tonight?" Darlene's heavily accented voice fills the room. "I'm gonna be teachin' you some steps and, since there's a bunch of you here, I'm gonna need y'all to break off into groups of ten. Each group will get its own private tutor, in case you're strugglin' a bit at first."

The room erupts in chatter as everyone breaks off into groups. In addition to Ritchie, Craig, Gina, and I, we've managed to lure Fred by mentioning Craig's employment at NASA, as I'd suspected might be the case. Filling out the remaining spots are Hugh, Helen, Jinny, George, and Roy. We all congregate near the appetizer table to form our lines, as instructed. I'm pleased to see Savannah, a volunteer at tonight's event, has elected to be our group's tutor.

"Alrighty!" Darlene's voice cuts through all the idle chatter. "Now that y'all are in your groups, I'm gonna teach you a step that you'll need a partner for. So everybody, grab a partner."

Hugh is smiling at me, and I can tell he wants to ask me to be his partner, but I really need to talk to Fred. Fortunately, Helen's had her eye on Hugh all evening and doesn't hesitate to ask the British doctor to be her partner. Roy also begins to approach me, but Gina, winking at me, steps in and claims Roy, which leaves me free to dance with Fred.

"I should probably apologize in advance," I say to Fred. "It's been years since I've been out dancing."

Fred, the thick lenses of his glasses reflecting light from the fake oil lanterns hung throughout the room, shrugs and replies, "Dancing is good for the limbic system."

"I'm sure you're right," I say as we take our places beside each other.

"The first steps we're gonna learn are for a dance called the honky tonk badonkadonk," Darlene calls out. "Gentlemen, drape your right arm over your lady's shoulder."

No words are exchanged as Fred and I learn the steps,

which involve a lot of walking and turning. At one point, during a turn, I spot Jolene loitering by the door. I'd nearly forgotten she wanted to speak with me. But by the time I come full circle, I notice she's gone.

Once Fred and I have settled into a pattern, I seize the opportunity to begin a conversation.

"Your wife didn't join you tonight?" I ask.

"No. She wanted to wash her hair," he replies in a monotone.

I chuckle. "I guess dancing isn't for everyone."

He frowns. "Svetlana likes dancing. But she also likes clean hair."

Not really sure how to respond to that and knowing I need to, somehow, bring the conversation around to Marjorie, I decide to launch right in. "Marjorie would have loved this class. I watched her dance at Helen's wedding. She could really move, even with a walker."

"Uh huh," Fred grunts.

"I'm sorry," I say, thinking a sympathetic approach might get better results. "It must be hard to talk about Marjorie. You two used to date, didn't you?"

"Uh huh," Fred repeats.

Trying hard not to get frustrated, I say, "It must have been horrible for you, hearing that she was dead."

His glasses slide down his nose as he frowns. As he glances off to one side, I notice that one of his eyes stays in place, staring straight at me. That must be the eye that got hit with the laser, I realize.

"Not really," he finally says.

His monotonous indifference takes me by surprise. "You weren't upset?"

"No. We broke up," he states matter-of-factly.

"Even so, you were once very close," I argue. "Surely you must have been a little sad."

"Not really," he repeats.

"You didn't feel anything? Nothing at all?" I press, suddenly feeling cold, despite the rising temperature in the room.

"I felt something," he admits.

"Really? What?"

I can feel him shrug. "Relief. I'm glad she's dead."

Stunned that Marjorie's ex-lover would volunteer to share his hatred of her with me, a relative stranger, I'm at a loss for words. Here I was, thinking Fred couldn't possibly be any more boring, when, all of a sudden, he'd shocked me with his blasé hostility.

It's my turn to feel relieved when Darlene announces we'll be learning a new dance, this time, without partners. As we all form lines across the dance floor, Fred excuses himself to use the toilet, and Gina falls in beside me, questioning me with her eyes. I widen mine in response, hoping she'll be able to interpret my bewilderment.

Following my tortured discussion with Fred, I can't help

feeling a modicum of sympathy for Marjorie. She seems to have been an unhappy woman, surrounded by people who didn't particularly care about her. I wonder which came first. Did Marjorie inspire hatred in other people because of who she was, or was she who she became because of other people's cruelty?

Either way, someone hated her enough to kill her. And if I don't want to let that radio show label me as the lead suspect, I need to find the real culprit.

It sends shivers down my spine knowing that whoever struck Marjorie on the head with that tortoise and drove her scooter into the pool could be standing here with me, in this very room.

I've barely finished the thought when everything around me, suddenly, goes dark.

Twenty-Three

The darkness fell so quickly, the ghosts of lights still haunt my retinas. The sound of my panicked breath drowns out everything around me.

My eye doctor in DC had warned me that I was showing early signs of glaucoma, but I never thought my vision would completely fail, all at once. I blink rapidly, trying to catch a glimmer of something. Anything.

"Lady?" Ritchie's shaky voice cuts through my haze like a foghorn. He's somewhere to my left. "Are you alright?"

"Ritchie?" I can hear the desperation in my voice. "No, I'm not alright. I think I've gone blind from the glaucoma!"

A hand settles on my arm as Craig assures me, "You're not going blind. The lights just went out."

"You can't see anything either?" I ask, wanting confirmation before allowing myself to feel reassured.

"No, I can't." Craig's hand squeezes my arm.

"Me neither," Gina chimes in. "And, just so no one gets any ideas, to whoever I bumped into, it was an accident. I put my hands up to keep my balance. I wasn't trying to get fresh."

"That's a darn shame," Helen replies. "I was hopin' you were someone else."

"Doesn't this place have an emergency generator?" Ritchie asks, sounding a touch nervous. "Where are the exit signs? Shouldn't those still be working?"

"It's going to be fine, sweetie," Craig comforts my son, while activating the flashlight function on his cell phone. "I'll go find the breaker. Does anyone know where it is?"

"Yeah, the box is next to the pro shop. I can show ya," Roy offers.

Having spent that whole exchange trying to turn on the flashlight on my own phone, and failing, I decide to stick with what I know. "While you're doing that, I'm going to check and see if there are any candles in the kitchen."

"Brilliant idea. I'll go with you," Hugh says from somewhere to my right.

"Y'all might need some help. I'll come too," Helen quickly adds.

Using the very faint light from the screensaver on my phone, I walk toward the doors leading into the hallway, bumping into people along the way. Darlene, the dance instructor, urges everyone to remain calm, as excited chatter begins to fill the room.

Once in the hallway, I can vaguely make out the shapes of Hugh, Helen, Craig, and Roy. My son-in-law and the former quarterback head right, in the direction of the fuse box. The rest of us turn left, heading down the long hallway to the kitchen.

"It's darker in here than the inside of a gator's belly," Helen observes. "Hugh, will you hold my hand, so I don't get lost?"

"Uh...sure," Hugh haltingly replies.

Since it *is* so dark, no one catches me rolling my eyes.

Thinking back to the altercation with David on Saturday, I think I remember seeing a box of candles on the shelves near the turtle-shaped mortar and pestle. Hopefully, whoever organized the kitchen thought to put matches nearby.

"Now that's peculiar," Hugh utters as we pass by the large glass front doors that serve as the main entrance to the Golf Club.

"What's that, sugar?" Helen asks.

"The lamp posts are lit," Hugh remarks. "It would seem the power is only out in this building."

"Maybe the streetlights are on a separate grid?" I suggest.

"Perhaps." Hugh doesn't sound convinced. "But in the

absence of a storm, system overload, or downed power lines, one doesn't often experience blackouts in relatively new buildings such as this."

"Are you fixin' to say you think someone cut the lights on purpose?" Judging by the tremor in Helen's voice, I'm guessing she's squeezing Hugh's hand a little tighter.

His brief, involuntary yelp confirms my suspicion. "Don't mind me. I'm certain there's a perfectly innocent explanation."

Any solace Hugh intended to offer has the complete opposite reaction in me. I begin to wonder about the particulars of Marjorie's death. Did someone sneak up behind her in the dark to deliver the fatal blow with a cooking utensil? Did she know what was about to happen? Was she scared?

When the kids were still very young, the boyfriend of a criminal Clint put behind bars cut the power and broke into our house in the middle of the night. I'd been petrified and clutched the covers, but Clint had been fearless. By the time I'd dialed 911, he'd already jumped the intruder and tied him to a kitchen chair with the tiebacks from the living room curtains.

Clint had always been my protector. I silently ask him to look after me again now.

Hugh pauses in the hallway, shining the screensaver on his own phone at a set of doors. "Which one leads to the kitchen?"

"The one on the right," I tell him. "It just swings open. Here, let me."

Using my shoulder, I push on the door, and, entering the kitchen, I'm blinded by a spotlight aimed right at my face. Before my eyes can adjust, the light shifts, aiming in the opposite direction and bouncing up and down as it moves away from me. At least I think it's bouncing. It's hard to see anything past the residual stars left behind by the initial burst of light.

"Who's there?" Hugh calls out.

Whoever is holding the flashlight doesn't respond. They just move farther away, toward the door that leads to the outside seating area.

Following a series of clicks, the overhead fluorescents blink on, flooding the room with light. Only then do I recognize the fleeing form.

"Detective Baptiste?" I can hear the surprise in my voice.

She looks around, as if searching for a way to deny what we'd all just witnessed.

"This isn't what you think!" she exclaims.

Before I can make sense of the situation, Helen screams, then crumples to the floor.

Following the direction of her gaze, my eyes settle on the prone form of her friend Jolene. She's lying on the floor next to the industrial sink, a pool of water forming around her hands. Glancing up at the sink, I notice it's full of soapy water with the power cord of an unknown appliance trailing into its sudsy depths.

"We're going to need an ambulance at the Egret's Loft Golf Club," I hear Hugh say into his phone.

As he relays our address to the police dispatcher, I move closer to Jolene's body. Even before I rest my fingers on her wrist, I know I won't find a pulse. Her eyes are open and staring, unseeing, at the ceiling.

Releasing her wrist, having found no signs of life, I notice that her hand is clenched in a fist. Gently working her fingers open, I see that she's holding what looks like a scrap of paper. Tenderly removing it from her clasp, I try to coax the wet paper open without tearing it.

It appears to be the header for some kind of an official document, with the logo of a medical company and the name of the letter's intended recipient.

Squinting to read the bleeding print without my reading glasses, it takes me a minute to work out what it says. Finally, I'm able to make out a name.

The letter was addressed to Ms. Drusilla Hackney.

Twenty-Four

My mouth opens in an involuntary yawn as I sit waiting for Detective Fletcher in the lobby of the police station early the following morning.

After he'd arrived at the Golf Club last night and sent his handcuffed partner off in the back of a patrol car, he'd conducted interviews with everyone who had been in the building at the time of Jolene's murder. Whether it was because he was still mad that I'd doubted him about his search of Marjorie's house or because he wanted to have more information before talking to those of us who found the body, he'd decide to speak to me last.

Flanked by my overprotective children, Ritchie and Eliza, Detective Fletcher's questions had all been very formal and professional. While I'd wanted to be supportive of his obvious efforts to improve his interrogation techniques, I couldn't help feeling annoyed by how antagonistic he still acted toward Eliza.

My irritation dissolved somewhat when he pulled me aside at the end of the interview and asked me to meet him here this morning. Intrigued, I'd instantly agreed, even though it meant getting only a few hours of sleep after a long day of golf, dancing, and stumbling across the dead body of one of my neighbors.

A wave of sympathy for Savannah washes over me. With no father in the picture, Jolene had been her only family. I'm thinking of ways to be supportive of the suddenly orphaned young woman, when I hear the door, the one separating the lobby from the main office, open.

"Hi, Madeline," Detective Fletcher says, standing within the doorframe. "Come on in. Thanks for coming so early."

Grimacing from the effort to lift myself out of the stiff lobby chair, I tell him, "It's no trouble at all. Before you tell me why I'm here, I did want to apologize for seeming to doubt you the other day. Of course, you would have checked Marjorie's house for the files. You've learned so much over the past few months."

Detective Fletcher's cheeks flood with color. "Don't mention it."

"Hear me out," I silence him. "I don't want you to think I'm not proud of all the strides you've made. When I think back to how...well...lost you were in the aftermath of Carlota's murder, it's truly amazing that—"

"No, really." Detective Fletcher squares his shoulders, and his voice lowers an octave. "Please, don't mention it."

Only then do I see the smirk on the face of the duty sergeant manning the front desk and the mortification on the detective's. It would seem that, in trying to make amends, I've only made things worse.

Attempting to backpedal from my blunder, I blurt out loudly, "I was very lost, too, when I moved into Egret's Loft. There are so many streets, if they weren't all designed in circles, I'd never be able to find my house."

"Just come in." He hurries me through the doorway before I can say anything else. Once we're safely through to the other side, the fifty-something detective whispers, "Look, Madeline, I appreciate you're trying to be supportive, but can you try *not* to embarrass me in front of my coworkers?"

"You're right," I admit. My kids always used to tell me I mortified them in front of their friends. Of course, they were teenagers then, not full-grown adults. But it's not my place to judge. "So why am I here, Detective? Did you manage to track down Drusilla Hackney?"

He shakes his head as he sinks into his desk chair. "No luck. Whoever she is, she doesn't live in Florida. She's not in any of the criminal databases. Heck, I couldn't even find a driver's license for her."

"Do you think Drusilla was really Marjorie?" I wonder aloud, warming to the idea. "Maybe it was a secret identity or something like that!"

"Before you get carried away," he cautions me, "I should point out that we have no evidence that's the case."

"Carried away?" I turn my head and look at him from the corners of my eyes. "So you knew before I did that Selena was the wife of a dead drug lord? Or that Helen had been in the Witness Protection Program?"

"Alright, alright. You've made your point." He sighs. "The fact of the matter is, I'm not any closer to knowing where we can find this Drusilla person. What kind of name is that anyway? Who would name their child that?"

"I had an uncle named Florence. My grandparents swore up and down it was a unisex name, but we all knew he'd been named after my great-aunt who died of Spanish flu. He was a great big man, but then, he'd have to be with a name like Florence."

Detective Fletcher stares at me, wide-eyed. "Was there a point to that story?"

I shrug. "Only that Drusilla was probably a family name."

"Alrighty then." He sits up straighter in his chair, looking around the empty room. "Why don't we get to the point of why you're here."

"I *have* been asking why you wanted me here," I point out.

He pretends to ignore me. "First, you have to give me your word that you won't tell anyone what I'm about to ask you. I'm serious. If you ever repeat any of this, I'll deny it. Do you understand?"

"Can I tell my kids?" I ask. "They know I'm here. I mean, my son-in-law, Tom, dropped me off on his way out of town. But the rest of them decided to stick around for another day after...well...someone else died. Anyway, they'll want to know why you had me come in."

"You can't tell anyone," he emphatically states. "Is that going to be a problem?"

Leaning forward, I simply shake my head. Intrigued, I don't want to say anything else that might prevent him from telling me the thing I'm not allowed to repeat.

"You know we brought in Sammy last night." When I nod, he continues, "I'm about to interview her about her presence at *two* crime scenes, and I was hoping you might be willing to listen in. You know, tell me if there's anything I miss."

"Oh, I don't think Detective Baptiste would appreciate me being in the room when you question her," it pains me to acknowledge.

"No, no. You won't be in the room," he assures me. "You'll be in the adjoining room, behind one-sided glass. She'll never even know you're there."

As curious as I am to find out what excuse the slippery detective will give for being found fleeing a murder scene, I am mindful of my friend's feelings. As a result, I feel compelled to ask him, "Are you sure you want me around? You just said the other day that you wanted to unmask Marjorie's killer on your own."

"I do. And I will," he insists. His eyes break contact with mine as he adds, "I could just use a little bit of help. I worked narcotics before moving to Calusa. Murder is a different kettle of fish."

"Alright then."

For the next minute, neither of us says anything. Assuming the conversation is over, I'm waiting for Detective Fletcher to take me into the room with the one-sided glass. I hope the chair in there is more comfortable than the one I'm sitting in now, I think to myself.

Though my thoughts have moved on, when Detective Fletcher speaks, it's clear his haven't.

"Look, I really shouldn't be asking you to do this. I'm completely breaking protocol," he acknowledges. "It's just, well, she's a trained police detective, so she knows how we go about getting people to talk. Not to mention, she has her union rep in there with her. I don't want to mess this up. And your husband seemed to talk to you a lot about his cases, so…"

It dawns on me how much he must trust me to make a confession like that. Feeling suddenly maternal toward him, I rest my hand on his wrist. "It would be my honor to help you in any way I can."

He clears his throat and abruptly stands up. "Okay, good. Let's get this over with, then."

Understanding that I now need to back off for the sake of his ego, I say nothing as he leads me across the station and into a room next to the one labeled "Interrogation Room." Stepping inside, it's like I'm entering a movie theater, with all the attention in the room focused on an enormous window cut into the wall. Detective Baptiste and a suited man, who I assume is her union rep, sit on the other side of the window. She seems to glare at me through the glass.

"You're sure she can't see me?" I ask, unconvinced.

"Not a chance," Detective Fletcher assures me before closing the door and leaving me alone.

Seconds later, I see him entering the interrogation room. He takes a seat across from his partner at the table. Before he can begin, Detective Baptiste points her finger, seemingly, right at me through the tinted glass.

"I know you're in there," she insists. "I bet you're getting a real kick out of this, aren't you?"

Inadvertently, I glance behind me to see if there is anyone else she could be speaking to.

Back in the room, Detective Fletcher squirms in his seat. "What are you talking about? Why would you think there's anyone in there?"

Detective Baptiste stares at her senior officer. "Do you really think I'm that much of an idiot? I know you have your little buddy, Madeline, watching all this from behind the glass. You're in there, aren't you, Madeline?"

I swallow deeply, nearly choking on my discomfort. Either someone lied about the window only going one way, or Baptiste is a better detective than I've been giving her credit for being.

"Enough," Detective Fletcher bangs his hand, theatrically, on the table. "You have some explaining to do. Why don't we focus on that?"

Surprised by his overblown response, Detective Baptiste sits in silence for what feels like several minutes. Finally, she turns to her union rep. He whispers something in her ear.

"Fine. Ask whatever you like," she says. "But I want to say, on the record, that I strongly suspect your friend Madeline, the one *not* sitting behind the mirror, is trying to frame me for murder."

Twenty-Five

"That's ridiculous," Detective Fletcher says to his partner, though his tone sounds less than certain. "Why would Madeline be trying to frame you for murder?"

"Haven't you heard the podcast?" Detective Baptiste demands. "The reporter makes a pretty compelling argument. None of the killings started until she arrived, and she's *conveniently* been involved in all the investigations. Come on, can't you see she's pulling the wool over your eyes?"

"Nobody's pulling anything over my eyes," Detective Fletcher petulantly replies. "There's no way she could have been involved in this latest killing. I spoke to everybody at the Golf Club last night. They all vouch for her being in the room the whole time. I checked."

Sitting alone behind the one-way glass, my heart sinks with the realization that Detective Fletcher interviewed me last because he wanted to see if I had an alibi for Jolene's murder. Which means, some small part of him has begun to doubt me.

A surge of intense dislike for Brock Leitman washes over me, but I'll have to worry about him later. Right now, I need to focus on the interrogation.

"Why don't you just walk me through what happened last night," Detective Fletcher suggests, pulling his trusty notebook out of his shirt pocket. "Let's start at the beginning. What were you doing at Egret's Loft?"

Detective Baptiste glances at her union rep. He nods.

"I got another text," she says.

I can't see Detective Fletcher's face, but I can hear the incredulousness in his voice when he asks, "You got another text from the dead woman's phone?"

"Yes," his partner confirms, adding, "but not the dead woman I think you're thinking of."

"Which dead woman do you think I'm thinking of?" he asks.

"Marjorie."

"That was the dead woman I was thinking of."

Detective Baptiste sighs. "I know. I was answering your question. You know what, never mind. The text I got last night wasn't from Marjorie: it was from Jolene. Or Jolene's phone, anyway. I ran a search on the number before I went to meet her."

"So, *two* dead women have been texting you?" Detective Fletcher sounds confused.

"Yes," Detective Baptiste confirms. "Only they weren't dead when they texted me. At least, I don't think they were."

"I see. Can you show me the text you got from Jolene?"

Detective Baptiste looks down at her hands. "No."

"You do realize there are consequences for impeding a police investigation," her partner warns. "Are you telling me you deleted *another* text that could have significant bearing on this case?"

"No." Detective Baptiste shakes her head. "I can't show you the text because I can't find my phone. I think it might have fallen out of my pocket or something."

"Interesting," Detective Fletcher says, scribbling frantically in his notebook. "And what did this *alleged* text say?"

Detective Baptiste opens her mouth to speak, but her union rep puts his hand on her arm. "I don't like your tone," he confronts Detective Fletcher. "My client is cooperating fully. And I've already put in a request with the cell phone company to get a copy of the text in question. If we can't keep this civil, I'll put a stop to all of this right now."

Sufficiently chastened, Detective Fletcher holds his hands up in surrender. "Alright, alright. Sammy, would you please tell me what the text said?"

The suited man interrupts with, "I'll ask you to refer to my client as Detective Baptiste."

"Oh for the love of..." Detective Fletcher stops and takes a deep breath. "Fine. Detective Baptiste, would you do me the honor of telling me the contents of your text message from the dead woman?"

After getting permission from her union rep to respond, Detective Baptiste says, "She said she had information related to Marjorie's murder, but she would only discuss it in person, just the two of us. She asked me to meet her in the kitchen at the Golf Club at precisely eight o'clock."

"That seems like an odd place to meet if she wanted it to be private." Detective Fletcher scratches his bald head. "Wouldn't the kitchen have been busy serving dinner?"

"I asked about that. Apparently, the restaurant's closed on Monday nights," she informs him. "Then she said to use the outside entrance to the kitchen, to avoid being spotted. She'd make sure it was unlocked."

"And you agreed to meet her there?"

"Yeah," Detective Baptiste confirms. "And that's exactly what I tried to do. I arrived at the Golf Club about five minutes to eight. As I was walking across the parking lot, though, all the lights in the building went out. Which was weird, because the streetlamps were still working."

This gets my attention. Walking down the hall with Hugh and Helen last night, I remember Hugh pointing out that the streetlights were still working. But there was no way of seeing them from the kitchen. So, in order for Detective Baptiste to have noticed that, she must have been outside during the ten-to-fifteen-minute window when the electricity was out.

"So the parking lot was lit?" Detective Fletcher asks. "Did you see anyone coming out of the building?"

Detective Baptiste shakes her head. "No. I just went back to my car, got my flashlight, and hightailed it to the kitchen. I had a bad feeling."

"Did you go through the building or use the side entrance into the kitchen?" her partner asks.

"I went to the side entrance, as requested. There was more light outside than inside at that point, anyway," she points out. "I opened the door—"

"Had Jolene unlocked it for you?" Detective Fletcher interrupts her.

"It wasn't locked. So, yeah. I figured Jolene probably unlocked it, but I couldn't say for sure who did it."

"Alright." Detective Fletcher jots down a few more notes. "So, the door was unlocked and you went into the kitchen. What happened next?"

"I called out for Jolene, but there was no response. I proceeded to walk into the kitchen. I almost tripped over a trash can at one point, so, as I was walking, I kept shining my flashlight at the ground. That's when I saw her."

Detective Fletcher has abandoned his notes by this

point and is staring, transfixed, at his partner. "What did you see, Sammy?"

"Detective Baptiste," the suited man corrects.

Neither detective pays him any attention. Baptiste leans forward in her chair and says, "She was already dead. I didn't see any blood or anything, so I don't know how she actually died—"

"She was electrocuted by a toaster," Detective Fletcher explains.

I had suspected as much after seeing an electrical cord, which was plugged into a wall socket, snaking into the sudsy sink. Perhaps Jolene's electrocution caused the power outage.

"But then," Detective Baptiste continues, "I heard voices in the hall. I recognized one of them as that meddling, old busybody Madeline Delarouse. I'd already heard the trailer for the *Serial Seniors* podcast. I panicked. I thought, if she saw me there, she'd try to frame me too! So, I started running toward the back door."

"But why would you run from Madeline?" Detective Fletcher sounds confused, and for a moment, I feel gratified by his belief in me. Until he opens his mouth again. "You had to know what she'd think of that. I mean, you're a police officer. Don't you see how bad that looks? A police officer running *away* from a homicide?"

"I wasn't running away from the body," Detective Baptiste insists. "I was running away from her."

"Why?"

"Why? Umm, okay. How about because, a) I didn't want any more questions. I already had enough after she saw me at the River Club on the day she found Marjorie's body. And b) because I think she's dangerous. Look at all the people around her that are getting killed or being accused of killing!" Detective Baptiste folds her arms in front of her chest and leans back in her chair. "Huh uh, no thank you. Not today, Satan."

The room dips into silence as Detective Fletcher sits back in his seat and strokes his chin with the fingers on his right hand. "I still don't understand," he finally says. "You say, both Marjorie and Jolene texted you and asked you to meet up hours before they died."

Detective Baptists narrows her eyes. "Yeah. And?"

Her partner shakes his head. "I just can't figure out why neither of them texted me."

In the privacy of the side room, I let out a deep sigh. Poor Detective Fletcher. He really needs to work on his confidence.

It's no surprise to me, after the altercation in the jail cell, why Jolene wouldn't have contacted Detective Fletcher if she knew something. She had tried to come to me, but I hadn't been available. A fact that fills me with no small measure of guilt.

What had she wanted to talk to me about? Did it have to do with Marjorie's murder? But then, what did Marjorie want to talk to Detective Baptiste about? No crime had been committed at that point, at least not one any of us know about. And who is Drusilla Hackney, the mystery woman who seems to be connected to both murder victims?

As I'm pondering these questions, I hear a beep on my cell phone. Checking the display, I see a message from Eliza.

I'm outside the station. You need to come with me now.

Puzzled by her urgent tone, I glance back inside the interrogation room. Though I'm still not convinced Detective Baptiste isn't involved somehow, I think I've learned all I'm going to from the conversation. I better find out what my daughter wants.

Being as quiet as possible, I sneak out of the side room and make my way toward the exit. Fortunately, no one seems to notice me as I exit the building. Eliza's car is illegally parked in front of the entrance. She leans over and pushes the passenger door open for me.

"Get in," she instructs.

"Is everything alright?" I ask, as the car screeches out of the parking lot. "Did Emmy eat something she shouldn't have again?"

"Emmy's fine," she says, her eyes glued to the road.

"Then what's going on?" I demand. My request is met with stony silence.

As we're about to turn onto the private road that leads

to the Egret's Loft gate, she reaches across me and releases a lever that causes my seat to abruptly fall backward.

"What in the world?" I exclaim, trying to sit back up. "You're frightening me, dear!"

"Everything's fine. Just please, stay down," Eliza orders me.

As I'm reclining back onto the seat, I see them. Half a dozen television news cameras, lined up in a row, their lenses aimed at the entrance to the retirement community. My heart begins to beat faster.

"Has something happened?" I ask.

Instead of answering, Eliza pushes a remote that opens the gates to the complex. A few minutes later, we're parked in front of my house. Ritchie is standing in the open doorway, looking nervously at the phone in his hand.

I hear a buzzing sound overhead and look up. It's some kind of remote-controlled toy, like the little helicopters Clint and I bought Ritchie when he was younger.

I point up at it. "Is that Curt's?"

"No, Mom. It's not a toy. It's a drone, and it has a camera. Don't look at it." Eliza gently takes my elbow and ushers me into the foyer of my house.

"A drone?" I ask. "Why would the military want their cameras in Egret's Loft?"

"It's not the military, lady. The drone probably belongs to one of the news crews," Richie informs me.

"You mean those TV people set up out front? Has word already gotten out that Jolene was murdered?"

Ritchie and Eliza exchange glances. It's Ritchie who finally speaks. "They're not here for Jolene. They're here for you."

"Me? Why would they be here for—" My chest tightens as the truth suddenly dawns on me. "Oh, the radio show came out, didn't it?"

"Podcast," Ritchie corrects.

Eliza shoots him a withering glance. "It did. Now, with the way the news cycles work these days, it'll probably blow over in a couple of hours. But I'm not going to sugarcoat things. It's not good. It's probably best you hear it for yourself."

Eliza nods to Ritchie, who unlocks his phone and hits play.

Twenty-Six

Carlota Moreno Hernandez had big plans for her golden years. The bubbly and personable seventy-four-year-old had helped plan and open the premier retirement destination of Egret's Loft—an all-inclusive residential resort, specifically for seniors.

The plan was simple. In the warmth of the year-round Florida sunshine, residents could spend every day golfing, boating, swimming, or any one of a hundred activities designed to entice the elderly into living an active retirement. In the evenings, they'd go home to one of the more than thirteen hundred modern-style, high-tech houses built in the community, each decorated to the specific tastes of the owner.

The plan worked. Not long after opening its palm-lined gates, Egret's Loft became the place to retire. In a matter of months, every home sold and a waiting list of those wishing to

SERIAL SENIORS

move in began to grow. For Carlota, who was unanimously elected president of the board, the future and her outlook were bright.

Until that future was stolen from her.

On a sultry November night last year, a fellow Egret's Lofter entered Carlota's home and brutally beat her to death with her own golf club.

(Theme song briefly plays.)

You're listening to episode one of the Serial Seniors *podcast.*

Carlota's horrific murder shocked the tight-knit community. Who killed her, they wondered, and why?

As Detective Pete Fletcher—a bald Inspector Clouseau kind of character—struggled to identify a suspect, another resident fell victim to the cunning killer. Harold Small, a disgraced oil executive, was poisoned and left in the swamp to be eaten by hungry alligators.

Petrified elderly homeowners, many with pre-existing heart conditions, demanded answers. Who was terrorizing their community and how many more people would have to die before the culprit was caught?

No one thought to look twice at the mysterious stranger.

In the middle of the investigation, yet somehow well above suspicion, was sixty-nine-year-old stunner, Madeline Delarouse, newly arrived in Egret's Loft following the death of her husband, a veteran of the Washington DC Police homicide division. Carlota was killed the same day Madeline moved in next door. With the blond-haired, blue-eyed looks of an aging film star and all the charms of a 1950s housewife, it didn't take long for Madeline to become a popular bocce ball player...and an avid collector of secrets.

Against the advice of law enforcement, Madeline set out to track down the killer herself. And she did, pointing the finger at former Dollars and Sense CEO Victor Collins. Weaving an elaborate tale of fatherly love and desperation, Madeline claimed Victor and his son killed Carlota to cover up the younger man's financial crimes.

Soon after, another murder struck the outwardly peaceful community. Classic car tycoon Carl Hancock was killed on his wedding day, choked to death by a champagne cork. Once again, Madeline enmeshed herself in the investigation, making herself an indispensable source of information for the lead detective on the case. Based on her insights, another alleged criminal was apprehended and life within the community returned to normal.

But it was only a matter of time before death came again to Egret's Loft.

Last week, mere days after Madeline returned from holiday, Marjorie Higginbottom—a prolific baker and heiress to a vast aluminum dynasty—was discovered dead at the bottom of a swimming pool. And, just last night, a retired US Marshal was killed; she'd been electrocuted with a toaster.

As the hunt for their killer kicks into high gear, Serial Seniors asks its listeners to consider the possibility that one person may be responsible for all the recent murders at Egret's Loft. Someone with a thorough knowledge of how homicide *investigations work. Someone who's endeared herself to the lead detective. Someone able to cast suspicion everywhere, except on herself.*

Someone like Madeline Delarouse.

It's a theory local police sources tell me they consider not only possible, but highly probable. But can they catch her before she kills again?

In the same vein as my award-winning podcast Everything's Deadlier in Texas—*which revealed the identity of the real killer in the infamous Griner case—this series seeks to expose a miscarriage of justice.*

As the people Madeline has accused of murder languish in jail—for crimes they claim they didn't commit—I'll follow the evidence to prove, once and for all, that all the deaths at Egret's Loft are the work of one clever, serial-killing senior.

(Theme song briefly plays.)

Coming up after this word from my sponsors, an interview with alleged killer Victor Collins, in which he reveals how and why he believes he was framed for murder.

Twenty-Seven

"Would you please turn it off?" I say through my hands, which are, at present, covering my face to hide my mortification.

Ritchie obliges. "Are you alright, lady?"

"Of course, she's not alright!" Eliza responds on my behalf. "Did you hear that load of nonsense? And who, exactly, are these *supposed* local police sources that think Mom is a murderer? I bet you dollars to donuts it's that Detective Baptiste. She's had it in for Mom since day one."

"It also doesn't hurt that blaming Mom takes attention away from the fact that she was at both crime scenes," Ritchie points out. "I agree. I think Baptiste is behind the whole thing."

"I did a little digging on her," Eliza says, warming to the subject. "Apparently, no one on the force in Miami could stand her. Okay, so they did say she was smart and had good instincts, but she got into trouble on more than one occasion for botching investigations because she was so eager to make a name for herself."

Ritchie frowns. "I thought we'd ruled out the idea that she was killing people just so she could blame someone else, then take the credit for solving her own crimes."

"I don't think we have the luxury of ruling anything out just yet," Eliza argues. "From now on, everything is possible. Including that Detective Baptiste is the real killer."

I lower my hands from my face. "Except I don't think she is."

"How can you say that?" Ritchie asks, dumbfounded. "You just caught her running away from a dead body, for Pete's sake!"

"Just hear me out," I entreat. "Eliza, were you able to get Detective Baptiste's cell phone records? I'd really like to see the language in the texts she got from Marjorie and Jolene."

"You know, in all the excitement, I forgot to check," Eliza admits, as she walks over to her purse and begins rummaging through the contents. "Last night I asked my guy to get me all of Baptiste's texts from yesterday as well. He should have gotten back to me by now. Yeah, he did. He found texts from Marjorie and Jolene. Hold on, let me send them to you."

Ritchie's cell alerts him to a new message seconds

before my own phone pings. All three of us stare down at our devices.

I read Marjorie's message first. It says, *I have important information about a crime. Need to discuss in person. Meet me at the swimming pool tomorrow morning at eight oclock sharp. Come alone. Dont be late.*

Trying not to grammatically judge a dead woman for leaving out her apostrophes, I open Jolene's message.

It reads, *I have important information about a crime. Need to discuss in person. Meet me in the kitchen of the Golf Club tomorrow night at eight oclock sharp. Come alone. Dont be late.*

"Umm, does anyone else notice anything strange about these texts?" Ritchie asks.

"They're practically identical." Eliza says what we're all thinking. "Right down to the missing apostrophes."

"But they were sent from different numbers, right?" I try to clarify.

"Yeah," Eliza confirms. "They came from different numbers, which were identified as belonging to Marjorie and Jolene. But if *we* think it's strange, don't you think Baptiste would have noticed the similarities?"

"Not necessarily," I say. "Detective Fletcher told me she deleted Marjorie's text right after she got it. Apparently, she was protecting her source. If she didn't have the two of them to compare, she might not have realized they were, essentially, the same message."

"So we're thinking someone other than Marjorie or

Jolene sent both messages?" Ritchie scratches his head. "Could Detective Baptiste have cloned their cells and sent the messages to herself as a kind of alibi?"

"You can clone a phone?" I wonder aloud, as images of Dolly the sheep dance through my head. "Why wouldn't you just buy a new one?"

Richie sighs deeply. "You don't clone the actual phone. Just the number and all the data associated with that number. That way, you can send messages and make it look like they're coming from someone else."

My eyes widen. "You can do that?"

"Yes. You can. And I'm thinking maybe that's what Detective Baptiste did."

"I wouldn't put it past her," Eliza states, then shakes her head. "But then, why would she have deleted the first message? If she sent it to herself to explain her presence at the pool, she would have wanted to hold onto it, right?"

"Good point," Ritchie admits. "But I still think she's responsible."

I'm not convinced. "Then how did she know about the streetlamps?"

"What do streetlights have to do with anything?" Eliza wants to know.

"They were still on," I explain. Seeing the blank look on Ritchie and Eliza's faces, I realize I'll have to go into more detail. "When all the lights went out at the Golf Club, Hugh noticed that the lights were still on in the parking lot. The inside lights were only out for about fifteen minutes, so anyone who noticed the streetlights would have had to be in the foyer or in the parking lot during that time. Detective Baptiste talked about seeing them on."

"When did you talk to Baptiste?" Eliza demands.

It occurs to me that I made a promise to Detective Fletcher not to disclose what happened at the police station this morning. "I, um…well, she didn't tell me. Per se. I heard it through Detective Fletcher." Technically, it's not a lie.

Ritchie's hands move to his hips. "You do know you're a terrible liar, right?"

"I know," I cave under the weight of his accusation. "I'm sorry. I can't talk about the specifics. Just believe me when I tell you, Detective Baptiste noticed the streetlamps."

Eliza throws her hands up in frustration. "Fine. We'll stop focusing on Baptiste. For now. Who else do we think could be the killer? I mean there were loads of people there last night for the line dancing class, weren't there?"

"It could be worth pointing out that the chef, David, was there last night," Ritchie mentions. "The restaurant was closed, but he was there making snacks for the class. And all the murders seem to be tied to the kitchen in some way."

I'd nearly forgotten. "Of course. The mortar and pestle. And now, the toaster in the sink."

"Ritchie, did you get a chance to talk to David?" Eliza asks. "Is he dealing drugs at Egret's Loft?"

"I tried to chat him up at the line dancing class, but Craig started getting jealous, so I had to walk away," Ritchie says. "I tried to find him again after the lights came back on, but he wasn't in the room."

"Did anyone see when he left?" Eliza, the only one of us who wasn't at the class, asks.

Ritchie and I both shake our heads.

"Okay. When was the last time you saw him?"

I try to remember. "I don't think I saw him after the honky tonk badonkadonk."

A line appears between Eliza's eyebrows. "The honky what? No, you know what? Never mind about that. The important thing is, if what you're telling me is true, David doesn't have an alibi for Jolene's murder."

"Do you want me to talk to him again?" Richie asks. "I'm scheduled to perform a surgery in DC on Thursday, so Craig, Curt, and I *have* to fly out tomorrow morning. But I can try to track him down at some point today."

Eliza shrugs. "You might as well. Try to find out where he went after he left the class. Even if he's not our killer, he might have seen Jolene before she died."

"You still think Detective Baptiste killed her. I can tell," Ritchie says. "Lady, what do you think?"

Sighing, I tell my kids, "I think this is all going to be devastating for Savannah. The poor girl's mother has just been murdered. We should really go over to pay our respects."

Eliza grimaces. "You know I love you, Mom, but what about the podcast? If they've heard it, do you really think they'll want you there?"

I hadn't thought about that, but now that I am thinking about it, the notion makes me feel defensive. "Helen must know it's not true. And Savannah. She was our teacher in the class last night. She'll know I was there, dancing, the whole time."

"You're right." Ritchie scowls at his sister. "We should go. Brock Leitman is *not* going to stop us from being there for your friends."

"I was just making sure. Don't shoot the messenger." Eliza walks over to the fridge, pulling out a can of Coke Zero. Between coffee in the mornings and sodas throughout the day, my daughter drinks far too much caffeine, if you ask me. I've brought it up with her in the past, but she always brushes off my concerns.

Looking at the can in her hand, I'm reminded of something Brock mentioned in his radio show. Before today, I wasn't aware that Marjorie got her money from aluminum.

Twenty-Eight

"I knew I should have put sunblock on my shoulders. It's so bright out here, I can feel myself burning," I complain as we walk along Cypress Point Avenue toward Jolene's house.

Technically, the house belonged to Helen's late husband, Carl. As a thank you for Jolene's years of service protecting Helen while she was in the Witness Protection Program, Helen had gifted the house to her friend only a few months ago, after Carl died.

"You don't need sunblock," Ritchie tells me. "The dress has SPF 50. That's why I got it for you."

"I know you said that," I say, "but I washed it. I don't know how to reapply sun protection to clothes."

Ritchie chuckles. "You don't have to reapply anything.

The fabric is the protection. It's designed to block out the sun."

"Really?" I shake my head in wonder. "What will they think of next?"

"We should probably be thinking about what to do if Savannah doesn't want us around," Eliza changes the subject. "Obviously, I feel terrible for her, but if she or Helen so much as hint that Mom is responsible, I might lose my temper."

"They won't," Ritchie assures her. "They know Mom. They can't possibly think she had anything to do with Jolene's murder."

Eliza doesn't seem convinced. She steps in front of me like a bodyguard as we approach the front door. After glancing warily at both me and Ritchie, Eliza knocks.

A moment later, Sydney opens the door. A look of surprise flits across her face. "Oh, I wasn't expecting to see you here."

I can see Eliza's fingers begin to clench and, hoping to avoid a scene, I quickly respond. "We came by to give our condolences. Is Savannah here? The poor dear, how is she holding up?"

Sydney adjusts the large, black-framed glasses perched on her delicate nose before answering in a low voice. "Not great. I don't think it's really sunk in yet that her mom's gone. I can't even imagine how she feels right now."

My husband, Clint, had been taken from me suddenly and unexpectedly. Knowing how long it took me to come to terms with his absence, I can honestly say, "I completely understand."

"Do you mind if we come in?" Ritchie asks. "We want Savannah to know we're all here for her."

"Umm—" Sydney turns her head to quickly glance toward the living room, "—yeah, sure. I mean, I don't see why not."

"Of course, you don't," Eliza retorts, smiling through bared teeth. "Because there's no reason why we shouldn't be here."

Sydney nods, seemingly oblivious to Eliza's defensive tone, and opens the door wider so we can all step inside. As we walk toward the living room, I hear Sydney ask Eliza, "Is Tom not with you today?"

"Tom? You mean my husband?" Eliza's voice lowers, the way it always does when she's getting angry. "No, he's not here. He went back to Miami this morning with *our children*."

Before Sydney can further annoy my daughter, Helen spots us entering the room and rises from the sofa where she'd been sitting next to Savannah.

"Bless your hearts for coming by," Helen says. "We're real happy you didn't think you had to stay away because of that nonsense on the radio."

"Podcast," Sydney corrects Helen, drawing sharp glares from both of my children.

Savannah, torturing the handkerchief in her hands, doesn't notice. "I just don't understand. Who would want to kill my mom?"

Walking to the empty side of the sofa, I sink down onto the cushions beside Savannah. "I'm so sorry for your loss. I hope you know I'd never do anything to hurt you or your mother."

Savannah, her watery green eyes streaked with red veins, puts her hand on top of mine and nods.

"Good Lord Almighty. We know that!" Helen exclaims. "Why, that reporter's about as worthless as gum on a boot heel. He needs to go back to New York City, where he belongs." Helen shakes her head in disgust. "Yankees are like hemorrhoids. Pain in the butt when they come down and always a relief when they go back up."

It doesn't feel like the appropriate time to remind Helen that she's originally from New Jersey.

"I told you they wouldn't believe a word of it," Ritchie whisperingly gloats to Eliza. "No one who's met Mom could ever think she'd kill anyone."

"Savannah, dear," I address the young woman gently, "I know this is hard. You loved your mother very much. And I want to find out what happened to her. We all do. I think she wanted to tell me something yesterday. Do you have any idea what that might have been?"

A solitary tear runs down Savannah's pale, lightly freckled cheek as she shakes her head slowly. "I'm sorry, no. She didn't say anythin' to me."

"When was the last time you saw her?" I ask. "How was she acting?"

Savannah wipes the tear away with her pointer finger. "Sydney and I were at the kitchen table yesterday afternoon, workin' on a family tree video for George and Jinny Myrtle—"

"A family tree *video*?" I ask. When my kids were in school, I had to help them complete family tree homework assignments. But those were all on paper, never on video.

"Yeah, we were editin' together pictures and home movies of all their family members. Stuff like that. Sydney's developin' a marketin' campaign out of it."

"Was your mother helping?"

Savannah sniffles. "No. She was in her room. I have no idea what she was doin', and then she burst out, took one look at us, and announced she was off to Naples to run an errand. Ran outta here faster than a scalded cat."

The location gets my attention. "Naples? What errand did she have to run in Naples?" I can't help wondering if the Naples errand didn't have something to do with Drusilla Hackney and the post office box registered under her name.

"She didn't say, and I didn't ask. Why didn't I ask?" Savannah softly laments.

"You couldn't have known what was going to happen," I try to reassure her. "I know this may sound odd, but does the name Drusilla Hackney mean anything to you?"

Confusion fills Savannah's face. "No. Should it?"

"Drusilla Hackney? Who's that?" Sydney asks.

I sigh deeply before responding to Sydney. "To be honest, I have no idea." I turn back to face Savannah. "Your mother had a scrap of a letter in her hand when...well, when she died. The letter was addressed to Drusilla Hackney. Are you sure you've never heard the name before?"

I don't bother mentioning that I'd also come across the name on bills at Marjorie's house. That evidence seems to have disappeared.

Savannah takes a moment to think. "I wish I had. But, no, it's not ringin' any bells."

"It means nothin' to me," Helen says. "Jolene never mentioned knowin' anyone with that name. Do you think maybe it was someone else she was watchin' over in witness protection?"

"Possibly," I concede. My original thought had been that Marjorie and Drusilla were the same person. I'd mentioned as much to Detective Fletcher. If I was right, maybe Jolene was targeted because she was the connection between the two personas: Marjorie and Drusilla. I turn to Eliza. "Is there any way we can find out the names of the people Jolene protected as a marshal?"

Eliza scoffs. "You're joking, right? No one's going to give you those names!"

"Can we at least find out if she ever worked with Marjorie?" I press. "I mean, Marjorie's already dead, what harm could it do now?"

Eliza slowly rubs her forehead. "Yeah, I suppose I could ask around."

"Don't you work at the IRS?" Helen's eyebrows move ever so slightly in what I assume is a Botox frown. "Why would accountants know anythin'?"

"I have friends in law enforcement," Eliza quickly replies.

Ritchie puts a hand over his mouth to cover a snicker, but immediately looks chastened when Savannah begins to softly weep.

Helen sits down and drapes her arm across Savannah's shoulders. "Vannah, darlin', you really need to try and get some sleep."

"We should go," I say. "But you know where to find us if you need anything at all."

Helen nods and I stand up from the sofa. As I'm about to leave the room, I'm surprised when Savannah grabs my hand.

"Promise me you'll find out who killed my mama," she pleads. "I need to know that they're gonna to be punished for what they did."

Taken aback by the strength in the timid young woman's gaze, I tell her, "I'll do everything I can, dear. You have my word."

Ritchie, Eliza, and I follow Sydney to the front door. She leads the way, almost as if we might get lost without her. Once there, Sydney opens her mouth, then quickly closes it again. I get the sense there's something she wants to say, but holding the door open for us to leave, she just gives Eliza the once-over and says to me, "Savannah will get through this. She's stronger than she looks."

I nod and step outside into the early afternoon heat. Eliza falls in step beside me as we walk back in the direction of my house.

"What do you think about Sydney as the killer?" Eliza asks. "Something about her seems off to me."

I chuckle. "I noticed that you didn't like her asking about Tom."

Ritchie joins in. "Yeah. Are you sure you're not just jealous that a younger woman is expressing interest in your husband?"

"No!" Eliza protests. When neither of us believes her, she adds, "Okay, maybe a little. She's just so perky and upbeat and clueless. It's annoying. Doesn't anyone else find that annoying?"

"I think she's kind of cool, in a trendy, hipster kind of way," Ritchie says.

As my kids argue over Sydney's character, my intuition

tells me that the young woman knows more about what's going on at Egret's Loft than she's letting on. But as perkily as she portrays herself, I also get the impression Sydney has a problem trusting people.

I need to figure out how to earn her trust and find out what she knows before anyone else dies.

Twenty-Nine

"That poor girl." Gina shakes her head, the bocce ball in her hand momentarily forgotten. "Teaching us how to dance while her own mother was being murdered."

After walking home from Savannah's house and attempting to eat lunch, despite having no appetite, Gina and I had decided to meet up at the bocce ball court to try to take our mind off things. If we thought we'd be able to do that, we'd been fooling ourselves. All we've talked about since arriving is the most recent murder.

"The whole thing is just awful," I agree. "Savannah's holding it together as best she can, poor thing. She may seem timid, but I think she's more of a fighter than we realized."

"Should we have invited her?" Curt, who begged to

come along so he could learn how to play the game, asks. "Though the theory that keeping busy helps speed the grieving process has been debunked, there is still adequate research detailing how grief can result in social isolation."

I ruffle his little blond head. "That's very sweet, dear, but it hasn't even been a day. I don't think we need to worry about social isolation just yet."

Gina, seeming to remember she has a ball in her hand, throws it toward the pallino. It lands wide of the mark, but she doesn't seem to mind. "All I can think is, I'm glad she wasn't in the room when you found the body."

I'm surprised the thought hadn't already occurred to me, but Gina's right. Savannah had only been down the hallway when her mother was electrocuted. It could just as easily have been her searching for candles in the kitchen after the lights went out. Anyone in that class could have, feasibly, stumbled upon the body. Anyone in that class could also be a suspect.

I take a step closer to Gina as Curt throws one of our balls. "Do you happen to remember who was in the room when the lights went out?"

Her eyes twinkle. "That's not what you're really asking though, is it? You're more interested in who *wasn't* in the room."

I smile at my friend. "You know me too well."

Curt tugs on the hem of Gina's blouse. "Your turn."

She kneels beside him. "How about we give you some time to practice, now that you know the rules."

Curt squints skeptically. "Are you sure you want to give me that kind of advantage?"

"I've been playing for years," Gina explains. "It only seems fair to let you warm up a little before we play for real."

"That's very sporting of you," Curt concedes. "I accept."

We wait for him to start throwing balls before continuing our conversation.

"Alright now, let me think back." Gina rubs her chin with her forefinger and thumb. "We know that Rob, Holly, and Hank were all in the room when the lights went out, because we heard them talking."

"You mean Roy, Helen, and Hugh. That's true. And either Craig or I were with all of them prior to the body being found. Which means they're in the clear. What about Fred? He left to use the washroom not long before the lights went out," I recall. "And he's been at the top of our list of suspects. Do you remember seeing him later on, after the police showed up?"

"I think I saw him wandering around when we were all waiting for the cops to talk to us," Gina tries and fails to remember more detail. "But I don't know how long he was gone or when he came back."

"Which means Fred would have had the opportunity to kill Jolene. The only question is, *why* would he? He had a motive to kill Marjorie; she nearly killed him. But did he even know Jolene?" I wonder aloud. Then a thought occurs to me. "Or does he know Drusilla Hackney? Maybe she's the connection."

"We still don't know who she is though, do we?" Gina asks.

"No one seems to know anything about her. Eliza and Detective Fletcher have been trying to track her down, but they haven't been able to find anything. Not even a driver's license. She's like a ghost."

"Oh, oh! Do you think maybe she belongs to that sovereign citizens group?" Gina's face lights up with excitement.

"The conservative nonprofit that went to the Supreme Court over campaign finance laws?" I attempt to clarify. "What do political contributions have to do with anything?"

Gina shakes her head vehemently. "No, no. You're thinking of citizens united. Totally different group."

"It's so hard to keep all of them straight these days. Who are these sovereign citizens, then?"

"Well, I saw something about them on an episode of *Bosch*," Gina explains. "Have you seen that show? Chantelle got me into it. It's pretty good. Anyway, they're apparently some kind of domestic terrorist group."

I frown. "Marjorie may have used premade cookie

dough, but that hardly makes her, or this Drusilla person, a terrorist."

"This has got nothing to do with Marjorie's cookies, hun, though what she did was a travesty," Gina declares. "No, these people are against big government. They don't have IDs or pay taxes because they don't think laws apply to them. Which means, no driver's license or anything. Just like this Delilah person."

"Drusilla," I correct her. "That seems a bit far-fetched, don't you think? I mean, I saw her medical bills. How could she get in to see a doctor without an ID? I can't even get an appointment for a mole check without proof of insurance and my Medicare card."

Gina ponders what I've said. "Yeah, okay. You have a point. In that case, I don't know. Maybe she's a kid and that's why nobody can find any information on her?"

"I think we're getting sidetracked by Drusilla," I observe.

"You're the one who brought her up to begin with," Gina points out.

"Well, now I'm un-bringing her up," I state, glancing quickly over at Curt to make sure he's not about to chastise me for making up words. He's so focused on throwing the bocce balls, I worry he might end up with permanent teeth marks in his lower lip. Since he's occupied, I feel safe continuing the conversation with Gina. "We'd been talking about who was in the room with us when Jolene was murdered. We should focus on that. I know Jinny was in the line dancing class, but I didn't see her right before the lights went out. Was she there?"

"Come to think of it—" Gina pauses, "—I don't think she was."

"Did you see her leave the room?"

Gina angles her chin down so she's looking at me through her thin, dark eyelashes. "I didn't need to. If she'd been in the room, she would have been talking."

Not wanting to disparage Jinny by admitting the accuracy of Gina's comment, I focus on a reason Jinny might not be our killer. "Jinny was mad at Marjorie for trying to send Paul off to jail, which is fair enough. But Jolene? Like Fred, Jinny didn't have any reason to kill her. Not one that we know of anyway."

"The same could be said about the psychopathic chef," Gina observes.

"Of course! I'd nearly forgotten about David," I admit. "He was in the room early on in the evening, setting out food, but I have no idea when he left. I was too focused on talking to Fred."

"The kitchen is his domain, and that's where I found the turtle that killed Marjorie," Gina says. "I know you think he's too suspicious to be a real suspect—and, by the way, the logic of that still eludes me—but both murders are tied to his kitchen."

"You're right. Ritchie's planning to talk to him this afternoon to see what he can find out," I tell her. "But we don't seem to be getting anywhere right *now*. We're not narrowing down our suspect pool at all. Any one of them could have snuck into the kitchen before the lights went out and then rejoined the group in all the confusion afterward. And then there's Detective Baptiste, who was in the kitchen, but claims Jolene was already dead when she found her."

"Yeah, right." Gina snorts derisively. "My money's on her. Or the chef. Something's not right about either of them, if you ask me."

Curt, having collected all the bocce balls, walks up to where Gina and I are standing. "I believe I've had adequate time to prepare my strategy for the game."

"Give us one second, dear," I say, not wanting my train of thought to get left behind on the platform. "I suggest we talk to everyone who was at the class to find out who was in the room when the lights went out, since it happened when Jolene was electrocuted with the toaster in the sink. So, if Jinny or Fred or David were in the room, then we know they couldn't have done it."

Curt touches my arm to get my attention. "The entire building lost power, and you're thinking it was caused by the toaster short circuiting after being submerged in water?"

"Yes," I confirm. "But it's nothing for you to worry

about. And please don't tell your Poppa you heard us talking about this, okay?"

Curt frowns. "Why?"

"Because he doesn't like it when my friends and I talk about…uh, unpleasant things."

Curt sighs. "I know *that*. I mean, why would you presuppose that an electrical fault which damages one circuit, in this case to the kitchen, would automatically trip circuits to the rest of the building?"

Gina and I take a minute to try and understand what my grandson just said. Giving up, Gina says, "You're gonna have to explain that to me again, kid."

"First of all—" Curt stands up taller, "—I find it appalling that the electricians didn't put in ground-fault circuit interrupters in the kitchen. Those would have prevented the potential for electrocution. We should inspect your circuitry, Grandmother, to make sure it's fully up to code."

"That sounds like fun," I lie. "But let's get back to what you first said. Were you saying that Jolene's electrocution would *not* have caused the power to go out to the rest of the building? Do I have that right?"

"In layman's terms, yes." Curt nods. "The statistical probability of that happening is low enough to warrant being deemed negligible."

Gina scratches her head. "So, what I'm taking from that

is—the murder could have happened at, pretty much, any time last night?"

"Affirmative." Curt smiles. "Now, who wants to be my opponent in a round of bocce ball?"

To Curt's dismay, neither Gina nor I immediately volunteer. We're both too lost in our thoughts.

If the time of death doesn't match up with the building's power loss, then anyone could have snuck into the kitchen and killed Jolene, at any time. And, if that's the case, no one would have had a better opportunity than David. Which means, I may have been wrong to have written off the knife-wielding chef so quickly.

Suddenly, a wave of worry for my son overwhelms me. Ritchie could be in the kitchen with the killer at this very moment.

While Ritchie is extremely intelligent and always calm under pressure at work, he does have a tendency to panic, just a little, when he thinks his life might be in danger. Which is why he generally shies away from putting himself in harm's way. In fact, one time, when we saw an intruder running through my backyard, he hid behind me while Eliza chased after the mystery man.

My instinct keeps telling me that David's not the killer. And, up until now, I've always trusted my instincts. But, realizing how much I have to lose if I'm wrong, I wonder if my obsession with solving murders is putting those I love at risk. And whether I can live with those kinds of consequences.

Thirty

My heart beats quickly and erratically as I tuck my golf club under my arm and push open the doors to the River Club.

Since Jolene had been murdered in the kitchen at the Golf Club, all meals have been temporarily moved to this location. Signs inside still prohibit access to the pool area, where Marjorie was murdered, but fortunately, the inside isn't considered a crime scene.

If these murders persist, I think, there'll be nowhere left to eat at Egret's Loft.

Though that's hardly my biggest concern. At the moment, all I care about is finding David and seeing what he's done with my son.

When I'd arrived home from bocce ball, I'd been disappointed to find that Ritchie wasn't there. With evident reproach for our investigative endeavors, Craig said he'd gone to speak with David to suss out whether the cook was selling drugs. My son-in-law seemed more annoyed than concerned, saying we'd meet up with Ritchie in half an hour or so, when we were all scheduled to have a last meal together before Ritchie, Craig, and Curt leave town in the morning.

Not wanting to worry Craig, I hadn't said anything about my new suspicions regarding the chef. But I knew I couldn't wait that long to make sure Ritchie was okay.

I'd immediately jumped into my golf cart and raced across the complex in an effort to save my son from a possible killer. Having faced death myself on a few occasions now, I'm familiar with the fear of knowing your life might soon be over. That pales in comparison to the terror I feel now, thinking of what could happen to my child.

Walking toward the kitchen, my fist tightens around the weapon clutched in my hand. As a last-minute precaution, I'd grabbed one of the golf clubs out of my bag before heading inside. If I'm going down, I want to go down swinging.

A cacophony of banging pots and chopping knives assaults my ears as I stand in the hallway. I take a deep breath before bursting into the kitchen. My sudden entrance draws a few frightened looks from kitchen staffers, but upon seeing me, their expressions soften. They must have thought I was their boss, David.

To my right, I see the young girl who'd been sent to fetch baking soda for me when Gina and I last tried to confront David. She's standing at the sink, her gloved hands submerged in water as she scrubs pots. I walk over to her.

"It's Sonya, right?" I ask gently.

She looks at me with wide eyes, before scanning the room nervously. "You shouldn't be in here. If David finds you..."

"Don't worry about me," I tell her, displaying the golf club in my hand.

Her lips spread wide in a smile. "In that case, what can I help you with?"

"My son came in here a little while ago," I explain. "He's about six feet tall with blond hair and blue eyes. Have you seen him?"

"Wow, the hot guy's your son? Is he single?" she blurts out.

"You're a very attractive young lady," I assure her. "But—and please don't take this the wrong way—you're really not his type."

The smile disappears from her lips. "Yeah, someone that looks like him probably dates, like, swimsuit models."

"Oh no, nothing like that," I correct her. "He's married. To a man."

Realizing that Ritchie's disinterest would have nothing to do with her looks, Sonya's smile returns. "Oh! That's cool. I mean, it's cool that someone of your generation would be supportive of that. You know?"

Though I'd tried my best to keep from hurting her feelings, she chose not to return the favor. I'm an older woman, so, of course, in her mind, I must be a bigot. Kids these days, what can you do? I sigh deeply. "Do you happen to know where my son is?"

"Yeah, sure. I saw him talking to David. They went out onto the patio about fifteen minutes ago," she tells me, pointing to the kitchen's side door. "They're probably still out there."

After thanking her, I cross the room quickly, throwing open the side door and stepping out into the dusky sunlight. A large hedge is directly in front of me with a paved path forking out in either direction. To the left, I see about a dozen tables that are starting to fill up with early bird diners. To the right, there's a bend in the path that, I think, leads to the dumpsters.

Hearing noises coming from the right, I rush to round the bend, the golf club raised above my head.

"Ritchie!" I exclaim. My son, wearing gloves and an apron over his clothes, is bending over a large trash bag. David looms behind him, holding up the lid of a large dumpster. "What's going on?"

Ritchie straightens up to his full height, his eyes focused upward on the head of my nine iron. "We're sorting through the trash to pick out the cans and plastics. You know how I feel about recycling. What's with the golf club?"

"What, this old thing?" Realizing that my son is safe and sound, I suddenly feel very silly. I lower the club so that the head is touching the ground. "I...uh, I hurt my ankle. I needed a cane and didn't have one at the house."

David frowns, his thick eyebrows drawing dangerously close together. "Yeah? So why were you holding it over your head?"

Good question, I think, while struggling to come up with a plausible explanation. "I was...umm...using it to push back some of the hedges there. You really should get a gardener back here for a trim."

From the look on David's face, I can tell he doesn't believe me. Even my own son looks unconvinced. Lying is definitely not my strong suit.

"Look," I begin. "To be perfectly honest—"

David cuts me off. "Don't worry about it. I know why you're both here."

"You do?" Ritchie whips around to face David.

"Of course, I do. I'm not an idiot," he tells Ritchie. "You can quit pretending you care so much about the environment."

"Actually, I *am* really big on recycling," Ritchie says.

"He is," I back up my son. "Has been since he was little."

David slams the lid down onto the dumpster. "Enough!

I've heard all about your little 'investigations.' Just admit it, you're here because you want to find out if I have an alibi for that marshal chick's murder, right?"

"Well, since you brought it up...do you?" I ask.

"Not that it's any of your business, but I have nothing to hide, so I'll come clean. I was in the janitor's room all night."

"Was anyone in there with you?" I try to ascertain whether there's a witness who can back up his claim. Then, realizing the implication of my question, my face flushes with embarrassment.

He smiles wickedly. "For a woman your age, you've got a dirty mind."

I can feel my cheeks getting hotter. "I didn't mean—"

"I know what you meant." His smile disappears. "And the answer is no. I was in there alone. Someone put me in there after they knocked me unconscious."

"Oh my goodness, are you okay?" My maternal instincts win out over my inquisitive nature.

"Not really. My head is killing me." He rubs the back of his head with his right hand. "I've got a massive lump. Feel it if you want," he offers.

Since Ritchie is in closer proximity, he volunteers himself. "Jeez, you should really have that checked out. You could have a concussion."

David shakes his head. "No way. I don't have time to go

to the hospital. In fact, I really need to get back into the kitchen before the early bird dinner rush kicks off."

"Of course, we don't want to take up too much of your time," I assure him. "But could you tell us what happened? Did you see who hit you?"

"Naw. They hit me from behind. I was heading to the kitchen to grab some Texas sausage kolaches for the buffet—"

"Kolaches? Aren't those a Czech dish?" Ritchie, who is a very good cook himself, asks.

David's eyebrows draw together. "I'm trying to explain what happened, and you're asking about the culinary origins of kolaches?"

"You're right," Ritchie concedes. "Not important. Please continue."

"So," David draws out the syllable, "one minute, I was going to pick up some *pigs in a blanket* from the kitchen. Next thing I know, I'm waking up this morning in a broom closet. That's all I know."

"Do you remember, roughly, what time it was when you were attacked?"

David rubs his forehead, a pained look on his face "I don't know. Around eight, I think. My shift was supposed to end at seven-thirty, and I remember being annoyed that I was still working."

It occurs to me that, based on the timing, he must have been knocked unconscious shortly before the lights went out. He could help us determine whether Jolene was already dead when that happened. "One last question. Were you already in the kitchen when you were struck?"

To my disappointment, he says, "No. I was still in the hallway. And before you ask, I never saw the dead woman. Before *or* after she died. Look, I've answered all your questions and now I really need to get back to work."

Without waiting for us to reply, David stomps past Ritchie and I in an aromatic cloud of onion and garlic.

"Well," Ritchie says after David is out of earshot. "What do you think?"

I take a moment to think before answering. "First of all, I think I need to have a serious talk with Detective Fletcher about the importance of checking rooms after a murder has been committed. If David was in the building, someone should have found him before he woke up the next morning."

"Yeah, yeah." Ritchie waves off my diatribe about proper police procedure. "But what do you think about David? Do you believe him?"

"I don't know," I admit. "It does seem a bit convenient that his alibi doesn't rely on any witnesses. Then again, he does have a lump on his head, right?"

Ritchie nods. "Oh, yeah. And I don't think it's likely to have been self-inflicted."

"I suppose we'll have to take him at his word for the time being," I remark.

"Speaking of time." Ritchie glances down at his watch. "We're late for dinner."

Not wanting to keep the others waiting, Ritchie strips off his apron and gloves, and we make our way around the building to the restaurant entrance.

Spotting Eliza, Craig, and Curt already seated at a table, we begin walking toward them. Halfway across the room, it dawns on me that all conversation in the restaurant has ceased, and everyone's eyes are focused on me. One woman, whom I've never met, shakes her head, then whispers something to her friend.

Holding my head high, I try not to notice the hostile atmosphere in the room.

I sigh. Who could have guessed, in this day and age, how popular a radio show would be?

Thirty-One

"Well, that was a bit awkward," Ritchie says as he types in the code that unlocks my front door. "Now, I know how a seal would feel in a tank full of sharks."

We've all just arrived back at my house after a rather uncomfortable dining experience. The only people who looked at us with anything other than accusatory glares were the waitstaff. And they probably just didn't know what all the fuss was about.

Curt rushes into the house first, heading for the garage. At dinner, he wouldn't stop talking about how much work he still has to do on his x-ray machine before leaving town in the morning.

Eliza waits for me to go inside next, then follows me in. "Something really needs to be done about Brock Leitman."

Craig raises a well-groomed eyebrow. "What are you suggesting?"

"Don't ask her that," Ritchie scolds his husband. "Do you want us all to be accessories after the fact?"

Eliza plants her hands on her narrow hips. "Seriously? I'm not planning to kill the guy, if that's what you're implying."

Ritchie mimics her stance. "Really? Then what else are you planning to *do* with him?"

"I'm not planning on *doing* anything to him," Eliza retorts. "I was just thinking it could be useful to tap into his phone. Find out who's been feeding him all these lies he's spreading."

At this point, Ritchie and Craig turn to look in my direction. They know I've been less than supportive when Eliza talks about plans that involve the infringement of another person's civil liberties, regardless of how well-intentioned and helpful the information obtained might be. They're expecting me to chastise Eliza for the mere suggestion of tapping into someone's phone, but I disappoint them by not objecting.

Truth be told, I've only been half-listening to their conversation. Standing in the foyer of my house, I'm staring out into the backyard. "Did one of you turn the lights on in the swimming pool?"

All of the devices in my house are fully automated, something the builders thought would be helpful for active elders who might or might not have a tendency to leave appliances on when they left a room. The oven turns itself on and off at prescheduled times. The electrical sockets all have sensors that deactivate the flow of energy when there's no motion detected for longer than half an hour. And, after some minor modifications by Curt, the refrigerator does everything from offering me recipes to reminding me of my scheduled activities.

The lights are much the same. They're all set to timers that Ritchie adjusted after I first moved in. He told me I can also turn them on or off with my phone, but, call me old-fashioned, I prefer light switches.

At the moment, I'm staring at the pool lights, because they're not connected to a timer and have no reason to be on. I'd read a horrible news story once about how a child had been shocked by faulty lights in a swimming pool, so I refuse to turn mine on, especially when my grandchildren are around. Ritchie and Eliza know all about my aversion. So who turned them on?

My kids look at each other and then back at me.

"Do you think there's someone in the house?" Ritchie whispers.

Eliza rolls her eyes. "The lights are on outside. Why would anyone be in the house?"

"Why would anyone be in the backyard?" Ritchie challenges her. "They'd need to open a gate to get into the pool.

If they're willing to open a gate, they'd be willing to open a door."

"It's probably just a glitch in the timer," Craig argues, trying to be rational. "Even if you don't have that one circuit turned on, it's probably still connected to the main system."

Ritchie glances around the room nervously. "I don't know. I think we should check the whole house. Especially the closets. That's always where bad people hide."

"Oh really? What bad people have you found hiding in your closet?" Craig asks, smiling.

Ritchie sighs. "Not *my* closet. But, in movies, that's always where they hide. Have you not watched any of Jamie Lee Curtis's earlier work?"

"I love you, but you're a mess," Craig teases my son. "I almost hope someone comes out of the closet and kills you, just to get you to shut up."

"But then I'd be right!" Ritchie exclaims.

"You'd also be dead," Craig points out.

"Why should I be punished for being right?"

"You're not being punished for being right," Craig explains, "you're being punished for being obnoxious!"

"Enough!" Eliza interrupts their banter. "There's no one in the house, alright. The security camera on the kitchen counter would have alerted us if someone came into the house."

Ritchie opens his mouth to argue, but Eliza doesn't give him the chance.

"Mom, stay here and protect your scaredy cat son, yeah?" she orders. "I'm going to go check out the pool."

I put my hand on her arm. "You shouldn't go out there alone. Are you sure you don't want me or Craig to come with you?"

Eliza takes an elastic band out of her pocket and ties her long blond hair back off her face. "It's fine. I'll be right back."

Ritchie draws in a sharp breath. "Don't say that! In movies, the person who says that is always the next to die!"

Eliza turns to Craig. "I'm starting to agree with what you said earlier."

Before Ritchie has time to get offended, Eliza is striding past the kitchen, across the dining room, and over to the sliding glass door in the rear of the house. She makes a show of unlocking the door, before slowly easing it open.

"There's no one out here," she assures us but, before stepping outside, she pauses. "Huh, that's strange."

"What's strange?" Ritchie, wide-eyed, asks.

"It looks like there's something stuck in the pool filter," Eliza says. "I'll go pull it out."

"Be careful, dear," I call out, but I can't be sure she's heard me.

Through the window, we see Eliza kneeling beside the pool, tugging at something pink. My first thought is of Jinny. It's the only color she wears. Has she been in my pool?

Unable to contain my curiosity, I walk closer to the back windows. Craig follows me, trying to shrug off the hand Ritchie's using to clutch his shoulder.

"What is that?" Craig asks, as Eliza, her back toward us, holds up a long piece of pink fabric.

"Is it a scarf?" I ask.

Craig shakes his head. "It looks like it's made of plastic, doesn't it?"

Eliza turns to face us. "I think it's some kind of pool float, but it's been punctured. In a lot of places, actually."

My mind automatically flashes back to another day at another pool. When Curt and I found Marjorie's body, there was a pink flotation device initially hiding her body from view.

I swallow my apprehension. "Could it have been shaped like a flamingo?"

Craig and Ritchie look at me oddly as Eliza examines the item in her hand. Instead of answering my question, she stands up and marches toward the sliding glass door, the pink vinyl float dripping pool water across my patio.

"Alright, Mom. How did you know it was a flamingo?" she demands.

I glance at Ritchie's pale face. I don't want to make him any more nervous. "Would you believe me if I said it was just a lucky guess?"

Ritchie and Eliza, in unison, say, "No!"

"There's no need to shout," I complain. "The reason I thought it might be a flamingo floaty is because Curt and I saw one just like it at the pool the day we found Marjorie's body."

"What?" Eliza erupts. "Why didn't you mention it earlier?"

"Why would I?" I ask, genuinely confused. "I didn't think a pool toy had anything to do with Marjorie's death. The killer could have hardly bludgeoned her to death with it, now could they?"

"Fine. I'll give you a pass on that one. But you do realize what this—" she holds up the shredded mass of vinyl "—means?"

Ritchie looks over his shoulder. "That we *really* need to check the closets?"

Craig groans. "Oh my gosh, enough with checking the closets already!"

Ignoring both of them, I answer Eliza's question. "It means whoever put this in my pool is probably Marjorie's murderer."

Eliza drops what's left of the floaty on the back patio. She reenters the house, shutting and locking the door behind her. "I'm going to call Detective Fletcher. At the very least, someone's guilty of trespassing. Maybe he can dust the patio door for prints or something."

As my daughter digs through her pockets for her cell phone, my own goes off in the little purse that's hanging from my elbow. In all the excitement, I hadn't had a chance to put it down after coming home from dinner.

Craig takes off in the direction of the garage. "I'm going to check on Curt. Just to be safe."

Ritchie's face loses all its color. "Safe from what?"

If they say anything else, I don't hear it. I'm too busy staring down at the phone in my hand. I have a text message from a number I don't recognize. It's short and sweet and lacking in apostrophes.

Back off now or youll be next.

"Mom, are you okay?" Eliza asks.

When I don't answer, she walks over to stand beside me, reading the message over my shoulder.

"You've got to be kidding me!" she exclaims. "I know that phone number. It's the number Marjorie and Jolene sent messages to before they died. This message was sent from Baptiste's phone."

Thirty-Two

When a loud knock sounds at the front door early the next morning, I've already been awake for what feels like ages.

Ritchie, Craig, and Curt left about an hour ago for the airport, but I was up long before emerging from my bedroom to say goodbye. My eyes seemed to be glued open through most of the night, staring at the ceiling and thinking about the mangled flamingo floaty and the threatening message sent from Detective Baptiste's phone.

In her interview with Detective Fletcher, the junior detective had said that she couldn't find her phone. It was lost, she'd said. Had she found it in the meantime? Had she never lost it at all? Or did someone else, the real killer, have it now?

I'm still pondering these questions as I walk to the front

door. After Eliza called Detective Fletcher last night, he'd come over and collected what remained of the flamingo so he could run some tests. He hadn't been hopeful of finding anything, not after the evidence had been submerged in chlorinated water, but he promised to come by this morning to update us, regardless.

Expecting the detective, I'm surprised when I open the door and find Hugh and Viviana standing on the other side.

"Good morning," I say to them, trying to think of a reason they might have decided to show up unannounced. Thank goodness I did my hair this morning. "I just put on a fresh pot of coffee. Can I offer you a cup?"

"That's very kind, but we don't want to inconvenience you," Hugh declines.

Viviana tilts her head. "Speak for yourself. I never turn down coffee."

I usher them into my house, still having no idea why they've come. After the reception my family got at the River Club last night, I certainly hadn't been expecting any social calls.

"Here you go," I say, handing them each a steaming mug of fresh coffee. "And here's milk and sugar. I'll let you help yourselves. Can I get you anything else?"

"No, no," Hugh insists. "We don't want to put you to any more trouble."

Viviana takes a long sip from her mug before saying, "We're actually here to try to help get you *out* of trouble."

Her words take me by surprise. "I'm afraid I don't understand."

Hugh taps the side of his mug with his fingernail, his eyes avoiding mine. "Well, it has come to our attention that there may have been a less than favorable portrayal of you in the media recently."

"She's a grown woman, Hugh. We can be blunt," Viviana remarks in light, rapid fire delivery. "Everyone at Egret's Loft has heard about Brock Leitman's podcast, and more than a few residents are wondering if you're a killer. There, now. The elephant has well and truly been identified as being in the room."

It takes some effort not to choke on the coffee I'd been sipping. "None of it is true, I assure you. That young man deserves a very stern talking to."

Viviana smiles, the crow's feet around her eyes deepening. "That's where I come in."

"Viviana worked as a defamation lawyer for nearly forty years," Hugh explains. "We got to talking to Gina last night, and we all agreed that you need to strike back at this muckraker. Gina wanted to come along this morning, but she had a routine appointment with her cardiologist."

Viviana nods. "It's not easy getting an appointment with Dr. Hengle, but he is the best."

Even though I'm aware I'm getting sidetracked, I have to ask, "Do you know if he's taking new patients?"

"He owes me a favor." Viviana winks. "I'll see if I can get you an appointment. Do you have a preference on days or times?"

"Oh no, I'll take whatever he has available," I assure her. "Thank you so much."

"Not to be a bore, but we've strayed a bit off topic," Hugh points out. "Viviana was telling me she can easily draft up a cease-and-desist order. She can have it delivered to Brock Leitman later today, if that suits you."

A lump that is my pride fills my throat, threatening to choke me.

"That's very generous of you, and I certainly appreciate the offer, but I'm afraid I can't afford to hire an attorney. My kids paid for this place," I admit, relieved that Eliza went out for a run, so she can't hear what I'm about to say. "I can't ask them to spend any more of their money looking after me."

Viviana's eyes widen. "No, you've got it all wrong. I'm not going to charge you anything! I only want to help because, in my life, I've rubbed up against plenty of injustice. From what I've heard, you've made this community safer by helping catch killers. It's only right that someone steps in now to protect you."

I'm hesitant to accept. "Are you sure? That seems far too generous."

"Absolutely," Viviana forcefully declares. "Young Mr. Leitman needs to learn that he can't make accusatory statements, which have the potential to damage someone's reputation, without proof."

"I don't know what to say." I'm feeling overwhelmed by my neighbors' kindness and generosity. "Thank you so much."

Viviana waves off my gratitude. "Not at all. I've drafted so many cease-and-desist orders throughout my career, it'll take me less than half an hour to write one up for you. You can even come with me, if you want, when I deliver it to his hotel this afternoon."

Eliza would probably be alright with me confronting the reporter if I have an attorney by my side. "Well, I *would* love to see you put some manners on him."

"It's settled then. I'm your new attorney." Viviana raises her coffee, and we clink mugs.

"Mom," Eliza calls from the door. "You have a visitor."

"I actually have two," I reply. "I'm talking to them right now."

"Wait, what?" Eliza, sweat glistening on her face and arms, walks into the kitchen. "Detective Fletcher's here. He was outside when I got back from my run."

"Good morning, I hope it's not too early," Detective Fletcher says, following my daughter into the kitchen.

"Not at all," I assure him. "Detective, I don't know if you've met Hugh Darcy and Viviana Arenas. They came to help me deal with the ridiculous allegations that reporter is making against me. Can I get you some coffee?"

"Help how?" Detective Fletcher asks, ignoring the offer of a caffeinated beverage. The tone of his voice suggests he's nervous about whatever we might be planning.

Eliza shares his concerns. "Mom, we talked about this."

"We did, dear. But things change," I tell her. "Viviana has graciously offered to be my attorney to stop Brock Leitman from making more libelous allegations against me."

"You mean slanderous," Viviana corrects me. "Libel is written, slander is spoken."

"You know, I always get those the wrong way round," I confess. "Same with burglary and robbery. I can never remember which is which."

"Burglary is when force is involved, right?" Hugh asks.

Eliza and Detective Fletcher, in unison, say. "No, that's robbery." And then, for the first time ever, the two exchange smiles. Though it only lasts a moment, the sight warms my heart.

Detective Fletcher clears his throat. "As much as I'd love to stay and chat, I have to get back to the station. I just wanted to let you know that, as expected, we didn't find any prints or DNA on the flamingo floaty. I'm sorry, Madeline."

Hugh and Viviana look at me, confusion on their faces, but I don't get a chance to explain.

"Well, what are you going to do about Baptiste?" Eliza

demands to know. "The text message came from her phone."

"There's not much I can do. Sammy had already reported her phone missing before the text was sent to your mom," Detective Fletcher half-heartedly defends his partner. "Look, I know her presence at both crime scenes looks a bit suspicious—"

"A bit?" Eliza scoffs.

"Alright, a lot suspicious," Detective Fletcher concedes. "But, even if I did think she was guilty, the only evidence we have on her is circumstantial. She was at both crime scenes, yes. But she had explanations for why she was there, and cell phone records back up her story. I'm not saying I'm ruling out the possibility that she's the killer, I'm just saying I need proof, not speculation. Especially when there's a plethora of other suspects—Fred, Jinny, David."

The room goes silent. Eliza, head tilted, stares at the detective. "Alright. You make a very good point."

Detective Fletcher stands taller, a slight twitch tugging at the edges of his lips.

I'm so proud that the kids are learning to play well together.

"I'm not really sure what a flamingo floaty has to do with anything," Viviana cuts in. "But, as Madeline's new defamation attorney, I'm curious about Detective Baptiste. Do you think she's the police source who's been feeding false information to *Serial Seniors*?"

Detective Fletcher shrugs. "Your guess is as good as mine. All I know is, it's not me. Oh, and before I forget, we got back Marjorie's time of death from the coroner. She was killed Friday morning around six o'clock."

I take a moment to process the information. The text sent from Marjorie's phone told Detective Baptiste to meet at the pool at eight o'clock. By then, Marjorie had already been dead for two hours. But I still have no idea how her body got from the Golf Club to the River Club or why it was moved.

"Do you know what time she ended up in the swimming pool?" I ask.

"No. I asked the coroner the same thing," Detective Fletcher proudly states. "He said it could be anywhere between twenty minutes and two hours. Which doesn't help. But now I really have to go. I'll be in touch."

Once we hear the front door shut behind the detective, Hugh speaks up. "This business with the pool toy and the text message you got last night. Forgive my impertinence for asking, but is someone threatening you?"

"Oh, it's really not a big deal," I try to reassure him.

"Not a big deal?" Eliza refuses to let me play it down. "Someone shredded a flotation device, left it in Mom's pool, and then texted her to back off or she'll die next."

"Oh dear!" Viviana exclaims. "And you think Detective Baptiste might be the one who made the threat?"

Eliza shrugs. "She's been antagonistic toward Mom since she transferred here from Miami."

"Madeline, what do you think?" Hugh asks.

All eyes turn to face me. "I think, if we want to have any chance of catching Detective Baptiste, we have to convince ourselves she's not the killer."

Hugh frowns. "How's that? Are you talking about playing some kind of psychological mind game?"

I shake my head. "Oh no, nothing like that. I mean we have to allow for the possibility that someone else is our murderer. You heard the detective, there are multiple other suspects to consider. So, we have to be able to prove that none of the other suspects could have killed Marjorie and Jolene."

As my words settle in, Eliza and Viviana smile.

Hugh looks worried. "And just how do you plan on doing that?"

Thirty-Three

"Do we *really* have to do this?" Gina whines. "If I'd known this is what you were going to ask me to do, I might have asked the doctor to run another stress test on me."

"Did he say you needed another one?" I ask, concerned.

"Heck, no," Gina exclaims. "But anything's better than having to talk to Forest."

"His name is Fred," I correct her as we walk along the circular street toward Fred's house.

After Viviana and Hugh left my house an hour ago, I'd immediately texted Gina to come find me as soon as she got back from her cardiology appointment. It was a deliberate choice on my part not to mention that I was going to drag her along for a conversation with Fred. I knew she would have turned me down.

"You know I wouldn't ask you if it wasn't important," I continue. "In order to clear my name, I have to prove that the killer couldn't be anyone other than Detective Baptiste."

Gina scratches her head. "Wouldn't it be easier to prove she *is* the killer, rather than try to prove that everyone else *isn't*?"

"Normally, yes. But the rules are a bit different when you're accusing a homicide detective of murder," I tell her, waving to young Paul as he passes us in his grandparents' golf cart. "That would be like me trying to point out a flaw in Mary Berry's lemon drizzle cake recipe. Whose judgment do you think the average baker would believe?"

"What does baking have to do with anything, hun?"

I shrug. "I was making an analogy. You know, Marjorie loved to bake—"

"Nope," Gina corrects me. "All she did was reheat cookies someone else made. That's not baking."

"You know what? Never mind," I tell her. "We're going to talk to Fred. End of story. So, there's no point dragging your feet. The sooner we get there, the sooner we can leave."

"That's the best thing you've said all morning," Gina replies. "And who knows, maybe he is the murderer. He could try to kill us! That would be exciting."

I want to chastise my friend for thinking that way, but when I see her grinning, all I can do is smile in return. As much as Eliza would hate to hear me say it, the two brushes I had with death since moving into Egret's Loft left me feeling more alive.

"Here we are." Gina stops in the road in front of Fred's house. "If I fall asleep while he's talkin' don't wake me until you're ready to leave."

"Just *try* to be nice," I tell her as we walk up the driveway.

With one final glance at Gina, I press Fred's doorbell and hear Elton John's "Rocketman" playing from the speakers inside the house. Through the frosted glass panels, we see a woman briskly approaching the front door.

She's yelling to be heard over the pop rock song. "Fred, is that you? This doorbell is ruining my favorite song. Can you please—" She pauses, mid-speech, when she sees Gina and I standing on the other side of the door. The music from the doorbell stopped the second she opened the door. "Oh, I'm sorry. I thought you were my husband. Can I help you with something?"

Svetlana Burrows, with bright hazel eyes and golden-brown hair, is even more beautiful than I'd expected. She's also much taller. Even in bare feet, she stands a good five inches taller than me. Dressed casually in loose cashmere sweatpants and a white tank top, the forty-something woman radiates confidence and composure. Though her Slavic roots are evident in the elegant bone structure of her face, she doesn't even have a trace of an accent when she speaks.

"Hi, my name is Madeline. I live on the other side of the lake. I was wondering, is your husband home by any chance?" I ask, self-consciously smoothing out the fabric of my sun protective dress.

"No, he's not," she says, then squints her eyes. "Hey, aren't you the woman from the podcast? The one that supposedly killed several residents here?"

Blood rushes to my head, warming my cheeks and making speech temporarily impossible.

"Technically, yes," Gina answers for me. "She is the woman from the podcast. But you can't believe a word of what that reporter says. Mandy never killed anyone."

Svetlana targets me with her sharp eyes. "So, you're not some kind of psychopath?"

Something about her Eastern European heritage intimidates me. People from that part of the world just *seem* tougher. Maybe because they make excellent villains in action movies. I would know, Clint made me watch enough of them.

I clear my throat and return her stare. "No. I'm not a psychopath."

"Hired assassin, then? You could come in very handy. Do you offer group discounts?"

Gina and I look nervously at each other. Maybe Fred isn't the one who killed his ex-girlfriend after all. His much younger wife seems like *she* may just be crazy enough to kill.

"Svetlana, darling. You should not to tease my neighbor," a heavily accented voice calls out from inside the house. Behind Svetlana, I'm surprised to see Natasha—the elegant Russian woman who lives next door to me—walk into view. "You know our humor is not so funny for the Americans."

Svetlana says something in Russian. Natasha answers. Svetlana suddenly smiles at Gina and me. "Won't you please come in?"

As I step into her house, I'm wondering if I shouldn't have brought Eliza instead of Gina on this fact-finding mission. Gina may be my best friend, but my daughter carries a gun.

"Can I get you something to drink?" Svetlana offers once we're seated on one of her buttery soft, white leather sofas.

"Coffee would be lovely," I say.

"I'll have a vodka tonic," Gina says.

Frowning at my friend, I point out, "It's ten o'clock in the morning!"

Gina shrugs. "It's five o'clock somewhere in Russia."

As Svetlana heads into the kitchen to make our drinks, I focus my attention on Natasha, who sits down in the armchair beside me. Though my neighbor may come across as dainty and dignified, I know from our past conversations that she can be icier than an un-defrosted freezer. But she's always been brutally honest with me, and I like her, even if I know she has an overdeveloped sense of vengeance.

"I didn't know you and Svetlana were friends," I say, trying to open a dialogue. "How long have you two known each other?"

"Not long," Natasha tells me. "But she ask for my help. What can I do?"

I lean in toward her. "What does she need your help with?"

Before Natasha can reply, Svetlana returns with two glasses. "Here's your coffee." She hands me a mug and then holds out a tumbler for Gina. "And here's your vodka tonic. Sorry, I didn't have any tonic."

Gina accepts the glass but holds it at a distance. "So, it's just straight up vodka then?"

"Yes," Svetlana bluntly replies. "Now, would you mind telling me why you're here?"

I take a deep, steadying breath. "To be honest, we came here because we wanted to see if Fred had an alibi for Marjorie's murder. We're not implying he had anything to do with her death, but it could help eliminate him as a suspect if we knew his whereabouts early Friday morning."

"And if I were to tell you he wasn't here all night, then what?" Svetlana asks.

My heart starts beating faster. Maybe I'd been wrong about Detective Baptiste after all.

Natasha says something in Russian, then, seeing my confusion, switches over to English. "You must tell truth, Svetlana."

The younger woman sighs. "Fine. Fred and I went to the hospital Thursday night. He'd picked up some mortadella at the grocery store, not realizing it had pistachios in it. He had a severe allergic reaction, and the hospital made him stay overnight for observation. He wasn't released until around noon on Friday."

If what she says is true, there's no way Fred could have killed his ex-girlfriend, Marjorie. But something isn't sitting right with me about her admission. "Pardon me for asking, but why were you hesitant to alibi your husband?"

Svetlana glances at Natasha, then exhales deeply. "Not that it matters, but sometimes I wonder if I wouldn't be better off without Fred."

Gina opens her mouth to speak, but, afraid of what she might say, I cut her off. "Marriage can be difficult sometimes. I'm sure we've all felt that way about our partners from time to time."

Svetlana shrugs. "I suppose. But what if you started feeling that way about your partner all the time?"

I find her frankness refreshing, if a tiny bit uncomfortable. "I would wonder what was causing you to feel that way."

"He's not who I thought he was. When I first met Fred, I thought he saw me as an equal," Svetlana says. "But I'm starting to realize I'm just arm candy to him."

"Svetlana has PhD in aerospace engineering," Natasha explains. "But Fred doesn't want her to work. He just buy her jewelry and tell her she should be happy being show pony. It is very frustrating experience for her."

So much for Gina's assumption that Fred ordered his bride out of a catalog. I'm reminded, once again, that outward appearances can be deceiving. There's always so much more going on inside people than you can see on the surface.

"I am frustrated with Fred. There are days I almost hate him," Svetlana admits. "But if you came here hoping to prove he's a murderer, you're out of luck. For all his faults, Fred's not a killer. I'm absolutely certain of it."

Gina, sitting next to me on the sofa, reaches across and squeezes my hand. I squeeze back. We've accomplished what we set out to do—proven Fred couldn't be the killer.

Now only Jinny Myrtle stands in the way of us accusing Detective Baptiste of murder.

Thirty-Four

"**B**ingo," Jinny whispers, almost as if she doesn't believe it herself. But after a quick review of the numbers, her confidence builds and she shouts, "Bingo! I have bingo!"

She jumps up, knocking her chair onto the floor, and races to the front of the room.

"Thank goodness." Gina leans back in her own chair. "I thought it was never goin' to end."

As Gina and I had been walking back from Fred's house, we'd seen Jinny climbing into her golf cart. She said she was running late for her weekly bingo game at the River Club and invited us to join.

An hour later, we still haven't had the opportunity to ask her about her alibi for the morning of Marjorie's murder, and my time is running out. Viviana should be contacting me soon to say the letter for Brock Leitman is ready for delivery. Not to mention, it doesn't appear that my presence here is particularly welcome. I keep getting nasty looks from the other active elder ladies, all of whom seem to have heard Brock's podcast.

A beaming Jinny, her cheeks as pink as the track suit she's wearing, returns to our table carrying her prize for winning—two day passes to Disney World.

"This is so exciting! I never win anything. And George just loves going to Disney, don't you know. He could go on the rides all day long," Jinny gushes. "I prefer Epcot myself. It's like traveling around the world in a single day but without all the fuss of airplanes and food that'll give me a queasy tummy. I can't wait to tell George. Maybe we can go tomorrow, since all the kids and grandkids went home. Except for Paul, of course, he's still here. But he won't mind being left alone for the day. No, he most certainly won't."

Knowing I need to delay her departure until we've gotten some information out of her, I say, "Before you go, why don't we have a little drink to celebrate?"

"Oh my, a drink before lunch? What would George think? Then again, it's not every day you win two tickets to Disney, so this *is* a special occasion. What kind of drink do you have at this time of day? It's almost noon, I suppose. So it's not too early, eh? Oh, maybe I'll have one of those mimosas I hear the young girls talking aboot. And it has orange juice, so that does seem to make it more of a pre-lunch drink. Do you think the bar is open yet? Oh, I hope it is."

As Jinny's been talking, Gina and I have been leading her in the direction of the restaurant. If we'd waited for her to finish her thought, we might have found ourselves locked in another round of bingo. Fortunately, the bar is open when we arrive, and we're all able to order drinks.

Gina raises her champagne flute. "Congratulations, Janine."

"Jinny." The word slips out of my mouth. I've become habituated to correcting Gina, so much that I've started to develop a kind of mental muscle memory for the task. "This is nice, isn't it? After the week we've been having, it's good to have something to celebrate."

Jinny's enthusiasm, though still bubbling, suffers a slight setback. "It has been an awful week, hasn't it? First Marjorie and then Jolene." She shakes her head. "It simply blows my mind that we were all just down the hall dancing while that poor woman was being electrocuted. The lights went out, and I grabbed George's hand in the dark, and I just knew then something bad was happening, though I never would have guessed what it actually was, don't you know. I can't imagine why anyone would have wanted to kill Jolene. It's true, she didn't really try to get involved in the community, though that sweet daughter of hers, Savannah, certainly has. She and young Sydney have become quite good friends, haven't they? Have you noticed? It does warm my heart to see it. Sydney took it pretty hard last year when her birth mother contacted her out of the blue. Poor dear. Can you believe, she didn't even know then that she'd been adopted. It's good she's making some friends her own age, though not so much at the moment, I suppose. It's bound to be a tough time, what with Savannah's mother being killed and all. I heard one of the detectives was there when you found Jolene's body. Wouldn't that be something if a police officer had killed her! Though I really can't imagine that pretty, young detective as a murderer. She moved here to help look after her sick mother, don't you know. You wouldn't think someone like that would electrocute anyone, now would you?"

As with all the conversations I have with Jinny, my brain feels like it's overheating after the first five minutes. Gina, whose mouth had fallen open as Jinny was talking, seems to give up on trying to follow the discussion. She takes a long sip of her mimosa and signals to the bartender that she'd like another.

I force myself to focus. In all of Jinny's monologues, there's always a kernel of significance. For example, I just learned that she and George were in the room when the lights went out during the line dancing class. That would seem to give her an alibi, at least for Jolene's death. Now, I just need to find out where she was when Marjorie met her end. But there's something else Jinny might be able to help me figure out as well.

"I know things had been tense between you and Marjorie before she died," I say, "but you had been friends for a long time. Did she ever mention anything about a woman named Drusilla Hackney?"

Jinny doesn't answer right away. It's the first time I've seen her think before she speaks.

"That name sounds so familiar to me," she finally says. "I'm sure Marjorie mentioned it once or twice, don't you know. Maybe it was the woman who did her hair? No, I think her name was Betty. But don't hold me to that, since I never met her. It is a strange name, though. Drusilla. It'll come to me later. Who she is. But for now, I'll blame the mimosa for any lapses in memory, eh?"

"In that case," Gina says, "before you have any more of that mimosa, can you tell us where you were on Friday morning around six o'clock?"

I glare at Gina, but she doesn't seem to notice.

Jinny's eyes narrow and she sets her champagne flute on the bar. "Now, why are you asking me that? Is that when Marjorie died? Surely, you can't think I killed her." Jinny's eyes suddenly open wide and her pink lips pucker together in a small circle. "Oh no! Is this what the podcaster was talking aboot? Are the two of you in this together? Did one of you kill Marjorie, and now you're trying to stitch me up for your crime? That wouldn't be very neighborly of you, don't you know."

"No, of course not!" I try taking Jinny's hand in mine,

but she buries hers in the pocket of her tracksuit jacket. She looks nervous enough to bolt from the bar at any moment. "Don't be silly. We didn't kill anyone. The truth is quite the opposite, in fact. We're trying to *catch* the killer. How could you even think that Gina or I would murder anyone?"

"How could you think *I* would?" Jinny demands. "That's what this is aboot, isn't it? You want to know where I was, eh? Like an alibi. Oh, goodness me. You *do* want my alibi! Should I call a lawyer? I don't think I should say anything else without George here. Can I exercise my right to not say anything? Though, whenever I see people do that in movies and TV shows, I always think they have something to hide. I don't, though, you know. Have anything to hide. I'm just a little bit leery when it comes to police matters—what with everything that's been happening with Paul and the theft charges, don't you know. I don't want to go to jail. Especially for something I didn't do—"

"Simmer down, hun. Nobody's going to jail," Gina tries to reassure Jinny.

"Well, now that's not true," I correct Gina. "Somebody's going to jail."

Jinny sucks in her breath. "So, you *are* trying to send me to jail? You just can't. I wouldn't last ten minutes on the inside. I mean, look at me. Orange is *not* my color!"

I sigh, wondering how this conversation got so far out of hand. "I don't mean *you're* going to jail. I mean the real killer will go to jail once we find out who they are. That's all. But, yes, we would like your alibi for Marjorie's death, Jinny. Not because we think you killed her, but because we think your alibi might help us prove someone else did."

Jinny frowns. "I'm not sure I understand what that means…"

Gina nods. "She's right, it doesn't make a whole lot of sense when you put it like that."

My phone dings from the counter, alerting me that I have a new text message. The print is too small to read the whole message without my glasses, but I can tell Viviana sent it, because her picture came up. She's probably texting to say she's ready to deliver her letter to Brock Leitman.

"I don't have time to explain. But I'm asking you to trust me," I try to reason with a very jittery Jinny. "Can you please tell me where you were on Friday morning at six o'clock?"

"Well, now," Jinny says, toying with the metal aglet hanging from the hood of her thin jacket. "I don't suppose I have a reason to distrust you. No, I most certainly don't. And I like to think we're becoming friends, as well as neighbors. So, I don't see what harm it could do telling you where I was. And I have proof. You see, I normally would have been out for my morning walk by six, but I slept in late on Monday. Having the kids and grandkids here really took it out of me, don't you know. I didn't end up making it out for my walk until around seven o'clock, as the staff were just starting to arrive. I saw David, then Sydney—"

Gina stops her. "You were asleep when Marjorie was murdered? I thought you said you had proof of your alibi. How can you have proof that you were sleepin'?"

"I'll get to that," Jinny says. "You see, for the longest time George was complaining about my snoring. He said it was keeping him up at night, and so he finally signed me up for one of those sleep studies, don't you know. I wasn't too sure about it at first. I mean, it seemed a bit weird to have somebody watching me while I was sleeping. Not to mention all the wires they hook you up to. What if one of them got wrapped around my neck? I do tend to toss and turn—"

I hate to interrupt Jinny, but if I don't, we could be here all day. "You were in the sleep study when Marjorie was murdered?"

"Oh, no." Jinny shakes her head. "I went in for the sleep study about a month ago."

Gina sets her champagne flute down so hard I expect it to shatter. "Then what in the world does it have to do with where you were on Friday morning?"

"Nothing, really."

"Why bother telling us about it then?" Gina's voice reflects her growing impatience.

"Because that's when I got my CPAP machine," Jinny tells us. "It turns out, George was right to have me tested. I have sleep apnea, so the doctor told me to use a machine when I sleep. Paul helped me hook it up to an app on my phone. Kids really are very handy with the technology these days, don't you know. Did you know I can look at the app and see how long I slept and whether or not I slept well? Can you imagine that? A machine telling me whether I got a good night's sleep!"

"That's your proof," I deduce. "The app shows you were hooked up to the machine and sleeping while Marjorie was murdered."

Jinny nods and opens her mouth to continue extolling the virtues of modern sleep technology. Too focused on my thoughts, I don't hear a word she says.

All I can focus on is the fact that I've done it. I've proven that none of the other lead suspects could have killed Marjorie and Jolene. Detective Fletcher will have to take my suspicions about his partner seriously now. I can't wait to tell him.

But first, I have to get Brock to stop telling the world I'm a serial killer.

Thirty-Five

"Well, well. Changed your mind about that interview, have you, grandma?" Brock Leitman smugly whines. "I thought you might want a chance to tell your side of the story."

He's standing in the open doorway of a cheap motel room ten miles inland from Calusa. A pristine white tank top hangs from his lanky upper body. He doesn't appear to have seen the sun, or the gym, for quite some time.

"First of all, young man, I am not your grandmother," I rebuke him. "Furthermore, I wouldn't give you an interview if my life—"

Viviana rests one of her hands on my arm while using the other to offer Brock a sealed envelope. "Brock Leitman, consider yourself served."

Staring down at the envelope, he frowns. "Served? With what?"

"A cease-and-desist order," Viviana informs him. "You will immediately stop publishing any defamatory allegations concerning my client, or she will sue you for all that you are worth."

Gone is the fidgety and energetic Viviana I'd recently met. She's been replaced by a tough, no-nonsense businesswoman, who would only see the word "no" as the starting point of the negotiation. My mouth hangs open in admiration, and I want to applaud her stunning performance, but I do realize that would undermine my own cause.

"I specifically referred to any potential allegations as *theories*," Brock confidently replies, declining to take possession of the envelope. "Which, honestly, was done out of consideration on my part. Aside from being a serial killer, Madeline seems like a nice old lady. But, based on the evidence I've received from the police, I could have said a lot more in that first podcast than I did. Your client should be considering her own legal options, rather than threatening me with mine."

"I see," Viviana, whose envelope-holding arm remains firmly extended toward Brock, says. "In that case, I'd like to see the evidence you've been presented with. My client has the right to face her accusers. If you're telling me the police have provided you with information that they haven't given the so-called accused, we would like to see it."

Brock refuses to be intimidated so easily. "I'm sure you can understand that, as a journalist, I have to protect the information given to me by my sources—"

"Hold on now," Viviana stops him. "I just want to clarify one thing quickly. Did the police give you information in their official capacity? Or do you have a source who's been feeding you this 'evidence' you claim to have?"

"Would it matter?" Brock challenges her.

Viviana considers his question. "Perhaps. If the police are planning to bring charges, as your podcast might lead one to suspect, they'd have to give all their evidence to the prosecutor. Which means, I could file an injunction to stop you publishing your little show until I have copies of the evidence in question to use in Madeline's defense."

"Well, that won't be an issue then, because I got my information from sources," Brock gloats.

"Do you have one source or several?" Viviana presses.

Brock chuckles. "You really are desperate, aren't you? Using this whole confrontation as a pretext to find out what I know. You know what? I'll play along. It's one source. But a very well-placed and knowledgeable source."

Viviana taps her lip with the edge of the envelope. "Now, I admit, I didn't study media law when I was at Yale, but I think I read somewhere about a journalist getting in trouble for only having one source on a story. Do you remember that, Madeline? It happened a couple of years ago. If memory serves, the source lied, and the journalist lost his job."

"Subtle. Very subtle." Brock claps his hand in mock applause. "While I do admire your threat tactics, you should know that they won't work on me. My source is solid. I have nothing to worry about on that front."

"You've known this confidential informant for a while then, have you?" Viviana asks.

Brock places his left hand at the top of the door frame and leans into it. "I've been getting intel for a little over a month now. So, yeah. I've taken my time to go through everything."

"Please forgive me if this is a dumb question," Viviana requests. "My eighth-grade teacher always said there was no such thing as a dumb question, but I think we all know that's not true."

Brock and I both nod in agreement. At least there's one thing we can all agree on.

"Back to that question I mentioned," Viviana says. "How is it possible that you've been getting information from your source for over a month?"

Brock frowns. "Umm. Telephone. Text messages. Email. There are lots of different ways to communicate these days."

Viviana's laughter sends shivers down my spine. If

Brock thought he could outsmart Viviana with his second-rate sarcasm then he has an important life lesson coming.

"Very funny," Viviana congratulates him when she stops laughing. "Because older people struggle with technology, right? I suppose that's true. But you missed my meaning. If you only decided to do your podcast *after* you learned that Marjorie Higginbottom had been murdered, why were you already in communication with the local Calusa Police Department?"

Brock's elbow buckles, and he nearly falls, but he pulls himself back together quickly. "Who said I wasn't going to do a podcast before Marjorie was murdered? Maybe I was going to do something about the earlier murders and how people were being falsely accused."

It feels like I'm watching a particularly fierce tennis match, my eyes are bouncing so quickly between the reporter and the lawyer. Right now, they're settled on Viviana, waiting to hear her response. I would jump in to be her double, but she doesn't seem to need any help serving Brock's balls back to him.

"Is that so?" Viviana makes a show of contemplating this information. "And how did you find out about the other murders at Egret's Loft? Did someone come to you suggesting the story? I mean, you live in New York. That's a long way away from here."

"Not that it's any of your business, but people know I'm

a serious journalist," Brock brags. "After *Everything's Deadlier in Texas* came out, I had tips for stories coming in from all across the country. A fan of my Griner podcast wrote to me about the deaths at Egret's Loft and it caught my attention."

"But you didn't decide to come to Egret's Loft until after Marjorie was found murdered. Do I have that right?" Viviana seeks to clarify.

"Yeah, sure. I mean, I was already looking into doing a story, but I came down right away when I heard the heir to the Sturdy Foil fortune had been murdered here."

That must be the aluminum connection he mentioned in the podcast. I had no idea Marjorie's family invented Sturdy Foil. That's the tin foil I've always used in my own kitchen. I think it once had another name, but I can't quite remember what it was called when I was a child. I think it started with an H. Handy Wrap, maybe.

"If you don't mind, I'd like to make sure I have all my facts straight." When Brock nods, Viviana proceeds. "Over a month ago, you got a tip from a fan about crimes that had been committed, and solved, I might add, at Egret's Loft a few months ago. Then, you started getting secret, inside information from a police officer you'd never met—except over the phone and in emails—all pointing you to one suspect, my client."

A slight groove begins to appear between Brock's

eyebrows. "Yeah, so? Clearly, they were right to be concerned, because it wasn't long before someone else was killed."

"You mean Marjorie?"

"Exactly!"

Viviana slaps the envelope against her thigh. "Well, that really is something."

Brock glances at me, then returns his gaze to Viviana. "What's something?"

"For such a clever journalist, you really haven't thought any of this through. You do realize you've set yourself up as someone else's pawn in a very dangerous game, don't you?"

Any trace of confidence has been chased from Brock's face, but he's not willing to back down just yet. "You don't know what you're talking about. I'm nobody's pawn."

"I beg to differ," Viviana tells him. "I'm going to go out on a limb here and say your police source is Detective Samantha Baptiste. You don't have to confirm it for me. Just know that I know. So, you were drawn down here to investigate a murder, before it even happened, by the one police officer who just happened to be present when two crimes were committed. Were you aware that Detective Baptiste is a suspect in both Marjorie and Jolene's murders? Or did your *source* not share that little tidbit?"

Brock's face has lost all of its color, and it looks like he might be sick.

I take the envelope out of Viviana's hand and toss it past Brock, inside his hotel room. "I think you might want to read that over after all, young man. Come on, Viviana. Let's go."

As soon as we're far enough away from Brock's hotel room, I turn to Viviana and gush, "You were absolutely brilliant! Cunning and terrifying," I add, "but also brilliant."

A blush rises on Viviana's cheeks. "Do you really think so? Lord, but it's been a while since I've done anything like that. I was so nervous, even my medication couldn't stop my hands from shaking."

"You were nervous?" I ask, surprised. "I never would have guessed it. Not in a million years. And I think you scared the bejesus out of that young man."

Viviana giggles. "That was fun, wasn't it?"

"It certainly was," I confirm, but my levity doesn't last long. "Something about this whole situation bothers me though."

"You're wondering, if the killer contacted Brock over a month ago, how long had he or she been planning to kill Marjorie?" Viviana successfully guesses.

"Precisely. Brock seems to have been lured here as a way to shift the blame for premeditated murder onto me. Which means our killer is smart, methodical, and patient. We've been playing catch-up the whole time, and we didn't even know it."

At that moment my phone chimes, emitting a special

ringtone Ritchie set up to alert me when someone was at my front door. Grabbing my phone out of my purse, I enlarge the image on the screen.

I watch as Detective Samantha Baptiste raises her hand and begins to knock.

Thirty-Six

My stomach feels queasy as Viviana pulls her car into my driveway. I'd asked her to get me back to Egret's Loft as quickly as possible, but I hadn't anticipated she'd take corners on two wheels and blow through yellow lights to do it. Between her speeding and my anxiety over what Detective Baptiste was doing at my house, I have to force myself not to be sick.

Quickly climbing out of the car, I take a deep breath of fresh air to calm my frazzled nerves. While there's no sign of the detective at my front door, there is a car I don't recognize parked behind Eliza's SUV on the street.

"Do you want me to come in with you?" Viviana asks, still seated behind the wheel of her car.

"No, thank you," I assure her. If Eliza is alone inside

with Detective Baptiste, I'm not sure I want any witnesses. "I appreciate all your help. I'll call you later."

I walk as quickly as my arthritic knees allow, my fingers shaking as I type in the code that opens my front door. The first thing I notice is the lights are all on inside. The second thing that hits me is the silence. I can hear my own heart beating.

"Eliza?" I call out, my voice uncertain.

"In here," Eliza replies from the direction of the kitchen table.

Rounding the corner, I see Detective Baptiste sitting across from where Eliza is standing. My daughter doesn't have her gun drawn, but the angle of her hip makes its presence known. At least things haven't gotten out of hand. Yet.

"Hello, Detective Baptiste. Is your partner here with you?" I ask.

"No. I'm not here on police business," she says, her eyes not wavering from the gun on Eliza's hip.

"She wouldn't tell me why she's here," Eliza informs me, her eyes locked on the detective. "Just that she had something she wanted to say to you."

"I see," I say, feeling slightly lightheaded following the adrenaline rush of confronting Brock and racing home at the speed of light. "Would anyone like some coffee?"

Eliza drags her eyes off the detective to roll them at me.

"Seriously, Mom? She's accused you of murder and you're offering her a drink?"

"Yes, dear. I am. It's the polite thing to do when you have a guest in your home," I lecture my daughter. "Detective Baptiste, can I get you anything?"

Detective Baptiste eyes me warily. "No, thanks. I won't be staying long."

"The sooner you tell us why you're here, the sooner you can be on your way," Eliza points out.

I sink into the chair next to Detective Baptiste. "You say you're not here in an official capacity. What is it you wanted to say to me, Detective?"

She looks down at her hands, clearly uncomfortable. "I came here to apologize."

"Apologize?" Eliza scoffs. "Because of you, everyone at Egret's Loft thinks my mom is a killer!"

"Not everyone," I correct her. There are still a few people who think I'm innocent. "Please continue, Detective."

"I came here because I know we've gotten off on the wrong foot. It's my fault. I admit, I've been a bit...hostile. But it's not for the reasons you think." Detective Baptiste's eyes beg me to understand. "I moved here to be with my mom. She's sick, so I had to put her in a care home. Then I came to Egret's Loft. I'd give anything to have her living in a place like this, but I'd never be able to afford it. I guess I hated myself for not being able to take care of my mom the way I want to. And that made me angry at you for having what she doesn't."

"Oh, please," Eliza sneers. "Are you honestly trying to make us feel sorry for you?"

"Eliza, I appreciate that you're trying to defend me, but let's hear her out," I say. "Detective, I'm sorry to hear about your mother. How is she doing?"

Detective Baptiste seems surprised by the question. "She's okay. The doctor says the slower pace here is doing her a world of good."

"I'm very glad to hear it. You're a good daughter for looking after your mother when she needs you. There's nothing a mother loves more than to have her children near her." I smile at Eliza. She smiles back. "Now, about your apology. I'm willing to accept that you're going through a rough time, but you must know that's no excuse for leaking false information to a reporter in an attempt to frame me for murder."

"Leaking information!" Detective Baptiste exclaims. "What are you talking about?"

"There's no point in denying it," I warn her. "I just went to see Brock Leitman, and he as good as admitted you'd been feeding him lies about me for the past month."

"Brock Leitman? The podcaster?" Detective Baptiste asks, her face a mask of innocence. "I've never talked to the guy in my life. Why would I tell him anything?"

Eliza snorts derisively. "Don't play dumb. You've made it

clear you think my mom is a murderer. It's not a stretch to think you'd share that opinion with a journalist. Admit it, you're his source inside the police. You're the one trying to frame my mom."

"Frame your mom?" Detective Baptiste echoes. "Can't you see someone is trying to frame *me*? That's the other reason I'm here. I was going to ask for help proving I didn't kill Marjorie or Jolene."

"Are you joking?" Eliza practically screams. "You arrested my mom, now you want her help? You've got some nerve. I'll give you that much."

As they've been going at each other, I've been trying to get a read on Detective Baptiste. On the surface, I have every reason to distrust her. She *has* been hostile toward me. She's accused me of being a serial killer. She locked me in a jail cell. She's the only suspect I have who doesn't have an alibi for either murder. Not to mention, she threatened me.

"Why ask for my help now?" I want to know. "Is it because your little text message threat didn't scare me off?"

"My what?" Detective Baptiste asks.

I search her face for signs of recognition but find none.

"You broke into my backyard, sliced up an alligator pool toy, and sent me a text to back off the investigation," I remind her.

Detective Baptiste shakes her head. "I have no idea what you're talking about. Why would I cut up a pool toy?

And I've never sent you any texts. I don't even have your phone number saved in my phone."

"You expect us to believe that?" Eliza demands.

"Believe whatever you want. I didn't do it," Detective Baptiste insists.

"But the message came from your phone number," I tell her. "The same number that received messages from both Marjorie and Jolene before they died."

"That's what I'm talking about, why I think someone is trying to frame me." Detective Fletcher's trademark aloofness has been abandoned. Her arms flail as she tries to explain herself. "I'm starting to think Marjorie and Jolene didn't send those messages. I think the killer might have sent them to make it look like I had something to do with their deaths."

Eliza settles her hands on her hips, one resting near the handle of her gun. "That would be a convenient explanation, now, wouldn't it?"

"Why in the heck would I set myself up to look like the murderer?" Detective Baptiste yells. "That doesn't make any sense!"

"Would you listen to yourself?" Eliza's angry eyes target the detective. "You admit to being a total jerk to my mom. You accused her of being a homicidal maniac, for crying out loud!"

"It's alright. Calm down, dear," I say, not realizing it was exactly the wrong thing to say.

"Calm down? You want me to calm down?" Eliza screams. "I'm sorry, I'm just having trouble processing this whole conversation. She called you a killer, Mom. Now, when all the evidence is pointing in her direction—when *she's* the one suspected of killing people, she wants your help? Please don't fall for this 'poor me' routine. It's pathetic."

Silence descends over the room, interrupted only by Eliza's erratic, panting breaths.

"She's right. I shouldn't have come." Detective Baptiste pushes her chair back from the table and stands up. "After the way I've behaved, there's no reason why you should want to help me. I'm sorry. For everything."

Detective Baptiste walks past me and, a few seconds later, we hear the front door close.

Eliza looks at me, a sheepish expression on her face. "I'm sorry I lost my temper, Mom. I just really hate the way she's treated you."

"I know and I appreciate it," I assure her. "But do you think anything she said was true?"

Eliza tilts her head to one side. "Not really. Do you?"

"I don't know," I admit. "When I mentioned the pool floaty to her just now, I said it was an alligator."

Eliza squints. "But it was a flamingo."

"That's right. It was. But she didn't correct me. It really seemed like she had no idea what I was talking about."

"*Or*," Eliza stresses the word, "she's a really good liar."

"That's a possibility. There's a good chance she's trying to distract us with misinformation to keep suspicion off herself. So how do we figure out whether or not she killed Marjorie and Jolene?" I wonder aloud.

"I've been looking into a few things while you were out," Eliza says.

"And?" I press.

Eliza surveys the room. "When you first moved in, you warned me that the walls had ears. I'm not saying I believe you about people listening in, but just in case, how about we go for a walk? I can tell you what I found on the security video."

"Sure, let me just grab my hat," I tell her. "But you'll have to take that ridiculous gun off your hip. That radio show has caused me enough trouble with the neighbors."

Thirty-Seven

"You went through all of the security videos and didn't see anything?"

Eliza and I are strolling along the sidewalk bordering the golf course closest to my house. It's late afternoon and, though the sun will be setting within half an hour, the humidity makes my skin sticky.

"That's not entirely true," Eliza argues. "I did see the floaty being thrown into the pool, I just didn't see who threw it. But that, in itself, tells us something."

"You mean whoever broke into the backyard knew where the cameras were?" I guess.

"Yeah. It's not much, but it's something."

"Except nearly everyone at Egret's Loft has cameras on their back patios. Most people know where they are and how to avoid them."

"Well, that was several hours I'll never get back," Eliza complains. "Hopefully, I have more luck tracking down Drusilla."

We pause for a moment at the intersection to let a golf cart pass.

"Did you ever hear back from your friend at the marshal service?"

"I did, but you're not going to like it," Eliza says. "They did a thorough search of all the cases Jolene worked on and the name Drusilla Hackney never came up."

I sigh, suddenly feeling very tired. "Another dead end. There seem to be a lot of them in this case. I'm having a devil of a time trying to figure out what's what."

"I know. It's frustrating, but at some point tonight, I should have the address of the post office box where the medical bills were sent."

"Really? How did you manage that?"

"I contacted a bunch of insurance companies until I found one that had filed claims under that name. They said it'd take some time to get permission to release the information, but I should have it soon. Once we have the address, I'll go ask the manager questions about who owns the box."

"Well done! Drusilla is tied to all of this. If we can figure out how, maybe everything else will fall into place."

"Let's hope so," Eliza replies. "My boss let me take the rest of this week off, but I'm going to have to get back to work at some point. With everything going on, I hate to leave you here on your own."

"I'll be just fine," I tell her, though I'm not sure that's true. In less than a week, I've found two corpses and been accused in a popular radio show of being a murderer. But there are a few people here who still believe in me. "I have Gina and Viviana."

"Oh my gosh, I forgot to ask. How did everything go with Brock Leitman?"

Remembering the altercation brings a smile to my face. "Viviana was brilliant. She really put the fear of God in him."

"That's great, Mom! Does that mean he'll stop doing the podcast?"

"He didn't really say," I admit. "But he's got to be wondering whether he should trust his source from now on."

When we arrive at the park, I see a group of active elders doing tai chi under the shade of some large palm trees. A few years ago, I took Clint to a class in DC. He fell over and nearly broke his nose. The memory is so real, for a brief moment, I think I see him amongst the practitioners. He's wearing loose white pants and his favorite Washington Nationals t-shirt. He steps forward into a repulse the monkey pose, his finger pointing to a spot at the edge of the group.

I glance in the direction he's indicating and see Jinny

doing her impression of waving hands like clouds. Sydney passes behind her, taking videos with her cell phone.

My eyes return to where Clint had been standing, but he's no longer there. Instead, I see Hugh Darcy standing in his spot.

I pull a bottle of water out of my purse—which feels heavier on my arm than normal—and take a long drink, wondering if I forgot to take my medication this morning.

"Mom?" Eliza sounds concerned. "Are you alright?"

After swallowing a large gulp of tepid water, I tell her, "I'm fine, dear. But I am a little tired. Maybe we should head back."

"Of course. Let's go."

She takes my elbow and we're about to leave when, from behind us, we hear Sydney call out, "Aren't you going to take the class?"

I can feel Eliza's shoulders tighten as we turn to face the young public relations specialist.

"It would be great to have a few more attractive people in the group," she flatters us as she approaches. "Is Tom with you?"

Eliza's hand tightens on my arm. "No, my husband is not here. As I said the last time you asked, he's back in Miami with our children."

"Oh, right." Sydney mimes slapping herself on the forehead. "It'd be great to have the two of you jump in there, though. What do you say?"

Before Eliza gets any more annoyed, I hurry to say, "I'm afraid not. The heat is making me a little lightheaded."

Her large glasses shift as her face fills with concern. "Oh no, do you want me to drive you home? My golf cart is right over there."

Eliza is quick to reply. "I don't think that will be necessary—"

But I interrupt her. "That would be lovely, thank you. Are you sure you don't mind?"

"Not at all," Sydney assures me. "I'll go drive it around and meet you on the sidewalk. It'll only take a minute." She rushes off.

"I know it's not a nice thing to say," Eliza begins, "but I *really* don't like her. Why's she always asking me about Tom? What's that all about?"

"Does it matter? You know Tom adores you," I remind her. "She just has a little crush. And besides, there's something I want to ask her."

I've only just remembered something Jinny said about the morning of Marjorie's murder. It had initially gotten lost in the barrage of thoughts coming out of Jinny's mouth, but seeing Sydney in the park brought it back to mind.

Before Eliza can press me for details, Sydney pulls her golf cart up to the curb and calls out, "Hop in!"

"Thank you so much for the ride," I say once I'm comfortably seated in the front passenger seat. "How are you doing? How's Savannah? I haven't had a chance to check in on her today."

"Oh, you know. She's still really sad." Sydney pushes her glasses higher on the bridge of her nose as she looks into the rear-view mirror to make sure Eliza is settled in the back. "I'm sure she'd love to see you though."

"The poor dear. It must all be such a shock to her."

"No doubt," Sydney confirms. "I can't imagine losing my mom."

"No, of course not." I turn so I can watch the expression on her face when I say, "Especially since you just found your birth mother. Isn't that right?"

Sydney doesn't even glance my way. She just stares at the road ahead of us. "Yeah, well. I don't know her that well, and she can't come visit. So…"

"But your adoptive parents live in the area, don't they? You went to stay with them after the party at the Golf Club on Thursday night, didn't you?"

Out of the corner of my eye, I see Eliza frowning. She's probably wondering where I'm going with my questioning.

"Umm, yeah. I did. They're not too far away. Just over in Naples."

"That's what I thought. You'd said you were with your parents early Friday morning. But I got confused when I was talking to Jinny this morning. She said she saw you Friday morning going into work."

That gets Sydney's attention. "What? No, that can't be

right. I wasn't here on Friday morning. She must have confused me with someone else. There were a lot of families here."

I nod. "That must be it. A lot of people had their grandchildren in town. When you get to our age, all young people start to look alike."

"Yeah. Well, she didn't see me, because I wasn't here," Sydney reiterates as she engages the golf cart's brakes. "This is you, isn't it?"

I was so busy with my interrogation I hadn't even realized we'd pulled up to my house.

"I have to get back to the class," Sydney says, urging me to exit her ride. "But I hope you feel better soon."

Once we're standing on the curb in front of my house, Eliza turns to me. "What was that all about?"

"I'm not sure," I admit. Once again, I have the nagging feeling that Sydney knows more than she's saying.

I don't have time to consider what Sydney might be trying to conceal because my eye catches movement in the shadows of the bushes near my front door.

There's someone there. I'm sure of it.

In the dying light, I can't make out who's trying to conceal themselves in the shelter of my foliage but there's one thing that's clear. They've been waiting for me.

Thirty-Eight

A crunching sound, like dried leaves underfoot, comes from the bushes.

Eliza grabs the purse from my arm and pulls out her gun.

"You hid your gun in my purse?" I whisper angrily.

Without taking her eyes off the bushes, Eliza whispers back, "You told me to conceal it."

"Yes, dear. But I didn't know you were going to *conceal* it on me! What if I dropped my purse and the gun went off?"

"It didn't," Eliza points out.

"But it could have," I insist, still speaking in hushed tones. "Not to mention I don't have a permit to carry a gun. I could have been arrested."

"Can this wait until later, Mom?" Eliza hisses. "Someone's hiding in your bushes. I think we have bigger issues at the moment."

"Please don't shoot!" a female voice calls out from behind my azaleas.

"Stand up with your hands behind your head," Eliza calls back.

The leaves shudder as a figure rises from behind the shrub. The flaming red hair makes the woman instantly identifiable.

"Savannah, what are you doing here?" I ask.

Her milky white face is even paler than normal, and her large green eyes seem to swallow her face. "I'm sorry, Miss Madeline, I didn't rightly know where else to go."

"You're always welcome here," I assure her, using my hand to push Eliza's gun down so that it's aimed at the ground. "But why are you hiding in the plants?"

Her gaze darts from side to side. "Would it be alright if we talked about it inside? I'd prefer it if nobody knows I was here."

I silently curse Brock Leitman. "Yes, of course. I understand that radio show has made people rather...skittish around me. You go around the house and come in by the pool, through the screen door. I'll let you in the back door."

"Thank you, Miss Madeline." Savannah bends over to pick up her backpack and then sprints toward the backyard.

Eliza types in the code that opens my front door, saying, "Savannah seems like a good kid, but I'm keeping my gun on me, until we're sure."

I shake my head. "You can't be serious. Why would she kill her own mother?"

"*Because* she's her mother." Eliza smiles. "I'm joking. But look—" she points to the rear windows where we can see Savannah scurrying across the back patio, "—she's not hiding from the cameras. That's a good sign."

"Savannah's no killer." I glare at Eliza for a second before walking quickly through the house to the sliding glass doors and opening them for Savannah.

"Come in, come in," I guide the young woman into the living room. "Can I get you anything? Would you like some water or anything?"

"No, thank you, Miss Madeline." Savannah remains standing, clutching her backpack. "I just really needed to chat with you and, what with my mama bein' killed before she could tell you what she found, well, I didn't want to go makin' the same mistake."

"Did you find something?" I sit down on the loveseat and indicate to Savannah that she should get comfortable on the sofa. Eliza hangs back, leaning against the breakfast bar.

"Maybe, but I'm not real sure what it means," she says.

"How about we try to figure it out together?" I suggest.

She nods. "When you came 'round the house, you said my mama had a letter in her hand when you found her. And that it was addressed to a woman named Drusilla. Drusilla Hackney."

I lean forward in my chair. "That's right. You said you'd never heard the name before."

"And that's all true. I didn't know who she was. But today, I was goin' through some of the papers in my mama's desk—" she pauses to unzip her backpack, reach in, and pull something out, "—and I came across this. I thought you'd want to see it right away. I don't know, I thought maybe it would help somehow."

She hands me a piece of printer paper. Eliza comes behind me to read it over my shoulder. It's a printout of what appears to be a death certificate. The decedent: Drusilla Hackney. Date of death: August 9, 1938.

"I don't understand," I admit. "If she died in 1938, why does she have medical bills in her name now?"

"Medical bills?" Savannah asks, almost to herself. "The letter you found with my mama was a medical bill?"

"Maybe there's another Drusilla Hackney," Eliza speculates. "Though this would explain why I couldn't find any current information on her."

"You've got the right Drusilla," Savannah tells us. "I'm sure of it now."

Eliza frowns. "What do you mean? How can you be sure?"

"On account of I didn't show you yet the other thing I found in my mama's papers." Savannah rummages through her backpack and retrieves a lined piece of paper with what looks like a handwritten genealogy chart. "After my mama found the death certificate, it looks like she started tracin' Drusilla's relatives. Apparently, the family invented Sturdy Foil. Well, it says here it was called Hackney Wrap up until the 1960s—"

"Of course!" I exclaim. "I knew it started with an H. My mother used to call it Hackney Wrap, when I was little, before the name changed. How could I not remember that?"

Eliza rests her hand on my shoulder. "I told you to start taking those B12 vitamins I gave you."

"As you can see from my mom's chart—" Savannah hands me the paper, "—Drusilla was Marjorie's great-grandmother."

Savannah's momentous reveal is interrupted by a pinging from Eliza's phone.

"I have an address!" Eliza says excitedly after checking her text messages. "The insurance company just sent me the address for the post office where the bills were going. If I leave now, I should be able to get there before they close for the night."

"Be careful, dear. I heard that it's supposed to rain again tonight. The roads might be slick, and I know you like to drive fast," I warn Eliza.

"Yeah, yeah," Eliza says, grabbing her car keys. "I'll call you as soon as I know something. You two stay here, and don't go anywhere until I get back."

After we hear Eliza leave, Savannah asks me, "Do you think someone killed my mama because she found out who was impersonatin' Drusilla?"

Not wanting to sugarcoat the facts, I tell her the truth. "Yes. I do."

Tears form in the corner of Savannah's eyes. She blinks them away. "But why?"

"Well, I didn't know what to make of the medical bills when I first found them in Marjorie's office," I admit. "I thought maybe they were just ordinary bills, but they disappeared while I was at the police station, and then I found a scrap of one of them in your mother's hand. I don't want to be insensitive, dear, but I strongly suspect those medical bills are why Marjorie and your mother were killed."

Savannah looks like she wants to cry, but she's fighting to act strong. "You think someone was using a dead woman's identity to make money off fake medical billin'? And Marjorie and my mama found out about it?"

"Sadly, yes," I confirm.

As she begins to softly sniffle I search my conscience, wondering if I should say the thing I've begun to suspect ever since Savannah pulled out the genealogy chart.

Though I don't want to make the poor girl suffer any more than she already has, I realize I have to tell her. For her own safety.

"And, I'm sorry to say, I think your friend Sydney might be involved somehow."

THIRTY-NINE

Thick pellets of rain strike against the kitchen window as I pour two cups of strong coffee. A slash of lightning illuminates the sky, and the overhead lights briefly flicker.

"I know I probably sound slower than cream risin' on buttermilk, but are you *real* sure Sydney had somethin' to do with all of this?" Savannah has removed her Vans sneakers and she's curled up on the sofa, hugging her knees.

"You're not slow at all. I know how hard this must be for you." I hand her a mug and sit down beside her on the sofa. "As I said before, I don't know all the facts yet. I'm still trying to work it all out in my head. But some of the puzzle pieces are starting to form a picture. You'd said Sydney was doing a marketing project. Video family trees, right?"

"Yeah. She asked for me to help her with them." Savannah pauses, her eyes growing wider. "Oh my gosh, does that make me an accomplice or somethin'? I swear I had nothin' to do with no Medicare fraud!"

Her accent has gotten stronger the deeper her distress grows.

"Of course, you didn't, dear. Don't you worry about that," I attempt to reassure her. "I remember Sydney telling me that Marjorie had helped her out with a marketing project. If it was the video family tree, that would explain how Sydney got the name of Marjorie's dead relative. But I doubt Sydney set up the billing fraud all on her own. Most likely, she had some help."

Savannah takes a sip of her coffee. When she looks up, her eyes are swimming in unshed tears. "Do you think Sydney killed my mama?"

"I honestly don't know," I tell her. "It's possible her accomplice committed the murders after Marjorie and your mother discovered what was going on. I just wish I knew who her accomplice was. How close was her relationship with David, the chef? She blushed every time she mentioned him."

"She was definitely into him, that's for sure. She thought the sun came up just to hear him crow," Savannah says. "But she wasn't really...his type, if you catch my meanin'."

"I may be old, but I'm not brain dead," I chuckle. "So

David and Sydney weren't involved romantically, but could they have been business partners in their illegal venture?"

Thinking back, I remember that David had no alibi for Marjorie's murder but claimed to have been knocked out and locked in a closet when Jolene was killed. It's possible Sydney gave him that lump on his head, the one he'd been so insistent that Ritchie feel, just to cover their tracks.

And then there was Detective Baptiste. Could she have been using fake medical billing as a way to raise money to care for her sick mother?

"Did you ever see Sydney talking to Detective Baptiste?" I ask Savannah.

"You mean the lady police officer that looks like a model?"

"That's the one."

Savannah thinks for a minute before shaking her head. "Not that I can recall."

A thought occurs to me. "Sydney would have had access to Marjorie's cell phone, since she worked with her on the family tree project. Could Sydney have gotten hold of your mother's phone at any time?"

Savannah frowns. "Probably. Why?"

"Both your mother and Marjorie supposedly sent texts to Detective Baptiste right before they died. But the messages were nearly identical. Someone else sent both of them." I snap my fingers. "Oh, maybe Sydney sent them to her partner, Detective Baptiste. That way, if anyone saw the detective there—while she was committing murder—the texts would explain her presence."

"That's devious." Savannah shivers. "Do you really think that's what happened, Miss Madeline?"

"I don't know, but who else could her accomplice be?" I twirl my wedding band, the one Clint gave me decades ago, around my ring finger. "Was there anyone else you saw Sydney spending time with on a regular basis?"

"Not really." Savannah shakes her head. "I do think I heard her on the phone talking to that podcast guy, Brock Leitman, a few times."

"Brock Leitman?" I'm overcome with the sudden urge to slap myself in the head. How could I not have thought of him? "Are you sure?"

"Well now, I didn't hear him talkin'. I could only hear Sydney's side of the conversation, mind you. But I assume it was him. She was goin' on and on about that podcast he did on the Griner case awhile back. She said that first podcast sent a woman to jail and that doin' another one, here, could accomplish the same thing."

"Brock and Sydney. Could it be possible they've been working together this whole time?" I wonder aloud. "Oh my goodness, maybe this isn't their first time doing this! What if they were also involved somehow in the Griner case? Do you know if Sydney ever went to Texas?"

Savannah leans toward me. "You bet. She was just there in November! She told me never to say nothin' about it, but she was goin' to spend some time with her birth mother."

I hadn't been expecting that. Maybe there *is* some kind of connection to the Griner case. "Her mother lives in Texas? Did Sydney ever tell you her mother's name?"

Savannah groans. "She sure didn't. Although..."

"Yes?"

"I'm pretty certain Sydney used two last names, like with a hyphen, on her condolence card. The one she gave me after my mama, you know..."

I rest my hand on top of hers. "I know, dear. I also know that your mother would be really proud of you right now. You're helping find out what happened to her. That would mean a lot to any mother."

Savannah nods as she wipes a stray tear from her cheek. "I need to find out who killed my mama. Whoever that ends up bein'. Do you really think knowin' the name of Sydney's birth mother could be important?"

"It's a long shot, but maybe. Do you still have that condolence card?"

She sits up on the sofa, putting her feet on the floor. "I sure do. It's on the shelf, back at my mama's house. Should I go get it? It'll only take a few minutes."

I look out the window. The rain is so thick I can barely see the edge of the swimming pool, even with the patio light on. "Maybe you should stay here for a bit, at least until this storm lets up."

"I hear what you're saying, Miss Madeline. But I'm done waitin' for answers. If we're this close, we might as well go the whole way. I'll be back in a few minutes."

Before I can argue against her decision, Savannah is out the back door and disappearing into the rain. Too anxious to remain seated, I stand up and begin to pace around the living room. As hard as it is to believe that Sydney, the girl everyone seems to like, is involved, I suppose I shouldn't be surprised. Clint wouldn't have made that kind of oversight. He never ruled anyone out as a suspect.

But I don't have the luxury of focusing on my mistake. I have to fix it, by figuring out who was helping Sydney. In my mind, I start going back through all my suspects, with the addition of Brock now in the mix, and try to recall who had alibis for which murder. I should probably write it down, so I don't get confused.

As I reach for a pen and paper, my phone rings. It's Eliza.

"Mom, hi. So, I went to the post office, and they gave me the billing address for the box. You're never going to believe this, it's registered to—"

"Sydney Walsh," I cut her off. There's silence on the other end of the line for so long, I have to ask, "Eliza, are you still there?"

"How, Mom? How did you know? Wait, did you know that before I drove all the way into Naples?"

Before I can answer her, thunder shakes the house, and

lightning shatters the darkness outside. Inside, the lights flicker and die.

"Oh no, not again," I complain.

"What?" Eliza's concerned voice echoes in my ear. "Are you alright, Mom? What happened?"

"Nothing," I say. "The storm just knocked the lights out."

"Uh oh. Go to the window and see if Viviana's lights are still on." Eliza instructs. Her voice is calm, but I can feel myself beginning to panic.

I squeeze my eyes into slits and concentrate on looking through the kitchen window to see if there are any lights on next door. "No, her lights appear to have gone out as well."

Eliza sighs deeply. "Alright. It's probably just the storm. Look, I'm on my way back and I need to focus on the road. When I get back, you're going to tell me how you knew about Sydney. I told you I never liked that girl."

"You did, dear." I roll my eyes. "Be safe driving in this weather."

Setting my phone down on the kitchen counter, I search blindly through the kitchen drawers for one of the flashlights Ritchie insisted on leaving in every room of the house. Finally, my fingers brush against the thick, rubber grip. Flipping the switch, the flashlight turns on.

A sudden, heavy banging on the front door surprises me, nearly making me drop the device onto the floor.

Taking a steadying breath, I aim the beam of light at the floor and walk quickly toward the foyer.

Poor Savannah is probably drowning out there in all this rain.

I throw open the door, expecting to see a mop of wet red hair. Instead, I see the hood of a pink rain slicker. I'm about to slam the door, when a hand shoots out and pushes the door further open. I stumble back from the force of the shove.

The hood begins to move until I'm staring at a large pair of black-rimmed glasses.

Sydney steps into the front room and pushes the door shut behind her.

"I'm sorry it had to be like this," she says, raising the barrel of a handgun.

Forty

"Sydney, where did you get a gun?" is all I can think to ask.

She shrugs. "This is Florida. Everyone has guns."

"And why are you wearing all pink?" I know they're ridiculous questions, but I'm trying to buy myself a little time to think. "You look like Jinny."

"That's the point," she says slowly, like a teacher who's trying to explain multiplication to a student who just isn't understanding. "If anyone saw me coming over here, they'll think they saw Jinny, not me."

"That's clever." I have to admit the wisdom of her thinking, even if it will make it harder to identify my murderer after the fact. "It's a shame you haven't been so smart about everything else you've done, though."

A hurt look crosses her face. "What's that supposed to mean?"

"I don't mean to criticize," I say, all too conscious of the weapon in her hand, "but you must have made some mistakes with that little medical fraud plan of yours, or Marjorie never would have found out. You wouldn't have had to kill her."

"That was unfortunate," Sydney admits. "But it was my first time doing anything illegal. How was I supposed to know that Marjorie used the same insurance company I was trying to rip off using her great-grandmother's name?"

"The insurance company found out and told Marjorie? How did they connect the dots? Granted, everyone knows insurance people hate to pay out claims. But I wouldn't think they'd investigate *that* thoroughly."

"I know, right?" Sydney animatedly replies. "But I actually don't think they figured it out, not intentionally anyway. See, I used Drusilla's social security number on the forms, but I used Marjorie's info—date of birth, place of birth, etc.—for all the rest. I think some minimum-wage worker saw the similarities and accidentally sent one of Drusilla's bills to Marjorie. I was at her house, working on the family tree video, when the letter came in the mail."

"When was that?" I ask, trying to get a clearer sense of when Sydney decided that Marjorie needed to die.

Sydney frowns. "Back in November. Why?"

I swallow the lump that's formed around my trachea. "You'd been planning to kill Marjorie for months?"

"No!" Sydney exclaims. "She wasn't supposed to have to die. I mean, yes, I did some planning, just in case. But I was really hoping it wouldn't come to that. You have to believe me."

"But you did kill her. I think that's pretty obvious at this point. What changed?"

Sydney sighs. "She kept trying to figure out what was going on. It wasn't hurting her in any way, but she just wouldn't let it go. When the insurance company refused to tell her anything, she started calling the post office to get them to reroute any bills for Drusilla. Eventually, she got a high-powered friend to pull some strings, and she was able to get a few more bills. She was starting to put the pieces together. If she went to the cops, it would have ruined everything. We couldn't let that happen!"

"We?" I take some comfort in knowing I was correct; she did have an accomplice. Figuring I have nothing left to lose, I hazard a guess at who she's been working with this whole time. If I'm right, it's someone who, Eliza said, had been accused of committing fraud in Florida before. "You've been working with your birth mother—the woman jailed in Texas for killing the Griner family—haven't you? Denise Kramer."

Sydney's mouth falls open in shock, but she recovers quickly. "Now who's the clever one? You're right, of course.

My mom got in touch with me last year, after that little turd, Brock Leitman, made his podcast and got her imprisoned for murdering the Griners. She wanted to apologize for putting me up for adoption when I was a baby. She said she was in a bad relationship at the time and had started doing some illegal things. That was no kind of life for a little girl. She thought I'd be better off."

My heart swells with sympathy for Sydney, even if she is a cold-blooded murderer. I'm beginning to suspect she was being used. "Your mother got in touch with you and then what? How long before she started asking for money?"

The gun in Sydney's hand begins to shake. "It wasn't like that. She needed cash to pay for a good attorney. The one the court appointed was a joke. She needed someone good, who'd be able to get her acquitted. She didn't kill those people; she swore to me she didn't."

The pieces are finally starting to form a picture in my mind.

"And when Denise found out you didn't have any money," I say, "she taught you how to commit medical fraud. You broke the law to help a mother you didn't even know."

"She would have done the same for me," Sydney says, quickly coming to her mother's defense.

"Oh my goodness," I blurt, as another thought occurs to

me. "You brought Brock Leitman here. You were the source that tipped him off to the murders at Egret's Loft."

Sydney smiles. "Now *that* was my idea. When I went to see my mom in November, and we were chatting about ways to deal with Marjorie—only if it became necessary, of course—I thought, huh, why not try to discredit Brock at the same time? I hated him for spreading his lies about my mom. So, I cloned the detective's phone and started sending him tips about all the other murders here. I figured, if somebody could catch him in a lie about these murders, it would make the case against my mom a lot weaker."

"That's true, it would," I admit. "But why did you tell him *I* was the murderer?"

She shrugs. "I heard somebody talking about how all the murders started after you showed up. It got me thinking you'd make a good scapegoat. But I promise, I never would have let you go to jail." Then seeming to remember the situation we're currently in, she adds, "you know, if I didn't have to kill you."

I return Sydney's shrug as I rack my brain for what to do next. I have so many more questions for her, and, if I can keep her talking, there's a good chance Eliza will get back from Naples and save me. Then again, Savannah will probably get here first, and I don't want to get her killed.

If I want to save myself *and* Savannah, I have to come up with a plan to draw the conversation with Sydney out long enough for Eliza to get here while also alerting Savannah not to come into the house.

"I have another question about the murders!" I practically scream.

Sydney waves the gun at me. "Why are you screaming? Is someone else here?"

"No!" I yell. "Am I screaming? I can't tell. My hearing aid battery must have died."

Sydney takes a step closer. "If you don't keep it down, I'll shoot you now and be done with it."

"Relax!" I scream. "No one can hear me over the storm. There's something I don't understand. Why did you kill Marjorie in the kitchen and then dump her body in the swimming pool?"

"Seriously?" she asks. When I pretend not to be able to hear her, she repeats in a louder voice, "Seriously? That's what you want to know? Fine. I'll tell you. My mom said, if I wanted to frame David for the murder, it would look more convincing if I also made it look like he was trying to cover his tracks."

"That's actually quite smart!" I yell. "But if you wanted to frame David, why did you send Detective Baptiste those texts from Marjorie and Jolene's phones telling her to come to the crime scenes? That made her a suspect too."

"I know." She smiles. "I did it on purpose. To create confusion."

I nod in appreciation. "It worked."

We'd all been sidetracked into suspecting David, Detective Baptiste, Fred, and Jinny of the murders. Though, thinking about it, I can't remember any way Sydney tried to implicate Fred or Jinny. She was just lucky in that regard. A lot of people hated Marjorie.

"I know you've been stalling, asking all these questions," Sydney tells me. "To be honest, I've been stalling too. I really don't want to have to kill you."

"You don't *have* to, you know," I point out.

"No, I really do," she argues. "Because if I don't kill you, then I'll go to jail. And how can I help get my mom get out of jail if I'm in jail too?"

I can see where she's coming from. I just wish it had taken her a little bit longer to realize.

"Do you, like, want to say a prayer or anything?" Sydney asks. "Before..."

"Yes, thank you. I would." I get down on my knees and pray that the roads between here and Naples aren't flooded. Where are you, Eliza?

I close my eyes and hear the sound of a round being chambered.

Forty-One

"Drop the gun and put your hands in the air!"

My eyes fly open, and I spin my head around to the sliding glass doors where Savannah stands, a rifle aimed at Sydney.

"Savannah! You have a gun too?" I'm suddenly wishing Eliza hadn't taken hers with her. It's an awful feeling being the only woman in the room without a weapon.

"I grew up in Alabama, Miss Madeline," she says, without taking her eyes off her target. "I learned how to shoot when I was eight."

"Put the gun down, Vannah," Sydney orders. "We both know you're not a killer."

"Don't you *dare* call me by my mama's pet name for me," Savannah snarls. "I thought you were my friend."

"I am your friend," Sydney says. "Look, I know you're

probably mad at me for killing your mom. I understand that. But she didn't leave me any choice. And neither did you."

"Me?" Savannah barks, her face growing very close in color to her vibrant hair. "You can kiss my go-to-hell. Don't even think about tryin' to blame *me* for what *you* did!"

Sydney shrugs. "All I'm saying is, if you hadn't left all the family tree info sitting in plain sight on your kitchen table, your mom never would have put it all together. I saw her rifling through the files when you were out of the room. I knew she was going to be trouble. Then, when I got a call from the manager of the post office in Naples that your mom was sniffing around, asking questions, I knew she had to go."

"That doesn't even make any sense," Savannah argues. "If you were worried about people findin' out what you were doin', why in the heck did you hire me to help you with the family tree stuff?"

"I admit, that was a miscalculation," Sydney concedes. "But the money wasn't coming in fast enough to help my mom. I needed to expand. I needed names and info on more dead people."

"Can you even hear yourself?" Savannah demands. "You had no problem killin' innocent, decent people to help some psycho criminal, who put you up for adoption when you were a baby? Has the cheese slid off your cracker?"

Sydney looks perplexed. "What do cheese and crackers have to do with anything?"

"It's an expression," Savannah snaps. "It means that you've completely lost your dang mind! If you ever even had one to begin with. The choices you've made are seriously callin' that into question."

"You watch your tone," Sydney warns. "All the choices I've made were to save my mom."

"Your mama? She killed an entire family for money. You only heard from her on account of she needed help, and no one else'd touch her with a ten-foot pole. Then she turned you into a killer, just like her."

"My mom loves me," Sydney shouts, her gun hand quivering.

Kneeling between two loaded weapons, I feel compelled to try and deescalate the situation. "Of course, she does, dear. Why don't we all just take a minute to calm down and—"

I don't think they even hear me. It's easy to be ignored when you're the only one in the group who's unarmed.

"Your mama doesn't love you," Savannah says, her tone softening. "She's been usin' you, and you ain't even got the sense to see it."

"You know, you should really think twice about hurling insults at someone who's aiming a revolver at you," Sydney growls.

"Oh, you mean that little pellet gun you've got?"

Savannah asks, seconds before her finger squeezes the trigger, and the bang of rifle fire fills the room.

"Savannah, no!" I yell, squeezing my eyes shut to avoid witnessing the bloodshed. I'm not sure my heart can take much more.

"Are you insane?" Sydney's voice cuts through my horror. "You could have shot my hand off!"

My eyes fly open, and I see Sydney standing in front of me, completely unharmed. However, the gun that had been in her hand moments before is no longer there.

"I wasn't goin' to shoot your hand off," Savannah refutes the allegation, as she chambers another round. "Though, I am seriously considerin' takin' your head off. Why, Sydney? Why'd you do all this for some woman you barely even know? You have a family. They love you. Weren't they good enough?"

Sydney holds her chin up defiantly. "You wouldn't understand. You don't know what it's like to feel like you don't belong."

"How do you think I feel now?" Savannah takes a step closer, raising the rifle to aim at Sydney's head. "My mama was all I had. I never had a daddy. She was it. She was the only family I had. And you took her away from me. Give me one good reason why I shouldn't shoot you dead right now."

With my heart lodged firmly in my throat, I slowly stand up, my knees cracking along the way. Raising my hands in surrender, I step directly between Sydney and Savannah's gun.

"I know how much you're hurting, but killing Sydney won't help," I try to reason with Savannah. "She's going to prison. She will pay for what she did to your mother. Don't ruin your own life, just to get revenge."

Savannah starts to cry, the rifle shaking in her hands. I walk over to her, and she allows me to remove the gun from her grip. I lean it against the sofa and put my arms around the young, distraught woman. As she sobs into my shoulder, I turn her around so I can keep my eye on Sydney.

But Sydney's not there.

Then I see movement on the other side of the foyer. Sydney took advantage of Savannah's despair, using the moment to scramble for her own gun, which had landed in the front room after Savannah shot it out of Sydney's hand.

Sydney jumps up, pointing the gun at Savannah and me.

"You'll never take me alive," she screams, closing one eye and tilting her head to take aim.

Just before she can fire, the front door flies open, slamming into Sydney and knocking her on the floor. The gun slides away from her, across the tiles.

Eliza and Viviana storm into the house as Sydney clambers toward her gun.

"I *knew* you were bad news," Eliza screams as she races over and kicks the weapon out of Sydney's reach. My daughter then drags Sydney to her feet and slaps handcuffs on her wrists, before turning in my direction. "Are you alright, Mom? Is anyone hurt?"

"We're fine," I say. "Thanks to Savannah. If she hadn't arrived when she did, I wouldn't be standing here right now. She saved my life."

"Thanks, Savannah. I seriously owe you one," Eliza says, trying to hide the tears forming in her eyes.

"Detective Fletcher should be here any minute," Viviana tells us, drawing her robe tighter around her body. "I called him when I heard a shot."

Eliza, her warring emotions spelled out on her face, walks over to Sydney. "Did you hear that? The cops are on their way to get you. Have fun asking about my husband in prison, you crazy witch."

Forty-Two

"Sydney seemed like such a nice, young girl," Gina says in between sips of coffee. "You know, she asked me if I wanted to do one of those family tree video things, and I was considering it."

Helen shakes her head. "She asked me, too, but I said no. I got eight dead husbands. My family tree'd have more branches than Bank of America."

"Sydney had us all fooled," Viviana says, pulling us back on topic. "Such a waste. She really could have made something of herself if she hadn't decided to start killing people."

My new friends are gathered around my kitchen table, reliving the events of the previous evening. Sunshine streams in through the floor to ceiling windows, erasing all but the memory of last night's storm.

Gina leans toward me and, in what, for her, is a soft voice, asks, "How's Savannah doing? She's got some guts, coming in here with a rifle and saving your skinny hide."

I glance at the door to the spare room, where I'd insisted Savannah sleep last night. "She's tougher than she looks. I think she's going to be just fine. With our help, of course."

"Absolutely," Helen agrees. "She may have lost her mom, but she has all of us now. And I'm going to sell Carl's house, may he rest in peace, and give Vannah the money to get her started."

"That's very generous of you, Helen," I say. "I'm sure it'll mean a lot to her."

Viviana clears her throat. "Speaking of money, I figure Brock Leitman will be offering a nice settlement to keep me from suing on your behalf, Madeline. You should do something nice for yourself. I was thinking we could all go on a cruise to celebrate putting a murderer behind bars."

"Oh my gosh, yes!" Helen exclaims. "I haven't been on a cruise since my third honeymoon."

"Would it be one of those ships with the casinos?" Gina asks excitedly. "I love slot machines. Leon and me used to go to Atlantic City once a month to play them."

"Oh, I don't know..." I hesitate, unsure about committing to the expense.

"You should go, Mom," Eliza calls out from the kitchen where she's raiding the refrigerator for orange juice. "If for no other reason than I think it'd do everyone good to get you out of Egret's Loft for a little while. People keep dying here, and Ritchie and I are running out of vacation days to come look after you."

"Fine," I capitulate. "I'll think about it."

The doorbell rings and I grab the arms of my chair to help me stand up.

"You stay there, Mom," Eliza instructs me. "I'll get it."

"Where do y'all want to go on our cruise?" Helen asks, as the sound of muffled conversation drifts in from the foyer. "The Mediterranean's nice this time of year."

Gina shakes her head. "Huh uh. Sorry, I don't fly. Maybe something closer to home?"

"We could go somewhere in the Caribbean," Viviana suggests. "Ships leave practically every day from Fort Lauderdale."

"I hope you're not planning to skip town before making a formal statement about last night," Detective Fletcher says, smiling as he walks over to the kitchen table. Eliza and Detective Baptiste trail slightly behind.

"Detectives, can I get you some coffee?" I offer.

"I wouldn't say no to a cup," Detective Fletcher says. "It's been a long night."

"Nothing for me," Detective Baptiste says, her eyes trained on the floor where they've been focused since she entered the room.

Eliza scurries off toward the kitchen. "You stay, Mom. I got it."

"We don't want to intrude." Detective Fletcher sits down at the table. "But I thought you would want to know. Sydney made a full confession last night. Not only that, but we went to her apartment and found evidence of the medical billing fraud on her computer. We also found cell phones belonging to Marjorie, Jolene, and Sammy...sorry, I mean Detective Baptiste...in her desk. We got her."

"What about Denise Kramer?" I ask as Eliza sets a mug in front of Detective Fletcher. "From what I can tell, she was the one who came up with the whole plan to begin with."

Helen pauses, her cup halfway to her mouth. "Please tell me you're not tryin' to make excuses for Sydney, that little, four-eyed monster. Let's not forget, she's the one who killed Savannah's mama."

I shake my head. "No, that's not what I'm saying. Sydney needs to face justice. But I think her birth mother should have to answer for some of it as well."

Detective Fletcher takes a large gulp of coffee. "That'll be up to the prosecutor, but we'll definitely recommend charges against both of them."

"What charges are you bringin' against Sydney?" Helen demands. "You better not have offered her some kind of plea deal. If you tell me she's goin' to be out of prison in a few years, I'll knock you into the middle of next week lookin' both ways for Sunday."

Detective Fletcher frowns. "No, she won't be getting any plea deals. She killed two people and committed fraud against old...um, active elder...people. Oh, and we're also pressing charges against Sydney for impersonating a police officer, since she was sending information to Brock Leitman, pretending to be Detective Baptiste."

"Alright, that's good." Helen settles down.

"I will need to get statements from both you and Savannah," Detective Fletcher tells me. "But it can wait a day or two."

"Thanks, Pete. I'll let you know when Savannah's feeling up to it. Can she and I give our statements at the same time?"

"Sure. Just give me a call when you want me to come by." Detective Fletcher downs the rest of his coffee and stands up. "Well, we better get back to it. You wouldn't believe the paperwork."

"I'll walk you out," I offer.

When we get to the door, I hug Detective Fletcher, and he walks outside. Before Detective Baptiste can follow him out, I rest my hand on her arm.

"I think you might have been right," I tell her. "We did get off on the wrong foot. Given that we've both been accused of things we didn't do, I was hoping we might be able to start over. Maybe you and your mother would like to come over for dinner sometime soon?"

She smiles. "Thank you. I'd really like that."

I smile back. "Excellent. I hope to see you again soon."

As the detectives' car pulls out of my driveway, I wave at them and close the door. Seeing that Eliza and the others are deep in conversation at the table, I decide to check in on Savannah before joining them.

Cracking open the door as quietly as possible, I see Savannah sitting on the edge of the bed with a piece of paper in her hand.

"How are you feeling?" I ask, slipping into the room and closing the door behind me.

"I honestly don't know how to feel right now," Savannah admits.

"I know, dear." I walk over and sit beside her on the bed. "You're going to be feeling that way for a while, I'm afraid."

Savannah nods. "I know. I just wish I could talk to my mama. There are so many things I want to ask her about. Especially now." She hands me the paper she's holding. "I didn't want to say nothin' last night, but I found this when I went back to get Sydney's condolence card."

I look at the blurry paper. "I'm sorry. But I don't have my glasses. What is it?"

"It's a letter that was in my mama's desk. The envelope had my name on it, so I opened it," Savannah explains. "She wanted me to read it if she died. I guess she always knew somethin' bad could happen to her, what with her job and all."

"Do you want to talk about it?" I ask. "If it's not too personal, of course."

"No, it's fine." Savannah waves away my concern. "I can't make heads or tails of it, so maybe you can help me figure out what it's all about."

Intrigued, I ask, "What does it say?"

"It says that, if I ever find myself alone in the world, I should seek out Audrey Murphy in Ireland. My mama said she'd explain everything."

"Do you know this Audrey person well?"

Savannah looks at me, confusion in her eyes. "That's the thing. I have no idea who she is. My mama never talked about her. Never. Why would my mama send me to a woman I've never met to get answers? And answers about what? Was there somethin' my mama was hidin' from me?"

"I don't know, dear." I take her hand in mine. "But I think you owe it yourself to find out. Was there an address for Audrey in the letter?"

Savannah shakes her head. "No, all it says is she lives somewhere in Ireland, probably in County Cork."

"Okay. That makes things a bit harder," I admit. "But we'll find her, don't you worry. And, if you want, I'll go over with you, if you decide you want to meet her in person. How does that sound?"

"Thank you, Miss Madeline. I'd be real grateful for your help."

As I sit beside Savannah, her eyes raw from crying, neither of us could have known that our journey into uncovering Jolene's secrets would take Savannah and I not only across an ocean, but straight back into harm's way.

End of Serial Seniors

Egret's Loft Murder Mystery Series
Book 3

Did you enjoy your time at Egret's Loft?

Why not continue your cozy mystery adventure by traveling with me to the coast of Ireland?

Keep reading for a preview of **Strange Winds**, the first book in my Raven's Wing Irish Murder Mystery series!

Thank You!

If you enjoyed *Serial Seniors*, I'd be incredibly grateful if you could leave a quick review.

Your feedback not only helps other readers discover the book but also supports my work in bringing you more cozy mysteries to enjoy. Reviews make a world of difference for authors, so thank you for considering sharing your thoughts!

Join me on social media for updates and info on new releases!

instagram.com/teharkinsbooks
facebook.com/teharkins.author

Acknowledgments

This book is dedicated to my brilliant and amazing brother. I feel so very lucky to be your sister.

I want to begin by thanking all the family members and friends who helped make these books possible—from reading drafts to giving helpful feedback to assisting me in choosing a cover design. I would never have the courage to put my writing out there without you!

And I *might* have been tempted to abandon my dreams of becoming an author without the support and encouragement of some incredible authors—Marc Reklau, Mark Dawson, and James Blatch. You're an inspiration and I'm so honored and grateful that you have shown your belief in me. Thank you!

I also want to thank my fabulous editor, Shannon Cave, for being so supportive while simultaneously making sure my novels make sense and are grammatically accurate. And a big thank you to Joe Montgomery, for sharing your patience and talent and for designing covers that I absolutely love.

Finally, as always, my deepest gratitude goes to Steve. If you ever get tired of hearing me talk about plot lines or excitedly recounting the events of my newest chapter, you never show it. I love you so much for that, and for always supporting me in my writing, no matter what. Thank you, sweetheart.

STRANGE WINDS

A RAVEN'S WING IRISH MURDER MYSTERY

T.E. HARKINS

BLURB

Find Audrey Murphy. She'll know what to do.

Those were my mama's final words to me. A cryptic message that led me from the beaches of Florida to a quaint, coastal village in the south of Ireland. All to track

ALSO BY: STRANGE WINDS

down a woman I've never heard of who, supposedly, has answers to questions I never even knew I had.

But as I sit outside the crumbling ruins of an ancient castle, working up the courage to go to Audrey's house, I see something. Or at least, I think I do. Out of the mist, a woman dressed in white materializes. She seems to need my help. Then, as quickly as she appeared, she vanishes. Like a ghost. Maybe my grief-stricken mind was just playing tricks on me.

Or maybe not...

Before long, the little village is buzzing with news of a brutal murder. And, as the only witness to the crime, I find myself squarely in the killer's crosshairs. Which means I'll have to get to the truth of what happened...or the next obituary in the local paper could just be my own.

Grab your copy of *Strange Winds (Book 1 of the Raven's Wing Irish Murder Mystery Series)* today!

EXCERPT

CHAPTER 1

Also By: Strange Winds

Why are you here?

The thought repeats over and over in my head. The last time I felt so trapped in a mental loop was when I heard Wham! on the radio a few months ago at Christmas. You can't go through a holiday season without hearing George Michael singing about how someone broke his heart at least a hundred times. The resulting earworm had eaten away at my brain well into the new year.

And now, sitting here in my rental car, late on a soggy March afternoon, staring at the crumbling ruins of an ancient Irish castle, my head is humming away. "Why are you here?" echoing to the beat of "You gave it away."

My journey began with a brief letter my mama left for me when she died. As a former US Marshal, hiding witnesses from violent felons, my mama must have thought about dying a lot. Otherwise, she wouldn't have left me a cryptic message about what I should do if she was no longer around:

If you're reading this, it means I'm dead. Find a woman named Audrey Murphy in the south of Ireland. She should still live somewhere in County Cork. She'll know what to do.

Those were the final words my mama left her only daughter. Not *I love you*. Not *I'll finally answer all the questions that I ignored, like who's your father.* Just instructions to travel from our new home in Florida to a country I know nothing about to seek out a woman I've never heard of.

As has been the case every few minutes since I lost her, I really wish I could talk to my mama.

To honor her wishes, and with the help of one of her friends, a kind and razor-sharp widow named Madeline Delarouse, I'd managed to track Audrey Murphy to a small village called Ballygoseir. She lives only a few miles from where I sit in front of this moss-ravaged castle on a cliff. The vacant eye of a steadfast stone window frame stares back at me like a bad omen.

Mist rolls in from the sea, thick and mysterious. As it wafts over the car, it leaves behind tiny liquid fingerprints on the windshield, making everything outside the warmth of my rented Ford Fiesta shift further out of focus.

Knowing I can't sit here all day, I'm mentally preparing to drive away, when out of the swirling, dense nothingness, a woman emerges. With translucent skin, golden hair the color of cornsilk, and clothed in a white gown, everything about the woman seems muted, ethereal. Her floor-length, chiffon-like dress seems to undulate, a combination of fabric and wind impersonating the waves of the ocean.

My heart beats faster, and my hand hovers over the rental car's gear shift.

The strange and unearthly woman seems to be heading straight for me. Her mouth opens in a terrible, ear-splitting scream.

Before I can decide whether to jump out and help her or speed away from the ghostly sight, the woman comes to an abrupt halt. Her fingers seem to pluck at imaginary strings in the air, reaching for something that only she can see. It's as if she's coaxing me to do something, though I don't know what she wants or needs.

Then, in the shake of a dog's tail, she vanishes.

Replaying the scene in my head, seconds later, I can't quite figure out whether she dissolved into the thick fog now devouring the castle ruins, or if she was yanked back by an unseen force, almost as if an invisible rope around her waist dragged her back into whatever nightmare she'd been trying to escape.

I don't know which scenario seems worse.

Shaking my head to reorder my thoughts, I try to convince myself I'd only been daydreaming. My mama always said I had a vivid imagination. That's why I'd gone into creative writing at the University of Alabama. And so, remaining inside the safety of my rental car, I persuade myself that the whole scenario was just a trick of the light at dusk, a long way from home. It's the atmosphere, nothing more, I tell myself.

I can't escape the overwhelming, if fanciful, feeling I'd been experiencing since the moment I'd left the airport in my rearview mirror—that this place has a kind of knowing. Driving down windy and narrow roads, with speed limits that border on the suicidal, past crumbling buildings and stone Celtic crosses, I carried with me the romantic notion that the land is carrying stories in its soil, with the present and the past locked in a struggle for dominance.

Was the woman really there? Or was she an echo reverberating across time to settle some long-forgotten score?

You need to pull yourself together, Savannah. I attempt to shake some sense into myself. *If the woman was real, she might need your help.*

Before giving myself the time to think better of it, I throw open the driver's side door and step out onto the gravel road. A thick blanketing of mossy weeds makes the ground slippery. Moisture seeps through the thin fabric of my Vans sneakers, sending shivers down the length of my arms.

"Hello?" I call out. "Is anybody out there?"

At first, the only response comes from the ocean, its thunderous waves crashing against the jagged stone of the cliff. I'm about to climb back into my car when I hear it. Loud and feral, the unseen woman howls a single word.

"*Help!*"

Grab your copy of *Strange Winds (Book 1 of the Raven's Wing Irish Murder Mystery Series)* today!